DON'T BE LIKE THAT

CYNTHIA A. KING

Dedication

To Pierre

Table of Contents

PART ONE

Bam! Bam! Bam! Loud pounding on the door woke Leslie with a start. She reflexively cast her arm over her husband's side of the bed to ask him what was happening, but his side of the bed was cold. Bam! Bam! Bam! The door rattled in its frame. *Paul? What the?* Leslie thought as she got up and opened the door. A rush of agents stormed inside, and one plastered a warrant on her chest as she hurried by. Leslie was dumbfounded.

She grabbed her phone to call Paul and ask him what was happening when Leslie noticed his missed call. She could barely hear it when an agent grabbed it out of her hand, saying it was evidence. Leslie sat like a stone as activity swarmed around her. Unable to produce the key to his locked office, they kicked the door in. *Why was the door locked? Paul never locked that door,* she thought. She watched them carry out his computer and break his beautiful antique desk into firewood. "Stop!" Leslie screamed. "STOP! WILL SOMEONE EXPLAIN WHAT'S HAPPENING!"

"It's in the warrant, ma'am." One of the older men came over to her. She looked at his feet and his wingtip shoes. She was barefoot with pink toenails.

"I have to talk to you?" Leslie said, sounding none too pleased. She narrowed her eyes at her opponent. "I Want My Lawyer. I'm here in my pajamas, the ones with the ripped knee, so I look like a slob, and you're tossing my apartment! Don't tell me that's not what you're doing. I watch Law & Order! I want my phone call."

"You're on your way to the Justice Center." He gave back her phone. "Ten minutes."

Leslie could only think of one person to get her out of this mess. She called her dad.

"Dad? Daddy? It's me. I'm going to jail! Paul did something wrong, and they think I'm in on it too. They're tearing this place apart." Leslie's voice started to waver.

"Where's Paul?"

"Paul? I don't know. That's the problem. He's gone, the money's gone, and I'm on the hook. They're taking me to jail! The Justice Center. Ok. I won't. Thanks, Dad." Leslie handed the phone back. "I'm invoking my right to legal counsel. My father and my lawyer will meet us there. I was advised not to say another word."

"Follow counsel. Whatever he said. Just stop talking." A nondescript man in a suit said. He wore a pair of wing-tipped shoes like the other detective. *Why can't I talk? I didn't do anything wrong,* she thought. It took all she had to bite her lips and remain quiet.

***

Leslie sat in a cell, waiting for her dad. It was going to be a long day. He had a couple-hour drive, and she asked for a lawyer, so she was stuck in this cell with these other women. One looked like she was going through withdrawal, shaking and covered in vomit. Another passed out, reeking of booze, and a big bruise started to color her face like a wildflower—*car accident. I hope nobody else got hurt,* Leslie thought, and the last girl, she didn't want to presume she was a prostitute, but she dressed like one.

The woman came and stood over Leslie. "Why're you in here, my sorority sister? Not tipping the nail tech?"

Leslie looked at her, wondering what she was talking about. She was sitting in her worn pajamas wearing sweat socks. *It's the blowout and manicure. I must look like all the wives their husbands complain about while she gives them head.* The simmering rage inside her boiled over. Leslie stood up, and the look she gave the woman should have caused her to worry.

"Why am I in here? Do you want to know why I'm here? I'll tell you why. I caught my husband with another woman and took my Tiffany carving knife and stabbed that rat bastard in the heart, and if he's still alive when I get out, I'm gonna cut his balls off and shove them down his throat. Any more questions?" Leslie snarled at her. "You haven't been with him, have you? 'Cuz that bitch is NEXT."

"Fuck you," the girl answered, but her tone was wary. *That bitch is crazy,* she thought and sat as far away as possible from Leslie.

Leslie leaned back and rested her head on the cinderblock wall. Somebody bailed the drunk girl out. It was just the two of them and the girl retching in the corner.

"Who are you waiting for?" The other woman asked.

"What's your name?"

"Diamond."

Leslie made a face at the obviously fake name. "I'm Leslie. I'm waiting for my dad and my lawyer. Oh yeah. And the FBI."

"Oh. The Feds. It looks like you're in for some big trouble."

"Looks like it. Who are you waiting for?"

"My boyfriend."

"Boyfriend? You sure about that?"

"What's that supposed to mean?" The girl's voice tensed up.

"It means if he bails you out, will you have to go out and earn it back?"

"Yeah," Diamond said, her voice tired and beat down.

"What if I posted your bail and gave you five hundred dollars? What would you do?"

"You gonna give me five hundred bucks?" She suddenly sounded interested.

"Hell no. I asked you what you would *do*. Run home to your 'boyfriend,' give him the money, and be back walking the track by dark?"

"No. I'd buy a bus ticket to my sister in Virginia. I'm not too fond of this city. I came here with a guy who promised I'd be a star. He said he could get me work as a back-dancer and hang out with famous rappers. He lied, and I didn't know what to do, so I went to the bus station. I thought I'd be safe there." She said with a laugh but no smile. "I must have looked pretty green because Raymond said he could help. He helped, alright. Now I have to work off my debt."

"You do drugs?"

"Not yet, but it's coming. I see how Raymond treats the other girls. He wants you on drugs; you're easier to control, plus you have to work 'cuz you owe him money. I do what I do so I don't cause no trouble, and right now, he's breaking this other girl. I'm next. I know it. It's getting closer and closer. This ain't no lifestyle for a sane person."

"If my dad gets here before Raymond, I'll post your bond, give you $500, and put you in a cab to the bus station. You promise me you'll get on that bus?"

Diamond looked at Leslie to see if she was bullshitting her. "Why should I trust you?"

"Because I stabbed my husband. I'm not real high on men right now. I'd stab Raymond just for the fuck of it."

"You didn't stab your husband."

"Not yet. He stole a lot of money from a lot of people, took off, and left me on the hook for it. I swear to God, I see that motherfucker I *will* stab him. What's one more if you're doing life?"

A guard walked to her cell. "Nelson? Your lawyer's here."

"Send him down here."

"Why?"

"Because I said so. Anything you overhear is against my rights. Send him down and get lost."

He left, walking as slowly as he could.

"Hey buddy," Leslie yelled at him. "Pick up the pace."

"How come you talk to him like that? Why aren't you afraid?"

"I'm a taxpayer. He works for me."

"Oh. White privilege." Diamond said.

"That's a myth. It's *green* privilege. If you have enough money, you can do whatever you want."

A large man in a suit approached and called out her name. "Leslie Nelson?"

"That's me."

"Your Dad should be here in twenty minutes. I'm Don Fraiser, the lawyer your dad retained."

"I need a favor."

"I bet."

"This is Diamond. We need to help her. You've got to get her out, give her five hundred dollars, and put her in a cab. Send her to the bus station so she can get home to Virginia. Diamond, you have one month to report to the D.A. Give him Don's card, and your legal trouble will disappear."

"Leslie, you don't even know her real name," her attorney pointed out.

"So what? She needs to get away from here, fast, or else she'll be lost to the streets. My dad will give you the five hundred. Now go to the desk and take care of her first."

"If you say so." He shook his head as he walked away.

"Really? You'd do this for me? How do you know I'll go? You don't even know my real name."

"I don't know. What you do after you get in that cab is up to you, but I don't think you like where you are. I'm giving you a way out. Please take it. Get the fuck out of here, go home, and start over. Whatever you did here, you did survive. If you get on that bus, you can have a life. If not, you'll probably be dead in five years."

By the noise of the guard's keys, they could hear him approach. "You get out of jail free today," he said to Diamond. As he unlocked the door, she grabbed Leslie and hugged her. "Thank you. Thank you. You have no idea what you saved me from. It's Christine. My name. Christine Moore."

"Christine, get on that bus. Keep Don's card. If you need me, call him. Now go."

She practically ran down the hall to freedom. The guard returned. "Got any plans for that one?" He jerked his head at the vomit-covered girl as he unlocked the cell. Leslie turned and looked at the girl.

"I wish I did."

"Follow me. You'll be in conference room B. Your father's here."

He opened the door for her, and she rushed to her dad.

"Oh, Dad, am I happy to see you." She hugged him and wouldn't let go. "Oh. Yeah. You owe the lawyer 500 bucks, plus bail."

"For what?"

"I helped someone out of a jam. I'll tell you the details later." The stress she'd been under caused Leslie to crack. Helping Christine was Leslie's way of avoiding thinking about her own situation. Tears leaked from her eyes and flowed down her face. Her father pried Leslie off and handed her a handkerchief. He looked to the guard who brought Leslie down.

"Would you please get us a box of tissues, and you can go. We need privacy."

After the guard left, they all sat down around the conference table.

Her dad put his arm across her shoulders and squeezed her. The lawyer started talking, but she was numb and couldn't process the information. They finally let her speak. She had to get the words out before she crumbled but didn't have much to say. Leslie said they took her phone, but Paul left her a message.

The night before the shit hit the fan, Paul called and left a voicemail saying he was sorry. The whole thing was so easy initially: moving money around to cover accounts wanting to cash out, he offered double-digit returns, and more money came in by word of mouth. So and so spoke to so and so, the money came in, and nobody was the wiser until the firm hired an accountant who took a good look at the books and noticed some discrepancies—significant discrepancies of missing money. The money disappeared into untraceable offshore accounts.

Paul's message said he was sorry to leave her holding the bag, but since she was unaware of what he was doing, she should be OK. I love you, Leslie. I would never hurt you on purpose, and I wish I could fix things, but it's too far gone. I will miss you every day for the rest of my life was the last thing he said to her.

The voicemail left the admission: Yes, he took the money, yes, he left her, and yes, she should give permission for them to pry into the dark corners of their financial lives because there was nothing to link her to the missing money.

The Federal Bureau of Investigation was still looking through old mail and trash, and she could not get back into the apartment or get clothes to wear. Leslie dissolved into tears, unable to hold it together any longer. A compassionate officer brought her a well-washed sweatsuit that had PROPERTY OF THE NYS *DEPARTMENT OF CORRECTIONS* stamped on it in big letters. She also gave her some socks and those rubber sandals issued to all prisoners.

Her father booked them at a hotel with two suites and a center room. She needed to go back to the precinct in the morning. Bill Phelps ordered dinner for them, but she couldn't eat it. It tasted like the ashes of her failed marriage.

"Dad, what am I supposed to do? I'm almost sixty. I have no job. No place to live. You're at the point in your life where you shouldn't have to deal with this shit. You're too old."

"I may be old, but my faculties are intact. There's not a lot of gas left in the tank, that's true, but since Mom died, I've been wandering around aimlessly with no purpose. Helping you is helping me. You'll always be my child no matter how old you are."

"Child. Me," she gave a little laugh. She threw her fork down. "The boys, Dad, the boys! How do I explain this to them? I don't even have their number. They have my phone!"

"I have it. I'll call the boys and fill them in." He dialed his phone, and to his surprise, the older grandson, Charlie, answered. Bill talked to him for a minute and passed her the phone.

"Charlie! Thank God you picked up. Grandpa told you what happened, but there's more. The FBI is picking me up tomorrow morning." She paused and listened. "I know. He's *gone*. He took his clients' money and left. I don't know why. He never acted any differently." She listened again. "No. Do not come home. Stay as far away from here as possible. I'll call you when I get my phone back. Tell William, too. Do not believe anything in the media. This place is flooded with press. I don't know. I don't know that either. I'll give you a call tomorrow when I have some news. Call Grandpa if you need anything. I love you, boys. OK. Goodbye." She passed the phone back.

"Go to bed, Leslie. Things will look better in the morning."

"You think?" Leslie asked with raised eyebrows.

Bill Phelps looked at his daughter, the pain evident on her face. "Go to bed, Les. I'll see you in the morning."

Leslie couldn't sleep; her mind ran in a continuous loop over the past thirty years. What didn't she see? What clues? What did she miss? Those thoughts operated on one level of consciousness but, on a deeper plane, ran the emotional pain. Leslie could not believe the man she loved and trusted all these years was a stranger. The ache in her chest felt like an anvil pressing the betrayal so deep she doubted anything could ever dislodge it. She fell asleep, but she got no rest from the questions roiling around her brain.

Leslie woke up early and went to the center room to see if there was a coffee machine. As she rooted around, she heard her father enter the room. "Hi, Dad. I'm going to make some coffee. Want a cup?"

"No, I just ordered some room service. Don is coming, and we need to be on the same page."

"I don't know anything. There's no page to get on."

A knock at the door interrupted their discussion. Leslie's Dad rose to get the door. The room service attendant pushed the cart into the room, and Don walked in as the room service person exited. Her father poured three coffees, and they sat around the table to talk.

"Thanks, Bill. Morning, Leslie. Were you able to get any sleep last night?" Don asked, a barrel-chested man who looked like he played offensive lineman in college only to have his physique go soft in middle age.

"Not much. I couldn't get my mind to settle down."

"It looks like it's going to be a long day. I'm here to prepare you."

"For what? I don't *know* anything."

"You know that. We know that, but a lot of people don't. First, the FBI is coming at nine to escort you downtown. Second, the press. The story broke last night, and with the internet, it's front-page news. They know your husband disappeared with one hundred and fifty million dollars of other people's money, and until we can prove otherwise, you were in on it. It'll be like fresh blood in the water, and the sharks are hungry. There might be people who lost money waiting for you. Angry people, so be prepared for anything."

"But I didn't do anything. I lost money, too. My retirement and savings."

"Yes, you did. Others might not be sympathetic. They lost pensions, investments, and maybe other things we haven't learned about yet. But here you are, with your fancy apartment and designer clothes. Look at your engagement and wedding rings. I'd take those off if I were you. We don't want to incite the crowd."

"But I didn't do anything."

"Hand me the rings. Why don't you shower and get dressed, honey." Her father extended his hand.

"Please dress down. No designer goods." Don said.

"I have these," Leslie pointed at her pajamas. "And a sweatsuit from the jail. Let me take a shower and get ready." There was a hair dryer, and Leslie used it to dry her hair but made no effort to style it. The sweats were massive, but at least not orange. A dingy gray from being washed too many times with big, bold PROPERTY OF THE NYS *DEPARTMENT OF CORRECTIONS* stamped across the shoulders and down the leg, there was no way she could hide. She looked in the mirror and didn't recognize herself.

Over the years, Paul had a hand in choosing her clothes and how she wore her hair, evolving her into a prototypical New York City married-to-money Manhattanite. Her presentation was crucial to Paul; Leslie wondered if he did it to project the image of a successful businessman's wife. *All I need is a bag with one of those stupid little dogs hanging out,* she thought. Here, the woman looking back at her seemed minor and diminished. Leslie's face flushed red with rage. *Goddamn you, Paul, you motherfucker. How dare you do this to me? If I see you again, I'll be going to prison for murder, that's for sure,* Leslie thought and composed herself. She was mad and decided to stay that way until this was over. She finished and went back to the table.

"Let me get you a fresh cup. Don wants to go over a few things with you."

Leslie took her coffee and mixed in some cream. "OK, Don," as she sipped her cup. "What happens next?"

Bill Phelps scooted his chair close to his daughter and hugged her. "That's my girl."

Don started in on being ready for the Feds and recommended that she act like her spine was made iron. "You lost as much as everybody else, maybe more. Your whole marriage has been a sham, and the father your sons thought they knew is gone. If you can help it, don't cry in front of anybody. Don't show any emotion at all."

There was a knock at the door. Her father let in one officer and two men in suits. Bill turned and looked at Leslie. "You ready?"

Leslie stood up and straightened her spine. "Let's go. It's showtime."

***

They exited into the lobby. Don looked at her. "I'm sorry, Leslie, but they have to put the cuffs on."

"Handcuffs? Am I being arrested?"

"Could we put them on the front and not behind her back?" Don asked. The officer nodded his okay. Leslie put her hands out in front, and he attached the cuffs.

"For right now, yes. It's just a formality. If there's any press out front, it looks like we are taking this very seriously. Paul Nelson stole a lot of other people's money. Keep your head down. Do not engage. The two gentlemen from the FBI will escort you to the car. Once you're in, they'll take their vehicle and escort you to the precinct, where your dad and I'll be."

The police car parked right in front of the hotel. *They certainly want to create a scene,* thought Leslie. There were only a few newspeople out front. Someone must have spent all night on the hunch her dad was staying at a hotel, calling them looking for Mr. Phelps and getting lucky. After exiting the lobby, Leslie saw a few camera flashes and people shouting, "Mrs. Nelson! Where's your husband?" The press yelled at her. "Mrs. Nelson!" the Federal Agent put his hand on her head to make sure she didn't bang it as he

12

guided her into the back seat, where she sat just like on TV. It was a favorite photograph the press used often.

It was completely different at the station. A crowd of media people and many people who were promised double-digit returns but ended up with double-digit goose eggs. The thought of her in jail sweats and handcuffs certainly made her look guilty, and she could feel the rage start to bubble.

"Mrs. Nelson! Do you know where your husband is?" "Mrs. Nelson! Would you like to make a statement?"

"Mrs. Nelson! Where's the money?" Media people of all kinds were waiting and screamed at her as soon as she got out of the car. She heard the click of many cameras. The Feds stood on each side of her, holding her by each elbow, and they started up the stairs. "Mrs. Nelson! Where's your husband?" "Mrs. Nelson! Are you in on it too?"

Leslie kept her head down as instructed, but when they reached the top of the stairs, they paused to open the door. Leslie couldn't help but turn her head to look back at the crowd. A man in regular clothes spat at her, landing on her cheek. She put her hands up and slowly wiped her cheek on the sleeve of her jailhouse uniform. One of the men yanked her around to enter the building, and as she turned, she locked eyes with the man who spit on her. He smiled at her with satisfaction until she took aim and spat right back at him, hitting him in the chin. The Feds jerked her around and pulled her into the building. *I wish I could see him wipe that look off his face along with the spit,* Leslie thought.

✳✳✳

Her dad was waiting for her, Don already in a room emptying his briefcase of details about her case. The Feds left her at the front desk and disappeared. The man in the wingtip shoes was there, apparently the lead detective.

They took mug shots and fingerprinted her. Leslie had about enough, and they hadn't even started. Once she was processed, they brought her to be with her dad in Exam Room B.

Everyone introduced themselves and sat down. Leslie looked around the room. It was painted a drab green with a big mirror that covered an entire wall. This was a room where they tried to sweat the guilty party into confessing. She loved Chicago P.D. She wasn't going to say anything until they took the cuffs off.

The detective and Don talked to each other over her head about details pertaining to her case. Don turned to her.

"Ready to start, Leslie?"

Instead of being scared and cowering, Leslie pushed back hard.

"No, I am not." She said defiantly. "Why am I here? Are you going to arrest me? Did I just get arrested? Is it all for show? Bullshit. If all this is 'for show,' it doesn't work for me. Read me my rights. What's that called? My Miranda rights? And what exactly am I charged with?"

Mr. Wingtip read her her rights. "You are being charged as an accessory to wire fraud and money laundering for now. More charges may be forthcoming depending on today's outcome." Leslie swore she saw him smile.

"Who is watching on the other side of the glass? Take these cuffs off since they are 'for show.' I am not saying a word until you tell me why I'm here."

Her father put his hand gently on her arm. "Les, we need to see where this is going before you get upset, honey."

"Fuck that. I'm a tax-paying citizen, and they work for me. I want some answers." She realized she had used foul language in front of her father. "Oops, sorry, Dad. I didn't mean to swear."

The FBI man named George decided to play bad cop. "Mrs. Nelson, don't be too sure about being a taxpayer. The IRS is also investigating your husband. And you, too." *Fuck you, Paul. What an asshole,* she thought. "FBI, IRS, I'd like to buy a vowel."

Mr. FBI jumped, startled some lady dared sass him; he bent close to her ear but spoke loudly. "Enough of this. We will discuss yesterday, and you're going to be very helpful. Very Cooperative." His breath smelled of mint with a hint of coffee. Leslie was grateful for the breath mint.

"I'll tell you, from my point of view, how it happened to me. But I want to know where I stand legally."

"Legally, you're a witness. You could be considered an accessory to wire fraud and held indefinitely because you're a flight risk, and that's why you were booked. An officer will accompany you home and get your passport. How it goes from here is your call." Mr. Wingtip said.

"Take these off, please," Leslie put out her hands, her wrists forward. They were removed, and she rubbed her wrists. "I'll tell you what happened yesterday morning. Yesterday, at six in the morning, there was a pounding on my door. I answered it, and all these people busted in, and someone who never identified themselves slapped me with a search warrant. They ripped through my house, kicked Paul's office door open, and destroyed a valuable antique desk. I didn't have a chance to look at the warrant, so I don't know what they were looking for or if they found it.

"I didn't realize Paul wasn't home, and he didn't say he wouldn't be the day before. I thought maybe he was at the gym. Everything happened so fast. You have my phone. Paul left me a message, but I didn't get it until yesterday morning. I thought I'd get Paul to come home and explain everything, but I saw he left a voicemail. He said a lot of things, but I couldn't hear it because it was so noisy. Then, some guy ripped it out of my hands. Get my phone. I want you to listen to the message. I'll put it on speaker so we can all hear it."

They waited a few minutes, and someone handed it to Detective Wingtip. He came over, the phone in a plastic bag marked evidence. "It's got to stay in the bag."

"Why?" Leslie asked, wrinkling her nose. "Are you afraid I'll contaminate it with my fingerprints? My fingerprints are all over it. After all, it is *my* phone. Let me get this out, and you can hear the message." Leslie got the phone out and put it on speaker. After it finished playing, she put it back in the bag with great care. "See. He confessed to everything and took off without my prior knowledge to parts unknown. I can't help you.

"Furthermore, he stole all *my* money and *my* investments. He stole 30 years of my life. He *erased* my life. My poor kids have to live with the fact their father left them without saying goodbye, and the guy who left wasn't their father. Their father would never do that, but that asshole did. Do you know what ices the cake? He ran off with another woman. He's a thief. An embezzler and a cheating rat bastard to boot. I got a lot of shit to take care of, so are we done here?"

The three men left the room. Leslie waved to the people behind the mirror. "Dad, what am I supposed to do? I'm broke. I'll have to sell the apartment. I'll be broke *and* homeless."

"We can talk about that later. Let's wait to see what happens here."

"Like what, Dad?"

"We can talk about that later, too."

"Wait a minute. Am I going to have to stay here *overnight*? I don't think so." Leslie's voice got loud and had a sharp edge to it.

"Don't be like that, Leslie. Calm down. They're just doing their job. We'll get you out of this as soon as possible."

When all was said and done, she was released under house arrest, but since she was unable to stay in her home, they released her in her father's custody. Once again, they told her it was for show. Paul committed a serious crime, and they wanted everything above board. Leslie had to wear an ankle bracelet that traced her every move. An officer will be stationed in the lobby, and leaving the hotel required her to call and receive permission. Leslie was tired and couldn't listen anymore. She trusted her dad was paying attention.

"Could we get something to eat at the hotel restaurant? I'm starving and they didn't serve lunch. Aren't starving prisoners against the Geneva Convention or something?"

Bill Phelps looked at his daughter and couldn't help but laugh. "The Geneva Convention refers to prisoners in times of war, Leslie."

"That's me, dad. They are holding me hostage." After they were dropped off at the entrance, they noticed a uniformed officer standing there. Leslie saw him and made a beeline for him. "Are you hungry? Would you like to join us for dinner?"

The officer smiled at her. "Unfortunately, I'm still on the clock, so I need to pass. Thanks for the invite, though."

Her father talked to their police escort. He said he would be there tonight, and a replacement tomorrow would get her passport. Right now, the ankle bracelet recorded her location there. If there was any movement, they would know and haul her back to jail, where she would stay.

They sat down at an empty table in the hotel restaurant. Leslie was starving. They each had a glass of wine and talked about where things would go from there.

"I have to leave tomorrow, but Jenny is coming to stay with you."

"Jenny? Why?"

"Because your family is going to help you through this. I'd worry if you were left alone to handle this media circus. Your sister is good at coming out strong, and you can't handle all this alone. She said she'd be happy to come and stay with you."

"Dad, she has a husband and a family. Jenny can't leave them. She has an obligation to her family."

"She also has a housekeeper, and the kids are in high school. They can drive her car, and Rob will be on call."

"I don't think she should be involved in this," Leslie said and sipped her wine.

"She's not involved. Neither she nor Rob gave Paul any money. She's coming in first thing in the morning. I wish I could stay, but I have some important business. Finish your wine, and let's get you to bed."

Leslie and her dad didn't talk on the way back to the room, and once inside, Bill kissed his daughter's cheek. Whether it was the adrenaline fading from her body or plain exhaustion, Leslie brushed her teeth and fell into a dreamless sleep.

The following day, her dad called room service. They brought breakfast and hot coffee. He needed to head out and speak to whoever was on detail and get an update on the changes. He gave her a big hug. "I love you, Les. We'll get through this. I promise."

"I know, Dad. I love you, too. I'm glad Jenny's coming. I'm still in shock Paul would do this to me, to us. He's, he was, my husband. He said he loved me, that he still loves me. I don't know what to do."

"Don't worry, Les. You'll get through this. We'll get through this together. I hate to leave, but it's important that I get home."

"I understand, Dad. I'm grateful you came. You got me through the worst of it. I'll wait for Jenny. We'll order one of each dessert and a bottle of wine while we wait. Oh, wait a minute. I don't have any money. The Feds took everything, even my credit cards. I can't pay for any of this. I'm poor, Dad. Poor."

"Don't worry about it. It's on my card, so stay as long as you want." He kissed her goodbye and left.

Leslie sat in a chair and looked for something mindless to watch on TV. She pressed the remote until she found a talk a show featuring fathers awaiting the results of paternity tests. It really didn't matter. Leslie couldn't help but think about her marriage and where the hell Paul went. *That miserable fuck,* she thought, and her mind wandered back to when it all started, searching for clues she missed. When did it start? What didn't she see? When did he change? Or he was always this way, and Leslie was simply collateral damage.

✳✳✳

During college, Leslie interned at a big-money Wall Street investment firm, where she met Paul Nelson, tax attorney. A highly sought-after single man, he was both rich in looks and money. Leslie was buried under paperwork in the very back, so far back from the C-suite she wondered when he had a chance to notice her, let alone get the idea to talk to her. It was probably by accident or mindless chit-chat since they both were on the elevator going down.

"Going to lunch?" he asked. Leslie thought he was just being polite.

"It is my break, but I'm only getting a slushy from the place on the corner."

He looked at her. She had dark hair and big dark eyes. A weakness of his. She was very pretty with a great smile, another weakness. "A slushy? I haven't had one of those in ages. What flavor?"

"Lemonade. They make a really good slushy."

"I'd love a slushy." They reached the lobby and exited the elevator. "Here. Show me where I can get a really good slushy, and I'll buy." He held the door open for her.

"I'll show you, but you don't have to buy."

They walked to the corner. She reached for the door. "In here." Leslie smiled. He'd probably never go into a place like this on accident, and definitely not deliberately. She made sure he wanted a lemonade and ordered two. Leslie spoke to the man behind the counter in Spanish, and while they waited, she bent over to scratch the bodega cat that silently appeared between them. "Hola, Nina." The orange cat purred loudly.

"You're her favorite customer. She stays away from everybody else. Here's your slushes." The owner's name was Mr. Alvarez, but he went by Al. He set them on the counter. Paul grabbed his wallet and, pulled out a black Amex, and set it on the counter. The owner shook his head at the card. Leslie handed him back his card and gave the man a twenty.

"He doesn't take cards for small purchases," Leslie said and handed him his cup.

"Sorry about that. I don't carry cash as a rule."

"Da nada. It's on me." She turned to exit.

"Adios, chica."

"Adios, Al." Leslie held the door open for Mr. Nelson, and they exited into the bright afternoon light.

"What do we do now?" He asked. "This *is* a really good slushy."

"I usually walk back to the office, lean against the building, and people-watch." Leslie looked at her watch, a Timex she bought at a drug store. "For about fifteen more minutes, and my break will be over."

He suddenly felt self-conscious about his Rolex. "I'm embarrassed I offered to pay and didn't have any money," he said as he leaned next to her against the building. "I'm even more embarrassed I never asked you your name. I'm Paul Nelson, by the way."

"Please. It was no big deal. Everybody knows who you are, Mr. Nelson. I'm Leslie Phelps."

"Please stop with the 'Mr. Nelson.' Call me Paul. Why did you speak to him in Spanish? He answered you in English."

"Yeah, I know. I'm trying to practice Spanish as a second language, for the heck of it. Conversational Spanish."

"Who do you report to? Learning a skill that's valuable and nobody's requiring you to do it? That shows initiative. You should get a raise."

Leslie laughed. "The H.R. department. I can't get a raise because I don't really work here."

"What does that mean?"

"It means my presence is part of a college internship program. I am unpaid labor for six weeks. This would be part of my degree, so I am indirectly paying you as part of my tuition to totally use and abuse me as unpaid labor."

Paul felt bad. There were so many people like her who worked-really worked. Not careers, plain old jobs. They had no financial advisors to move their money around. They had no need for one because after they made rent, tuition, and other expenses, there was not enough left to earn a commission worth pursuing. He personally never lived in such financial stress. Paul went to a prep school and spent summers out in the Hamptons with his grandparents. Leaning against the wall gave him a chance to look at the world at large and segments of society he would normally if he were honest with himself, ignore.

Leslie didn't seem bothered by it in the least. They rode the elevator; she got off two floors below theirs. "See you upstairs," she said with a little wave.

Paul got off the elevator at their floor. He saw no sign of her and went in his office. He closed the door and sat deeply in thought. He thought about her, how she was so composed about it all. Like little ants coming through a crack in the cement, every day, people knew their mission for the day and headed off to get it over with so they could be home by five for cocktails with the spouse. Paul usually worked past seven and had a car service drive him home. He poured his own scotch.

***

The next day, he went upfront to the receptionist on the pretense he was expecting a package, but his motive was to time it when Leslie took her break. He made the poor receptionist call around, looking for a nonexistent package. Paul stalled as much as he could, but he decided he must have missed her. He turned to go back to his office and ran smack into her.

"Oops. Sorry about that." He spoke. "Going out for a slushy? I need to run back to my office for a minute. Would you mind waiting for me in the lobby?"

"Sure." He hurried away. "Nancy, I'm going out for a minute. Do you want me to bring you back anything?"

Nancy. That was the receptionist's name, Paul thought. *I should probably learn some of these people's names around here. Couldn't hurt to be personal.* Leslie confused him. She was so nice to people, and they responded in kind. Leslie was nice when there was nothing to gain from it.

She waited for him in the lobby. They went to the bodega and got their slushies. He remembered to bring cash. Al spoke to Leslie. "You have a new boyfriend, Miss Leslie?" referring to Paul Nelson.

21

"Who?" Leslie said in surprise. "Mr. Nelson? No, he just wanted a really good slushy."

Paul was taken aback. Most girls giggled or blushed when he was around. He never questioned it before; girls behaved that way since puberty. Leslie acted like he was so far out of her league there was nothing to be gained by indulging in the delusion he had any interest in her whatsoever. Her complete lack of interest in him is exactly what made him interested in her. Paul was never short of women who wanted to be on his arm or in his bed. Maybe she thought she was so young he'd find her boring with no common interests. They finished their drinks.

"Oh, well. Back to the grind," she said.

"Hold up a minute. What time do you get off work?"

"Me? Five. I get home around six. Why?" she asked.

"Because I'd like to take you out for dinner this evening, but I'll be tied up until six. Is it too much to ask you to hang around until I'm finished? Kill some time? Go shopping, maybe?"

"I'm not sure, I'm supposed to get involved with a higher-up, or you're supposed to take up with an intern. There's an imbalance of power here. Things could get sticky for you. I could be a real psycho bitch, for all you know. I could ruin your career."

Like she could ever get enough power to do that, he thought. *The fact she's concerned about it, though, validates my instincts she's trustworthy.* "How about this? We have one dinner, as friends. I'll have my driver bring you home."

Leslie was quiet for a moment, evaluating the risks. He had more to lose than she did, plus she'd avoid the subway on a hot day like this. "OK, yes. One dinner. That's all. I'll meet you in the lobby at 6."

They got on the elevator, and again, she got off two floors below. "See you at six," she said as the doors closed.

She was sitting in the lobby reading a book when Paul arrived at 6:30. He rushed from the elevator with his jacket and metal briefcase in his arms. Paul raced over, afraid she stayed only to scream at him, 'Don't ever speak to me again!' And storm off in a huff. He was surprised she sat there, nonplussed, unaware he was late.

"You're late? Huh." She looked at her drugstore watch and shrugged. "I guess you are."

The sight of that watch irked Paul to no end, but he couldn't do anything about it. He wanted to drag her downtown, stop at Cartier, and find a suitable watch for a wrist as delicate as hers, but he was sure that would be his last contact with her and perhaps a restraining order to follow. Paul approached her cautiously. "Sorry about that. My conference call ran over."

"You know, that's the second time you apologized to me. Three strikes, and you're out." Leslie stood. "Where are we going tonight?" She packed her bag; he donned his jacket.

"I wasn't sure, but since it's a beautiful night I know the perfect place. He took her downtown to a rooftop restaurant, close enough to see the hospital down the street have a medical emergency helicopter land on its roof. Leslie enjoyed it very much. She was interested in everything but him. She talked to the waiter for ten minutes about the freshest dessert. The helicopter landing was fascinating. The meal was delicious. He finally interrupted her.

"I'm curious. Don't you want to know anything about me? We've sat here all night, and you haven't asked me one question. You're infatuated with everything but me."

Leslie laughed. "Order another round and we can talk."

"Done," and their drinks magically appeared.

Leslie took a sip and looked at him. "Why me?"

"I don't understand the question."

"Don't give me that bullshit. You have girls throwing themselves at you if you sneeze in their direction. Your building is full of available women. You're not wearing a wedding ring, so I am assuming you aren't married. Is my assumption correct?"

"Yes. Divorced."

"Children?"

"No."

"OK. Those questions are dealbreakers. If you had either I'd say, call your car and take me home. So again, I ask, why me?"

It was his turn to sit back and study her. "I honestly don't know. Maybe it's your calm disposition. We work in a high-pressure environment, and when things are down to the wire you act totally aware but unconcerned. You are extremely pretty, but there are a million pretty girls in this city. My answer would have to be your way with people. Like Al. He's Hispanic and instead of judging him for being an immigrant, you are curious enough to try to learn Spanish from him.

"The bodega cat loves you, and from what Al said she hides from everybody else. You talked to the waiter at length about dessert. You were in awe of the helicopter landing. You're right about women. I don't know if it's my looks, my job, or my bank balance, but there never seems to be a shortage of interested females. You, on the other hand don't seem to be attracted to anything I have to offer. I think that's why.

"We met on the elevator by accident, you took me to get a slushy and bought mine when I didn't have any cash. Most women would stand there and wait for me to buy theirs, but you already had the cash out and no expectation of me doing anything. What could have been an embarrassing situation for me wasn't because you took care of it. Why do you get off the elevator before our floor?"

"Well, Mr. Nelson," he gave her a look. "Paul, it's because I don't want any trouble. You know what happens in the boardroom, but I know what happens in the break room. All it would take is one person to see us together and start a rumor, and rumors spread like wildfire. Even if there's no substance to the rumor, it doesn't matter. Mostly because people are bored, they love to gossip. A member of the C-suite messing around with a college intern is one hell of a juicy rumor. It has legs so it could last all summer. I avoid any possibility of that occurring. I'm only here temporarily, but a rumor like that connected to your name might have ramifications that could come back and bite you in the ass when you least expect it, so I get off at seven and take the stairs."

"You get off on seven to protect *my* reputation?" He sounded stunned.

"Yeah, and mine. It wouldn't look good on my review if everyone's talking about me sneaking around with a man of position and power. I have my senior year left and I'm done. I've worked too hard to blow it now."

A thought came to Paul as she talked. "How old are you, Leslie?"

"Twenty-one. Why? How old are you?"

"Thirty-two." He calculated their age difference. It didn't really matter, but there was a gap. How big a gap he wasn't sure. She didn't seem young and naïve; she seemed wise and mature beyond her years. Still, there were lot of experiences after college he already grew past, and they were on her horizon.

They had already discussed the differences in their backgrounds. His all-boy prep school against her public school one. She grew up in a small town upstate where her family still lived.

He grew up in a tony estate in Connecticut, summered in the Hamptons, and graduated from Harvard. She spent her summers at a country club, but working at the Snack Shack by the pool, scooping ice cream and serving pizza. The only reason she was there was NYU gave her the best financial aid package and she wanted to experience life in the big city.

"You've been here three, four years. How do you like it here?"

"It's like any place else. It has its good and bad points. Good as in culturally, there's never a shortage of things to do or see. Bad? It's expensive. I live with two other girls in a one-bedroom apartment. Two people get the bed, one on the futon. It's not so bad, one of my roommates is in med school so she's rarely there, but if she is she gets the bed. She's so tired Frankenstein could crawl into bed with her. We're all very good friends, but if you want to be alone with a guy, you better go to his place."

Paul saw an opening and he took it. "How about you? Any special guy in your life?"

"Just you," she said with a laugh, and he choked on his coffee. "Sorry about that. I couldn't resist. When I decided to come here, my high school boyfriend wasn't happy about it. He thought I shouldn't go so far away, and if I did it meant I didn't care enough about him. So, I called his bluff and said I was coming here. He called my bluff and told me it was over if I left. I decided he was a jerk, issuing me an ultimatum like that. I wasn't bluffing, and that was the end of him. As far as anyone here, I've kissed a few but nobody thrilled me. Besides, I was having too much fun to get tied down. I've got some decisions to make this year. Do I find a job and stay here? Go back home and look for something, or maybe go out west and work on my masters."

Go out west? Good God. I'm no better than the guy from high school. I don't want her going anywhere, Paul thought.

"How about where you are now? Would you like me to see if I can find a place for you?"

"Thanks, but no. The idea of staying here is great, but I can't afford it. My major is business, which means nothing. Maybe I'll work in a bank. I'm good with numbers, and I've got time to figure things out. There's the college career placement program. Perhaps there's something there."

"I'm sure you won't have any problem whatsoever. Whoever hires you will be lucky you're on their team. The financial part. You could move out of the city and commute."

"I've lived here long enough to know it's not worth the commute. Why spend an hour each way to get to some job I'll probably hate in a year?"

"You're not interested in a career?" Paul asked, surprised. "You seem so good with people. You actually enjoy people."

"It's not that. I try to live in the moment, and if I'm around people, I try to enjoy it. Plus, I'm interested in people. Everybody has a story. As far as a career, I'm not that hungry. If you want to climb the corporate ladder, I guess you have to be cutthroat. That's not me. I'd rather work in a bodega. Why'd you become a lawyer?"

"Two reasons. My father was a judge, and I always looked up to him. Two, I like money. I'm good with it. I have a knack of making a lot out of a little."

"I suppose I could go home and work for my dad." Leslie said. "He's a developer. Like you, he can make money out of money, he takes outdated projects like strip malls and repurposes them. He took an abandoned one and created a physician's office park. Most physician's offices have those buildings with soaring atriums in the center, square footage you'll never make a penny off. Now, if you switch to a plaza, people can drive up to an office. Free parking, and you're not making a sick person walk in circles trying to find the office."

"Your father sounds like a visionary. There're so many empty plazas. It's genius. Puts them back on the tax rolls. Patients benefit and the doctors aren't paying on overhead on space they don't use." Paul registered her father's company for further investigation.

"I'm sorry, but this cheesecake isn't going to eat itself," Leslie said and took a bite. "Heavenly. Want a bite?" She extended the plate to him. Paul used his fork and took a bite. It felt intimate to him, sharing food. "It is heavenly."

It took a while, but they gradually relaxed. They shared the cheesecake. The two forks spooning each other on the plate could be taken as an omen to their futures.

Paul called the car around and drove her through traffic to her place near the university. He got out first, came around, and opened the door. He escorted her to the stairs and kissed her cheek. Leslie thanked him for a lovely time, and he said he'll see her soon. Paul watched as she entered the building, with a concern it might not be the right neighborhood for her. There was nothing he could do about that, either.

***

The next couple of days Paul was tied up in meetings. There was no way to get a message to her and he didn't want her to think it was because he found her boring and dull at dinner. He didn't know her phone number or address. Paul thought if showed up at her apartment and camped out waiting for her he'd spook her. He decided to get creative.

Later, after lunch, the reception desk called her upfront. There was a delivery for her. Waiting for Leslie was a large bouquet of flowers. Two or three women came over, curious about the flowers. Women love flowers and having them delivered to the office was exciting and romantic.

Leslie saw them and her eyebrows raised in surprise. "These?" she said and pointed at the large bouquet. "For me? These are for me?"

"Yes," said Megan, the receptionist said. "Who are they from?"

"I have no idea."

"Come on! Open the card!" said Julie, an administration assistant from another department.

"Here goes nothing." Leslie said and ripped opened the card.

"Who is it? What does it say?"

"Huh," said Leslie. "'Thinking of you.'"

"That's it? That's all? It doesn't say from who?"

"No. Just think of you."

"You have no idea? Guess! Do you have a secret admirer?"

"Sorry, guys. No idea. And no secret admirer. I'm either here or at my apartment."

"Any cute guys in your building? Anybody hanging around hoping to catch your eye?" Meghan asked.

"No clue. I have no idea."

"How are you going to get them home?"

"I can't take them on the subway. Maybe I'll leave them here."

"Can I have them, Les? Leave them up here?" Meghan said. If they were left here, she could pretend she's the one with a secret admirer.

Leslie reached out and took the vase. "No, I'll bring them in the back. Nobody's ever sent me flowers before, and I'd like to enjoy them. You can come visit any time you want."

There was a murmur of male voices that grew louder as a group of professional men moved toward the front. Upper management and partners, judging from the tailoring. Not an off-the-rack suit in the crowd. Leslie held the vase and waited for the crowd to pass. The last man to exit was Paul Nelson. He looked at her, glanced at the flowers, and winked. Leslie felt a flush from her collarbones to her hairline. She pretended to show the flowers to another girl. Once he was gone, she took the flowers to the break room and placed them in the center of the table. They were so pretty she left them there for everyone to enjoy.

✳✳✳

The next day they were leaning against the building drinking their slushies. "Oh, Paul. Thank you so much for the flowers. Everyone loved them."

"Everyone who?"

"The staff. I left them in the break room for everyone to enjoy."

Paul pressed his lips together and tightened his jaw. "Those flowers were for *you*."

"I know. I loved them. I thought it might give a few old ladies a thrill. Why? What's wrong with that?"

"I wanted you to have them at your desk so every time you looked at them, you'd think of me until every last petal dried up and fell off, but you'd keep the vase to put your pens in."

"Wow. All that. I don't need to see something to remind me of you during the day."

"You don't?"

"No. I don't. I think of you anyway."

Something happened in Paul. An internal shift where it was once soft and sloppy now turned firm and solid. He turned his head to looked at her profile, thinking how perfect it was.

Paul watched her check her drugstore watch. "Time to go. Break's over."

He held the door open for her. As they waited for the elevator to come, he said, "Meet me at 6?"

The doors opened and she got in. "Yes," she smiled.

"I'll wait for the next one," he said as the doors closed.

***

They saw each other a couple of times a week, either at lunch or out to dinner. Leslie looked forward to their moments and was afraid she was falling for him. *Like he'd actually be interested in me, some dumb college kid. He seems so much older and more sophisticated, and I'm like a newborn calf,* she thought. In spite of herself each time she saw him it only got worse. Leslie's time at his office was coming to a close. Her internship would be over, and she'd be back on campus. Leslie thought he'd forget her name by Christmas.

It was after six. Usually his lateness never bothered her, but her mind wouldn't shut off about their future. Her future, not his. Paul probably had

30

the next five years mapped out, but he wouldn't be as successful as he was by being wishy-washy. She felt like she already outgrew college, but she had to finish. It was only one more year.

"A penny for your thoughts?" Leslie was lost in her reverie and didn't see him approach.

"Oh, hi, Paul. I didn't see you. I must have been daydreaming," she said as she stood. They exited the building, and she stopped. He kept walking. After a few steps he asked her if she was coming. She hurried to his side. "Aren't we waiting for the car?"

"No. I thought it was a nice night for a stroll." He reached out and held her hand as they walked. It was like he read her mind. She was trying to figure out where to go from here and he took her hand. He took them downstairs to an exclusive dining room. There was a courtyard off the dining room with tables lit with by candlelight and big bulbs strung about giving it a very al fresco atmosphere. They were immediately seated.

"This place so cool." Leslie said, looking around. "I love the lights. It looks like Italy."

"When were you in Italy?"

"Never. Does it look like this?"

"Yes, I suppose it does."

"When did you go?"

"On my honeymoon."

"Ouch," Leslie said. "Sorry."

"Believe me, I'm the one who's sorry." He gave a little laugh. "I have a present for you." He handed her a box tied with a red ribbon.

Leslie put the box down. She pushed her hands forward. "I don't, I can't, I shouldn't. I mean I can't accept a gift."

"Why not?" Paul said, smiling at her discomfort.

"It wouldn't be appropriate. I mean, we're friends. Colleagues, almost. I haven't done anything to deserve a gift."

Paul expected her to respond like this. He laughed. "Yes, we are friends, that's true. Colleagues? I don't think so. I don't think I've seen you more than once in the office. When do you finish your internship?"

"Next week is my last week."

"So, we aren't really anything to each other." He looked her in the eye. Her eyes were large and luminous, her lips slightly apart, her features soft and delicate, and a red flush across her face. *She's so beautiful and she doesn't even know it,* he thought. "I think I'd like to change it. I'd like us to be more than friends. You have to admit we get along quite well."

"Yes, we do but I feel like a little kid around you. You're so worldly. You're light years ahead of me in life."

"I've had the time to do more, experience more, but so what? I'm like the bodega cat."

"What does that mean?"

"I imagine the bodega cat's been around a bit. She looks like he's been in a few scraps and hides herself away to avoid getting in anymore. You walk in and she lights right up. She comes over to you and starts to purr. Loudly. Like a boat motor. All she wants is some attention from you. That's all I want-some attention from you. Open the box." Paul told her. She did.

"What the fuck-" Leslie clapped a hand over her mouth and looked at him. "You want to give me a watch? A *Cartier* watch?"

"Yes. From the moment I met you. You wore that cheap dime store watch, and I thought how sad. You deserved so much more. Every time, you check the time I wanted to rip it off your wrist and get something more appropriate."

"My watch is fine. It keeps perfect time." Leslie put her hand defensively over her watch. Paul saw her do that and smiled.

"Just try it on. See how it fits." He waited until her watch was on the table and put the new one on her wrist. As he pulled his hand back, he palmed her old watch. He wanted to sneak it to the waiter with instructions to pitch it in the trash, but that might offend her, so he slipped it in his jacket pocket. Leslie put her hand out and admired the watch. It sparkled like a star under the dim light.

"Paul, this watch is stunning. I can't accept a watch like this. It's too much."

"It's perfect. Consider it a goodbye present from the office. Or a graduation gift from me. It belongs on your wrist."

The waiter brought their drinks and took their order. After he left Leslie looked at the table. "Hey. Where'd my watch go?"

"Don't worry. It's in a safe place."

"Paul, I've got a problem with this."

He looked over his glass at her. "You don't like it?"

"I love it. It's beautiful, but I'm some broke college kid. I wear a watch like this people are going to notice. I don't like being noticed. I like to be as ambiguous as possible. Wearing a watch like this is a beacon. People who don't know me might get the wrong impression. Like, 'if she can afford a watch like this, what else does she have?' I'd be worried about it if I took it off. Someone might steal it."

Sorry, sugar. You were born to be looked at, he thought. "I didn't give it to you to make you uncomfortable, I gave it to you because I like you. A lot. But you're right. It might be too extravagant for school. So, let's make a deal." He put her old watch back on the table. "If you accept it as a gift from me, I'll hang on to it. When we're together, you'll wear it. When you're on campus, wear that one. Deal?"

"Deal. But what if someone asks me about it?"

"Say it's a knockoff you bought on Canal Street."

The waiter brought their meals out with another round. She picked up her wine glass. "Here. Let's toast on it." He picked his up. "A toast. To us," Leslie said, a with resounding clink of her fluted champagne against his.

"I like the sound of that. To us." He tilted his glass towards hers, and they clinked them together again and laughed.

✱✱✱

She finished up her internship and headed back to campus. Paul did have her number and called every night. They didn't have too much in common, both at different stages in their lives, but it didn't get in the way. He asked thoughtful questions, and she answered them. She asked him the same questions and he gave thoughtful answers. On Saturday they spent the days doing touristy city things. Leslie, for spending so much time there, saw very little of it. Paul was an excellent guide and a perfect gentleman. They were walking in the park. He stopped and looked up. She followed his gaze but saw nothing.

"Well, doesn't that beat all," he said, still looking up.

Leslie stood closer and looked up. "There's nothing up there. You're crazy."

"You don't see it? Mistletoe," he took her in his arms and kissed her. He felt her relax and she started to kiss him back. *For someone who thinks she's naïve to the whole boy meets girl concept...*he lost his train of thought. He thought he was kissing her, but she was kissing him with the heat of a jet engine. All he could do was try to out-kiss her and slow this train down, but she wasn't allowing him to hit the brake. It was all he could do to stand upright. Paul broke them apart, took her hand and sat down on a nearby bench.

"Huh. I never saw that happening." He gasped.

"Never?"

"Not in my wildest dreams did I ever see..."

"Really?"

34

"I'm changing the subject. Let's figure out dinner. We could stop at a store, make dinner and see what develops."

"Why don't we see what develops and order order a pizza later."

"Yes. You wicked, wicked woman."

✳✳✳

She stayed on campus most of the time. Whenever they were near each other, sparks flew, and things caught fire. Plus, she didn't want to ditch her roommate Annie. They were very close friends and Leslie felt there was more than enough of her to go around. Paul didn't try to dictate to Leslie where she needed to be, and her senior year moved ploddingly along. The holidays were coming up quickly, and Leslie needed to plan. She wanted to spend the Thanksgiving holiday alone with her family to clue them in on the status of her love life, hoping to bring Paul home over Christmas to meet everybody. *That's if he decides he wants his life to go in that direction,* Leslie thought.

Paul planned on spending Thanksgiving Day in Connecticut. Usually, he lied and said he was going to friend's and spend the day in his underwear, watching football, and drinking beer. Leslie had changed him somehow. What he used to consider excruciating, spending time with his family, now was enjoyable. With Leslie, everyone had some interesting tidbits that made them unique. *You just have to it wait for them to disclose it. You can't bully it out of them,* she told him.

Leslie told her family about Paul and how he might be the 'one.' Her mother and sister Jenny wanted all the details, her father and brother headed off for more football. They were excited for Leslie, they secretly wondered why she never dated. That wasn't true. She dated, but never the same guy more than twice. When her dad passed by, she asked him what he thought about her getting serious with Paul. He asked enough questions to get Paul might be some mucky-muck high finance Wall Street lawyer, and he didn't care much for them.

"This boy breaks your heart; he'll have to deal your brother Billy. I'll tell you right now. I will not mix business with family. If he has any intention of pitching me the investment deal of the century, he's dead wrong. I don't need somebody's advice on what to do with my money. If he's using you to get to me, it's not gonna help him any. I don't do business with family."

"Thanks, Dad. I guess that's what you think of me- some twit not smart enough to figure out I'm being used."

"Of course not. I'm not worried about you. I'm worried about him. You seem to think I've no confidence in you. I do, 100%, but money does strange things to people."

✳✳✳

Paul and Leslie saw each more. Christmas break was starting, and Annie was doing the spring semester abroad, and KaSu was doing the semester in Germany. Paul asked Leslie to move in with him. Leslie said yes because she'd be living alone that last semester, and she would miss her friends dearly.

Paul came over and helped her pack. He lived in Student Housing one semester and moved into his fraternity house. He didn't understand why this place meant so much to Leslie. It looked like a dump to him. While he loaded up her things, she looked at the place. It had been home for what seemed forever. There were no plans for the roommates meet up and say goodbye. The fall was as far as committed an answer they got from each other.

Paul came in and, put his arm over her shoulders and squeezed. "Take all the time you want to say goodbye. It was a big part of your life." She stood a bit more and took her key off her key ring. Leslie needed to place it in the advisor's mailbox. "I'm ready. Goodbye, room. Come fat, it will be somebody else's apartment."

He arranged to have movers waiting to take her things and put them in storage while he took her to dinner. There wasn't that much. He watched her push her food her plate around but eat very little. "You don't seem happy, Leslie. Are you that sad about moving?"

"Not really, but I imagine it's like a snake shedding its skin. In order to grow, you need leave something behind. I'll be ok. You're the one with more changes. You're going home with me for Christmas, and meeting my family, and coming back to sharing your space after years of living alone."

"After we eat, let's go back, and I'll love you so hard you won't want to live anywhere else."

"I'd like that. I'm feeling a little, I don't know, unmoored. At sea? Unanchored?"

"Well, you're not. You're with me, and I love you. I promise you'll always be safe with me."

They walked back to his, now theirs, apartment. Leslie couldn't help but wonder about the expense of it. The address. A doorman. It had floor-to-ceiling windows overlooking the park and a second bedroom he used as an office. Paul offered her half the office for her needs, a sign of true love in NYC if there ever was one. He was true to his word. Paul loved her harder than she'd ever been loved before, and he held her in his arms until it felt like she melted into him.

***

The visit with her side, he didn't challenge the family motto 'to be happy with enough. Why do you need more?' Contrasted to his side, who had crabs flown in from Alaska for Sunday dinner. Paul felt very out of place. They all had years of riffs and voices back and forth with rapid repartee. Paul couldn't keep up with it. Leslie's mom, Denise, looked at him, she could tell he was uncomfortable.

She walked over and took his hand. "Let's go in the living room, it's a lot quieter in there."

They sat next to each other and talked. Paul could see a lot of Leslie in her. The way she embraced him was just like Leslie. She asked questions about his family; if they were close. His parents were deceased. When he told

Denise that she reached out her hand and took his. "I'm so sorry for you. I can't imagine how a young child could cope with that."

Paul had two much older sisters. His parents split up before he was born, reconciled, and she immediately got pregnant, but the marriage crumbled anyway. Paul could not remember a time when his parents were together for any length of time. Or any length of time without arguing. When it was his Dad's turn with Paul, he would pick him up, and they started to fight. It seemed to young Paul it was one continuous fight. It never resolved. His sisters Carla and Melanie were teenagers when he was small, but they helped buffer his parents. and his grandparents had a place on the shore, and he spent summers there.

His sisters took Paul with them wherever they went. He tried to get small and not talk, afraid they'd say, 'you're here?' and take him home, but they never did. They even took him on their dates, and if any guy had a problem with him being there, that was the last date he'd have with his sister. When Carla went to college, it was Melly who stepped up. When she left for school, he was older. He was old enough to recognize the empty wine and vodka bottles in recycling bin drove a lot of his parents bad behavior. Being older meant he was able to go away to prep school and avoid his parents completely.

When he was fourteen, his father quit drinking and remarried a teatotaler. They got along wonderfully, and Paul found himself furiously angry about his dry dad. Back when he needed a dad he was already three martinis deep to be of any use to young Paul. *How dare he? How dare he leave his mother? Didn't he know she was still drinking a bottle of wine after dinner after drinking all day? Crying because he was happy and she wasn't,* Paul thought.

His father sat him down to talk. His father never talked to him, and it made Paul nervous he wanted to now. His father apologized to him for being a shitty father and for his boozed-soaked childhood. Paul found out the reason he left was for his own sobriety. The arguments that lasted for years were around sobriety. His mother was not ready to admit she had problem, and his dad hit rock bottom and wanted out. His parents couldn't stay together. Their bad habits fed off each other, and his mother dug in. His dad could abandon them, Paul told himself he didn't care. Unfortunately, that was her downfall. Literally, she was shitfaced and fell down the stairs, dead before anyone found her.

His sister Carla got a garbled call from their mother that made the hair on the back of her neck pricker. She left work and ran home to get there before Paul and called their dad to come help. He got there before Paul met him in lobby, and took him out to dinner. Carla took over all the legalities of their mother's demise.

Paul was furious with his mother because she couldn't stop drinking, and his life was upended. He had to move in with his dad and stepmother, Roslyn when he wasn't away at school. She was very kind and tender to Paul. Whereas his mother was always dressed rather formally, Rose was much more relaxed. One Levis, the other Chanel. She let him explode when he hit maximum saturation. He'd lose it, blame her for the destruction of his family. Roslyn let him rage and storm off to his room, and when he returned to apologize, she always shoved a pan of brownies in his hands. Roslyn brushed off his bad behavior. He was grieving. She gave him space to vent, and when he was done, she'd have warm brownies waiting for him.

She told him a bit about her home life, but in the end, it was her mother, her developmental delayed sister Aggie, and Roslyn. Rose worked and supported the family. She made a promise to her mother she would take care of Aggie if her mother passed; Aggie would always be with family. Roslyn had a long-time boyfriend who drew a line in the sand. Her or me. Rose threw him out and slammed the door in his face. No one gave *her* an ultimatum. When her mother died, there was enough money for Roslyn to care for Aggie. She found an adult daycare center. It ran from 10 to 4, and Rose expected it to take an army to convince her it was a nice place.

The first day Aggie was so excited she wore her best dress. Roslyn took her arm and walked her around, explaining what was happening. A few old men said 'Hey cookie' to the new girl. Aggie blushed. One old man said, 'Look, a hottie.' Aggie told him not to be fresh. After about half an hour, one of the attendants came to take her to bingo. Aggie turned to her sister and said, "Goodbye, Rosie. I go to work now." And kissed her cheek.

Roslyn's office let her work 10:30 to 3:30, and she was allowed to bring work home, glad they didn't lose her. She handled the bookkeeping. Aggie had her own 'job,' just like Rosie. 'Working' provided Aggie with a purpose. She blossomed and made friends there. Aggie was too busy to miss her Mom. Three years later, Aggie passed in her sleep. Rose was frantic; her life had a certain rhythm and flow with her mom and her sister, and all that was gone. Not a devout Catholic, but Aggie's passing and the service following left her looking for a connection. To what, she did not know, but the priest recommended grief counseling the church offered on Tuesdays. Not sure it would do any good, she went anyway. Roslyn found stability there.

After the bereavement group was an AA meeting, and that's how she met his dad. Paul didn't know his dad went to AA. Paul learned things about his dad he never knew and got some newfound respect for him. With his mom, it was too late, but all his relatives looked after him like Rose did for Aggie. Everybody stepped up for him when needed. His early childhood was traumatic, but he thought everyone lived like that. When he realized how fucked up his parents were, he was angry, but his sisters were there. When he thought his Dad had walked out on him, boarding school meant he didn't have to face it everyday. His mother's parents knew the reality of his home life. He spent summers with them to avoid the constant drama surrounding his alcoholic parents.

***

PART TWO

"How do you think it went?" Leslie asked Paul in the car on the way home. "I think they liked you."

"I loved your mom. Billy seemed like a good guy, and his wife Stephanie, too. I'm not sure, I'm good enough for your father's little girl, though."

"Don't feel bad. Nobody is good enough for his little girl. Jenny's his little girl, not me. He liked you fine."

"He said as long as I promised to never bring up money, we'd get on fine. He won't do business with family. That was weird, but OK. Once I agreed to that, he was a good. Nice. We shared some of his finest scotch and went out and smoked a couple of Cubans. How does a man who comes off so economically middle class in his personal life have the finest of Scotch and Cuban cigars?"

"Oh, my dad has his vices. Same things other guys do, but with a better class of booze."

Paul thought about how Bill Phelps spun his place in life as a staunch member of the middle class, yet Paul smelled money. It was uncanny how one sweep around the room he could tell who the players were. The Phelps were prospects. He'd look into it after he married Leslie, loving her was a bonus.

They returned to his or rather their apartment. He gave her a diamond ring for Christmas but she wouldn't take it. "I can't believe that's your gift. *An Engagement ring.*"

"Most girls would be overjoyed, but not you. Just take it. We can discuss the date in the future."

"No. I'm finishing up this part of my life. I don't want the weight of that," Leslie said, pointing at the ring. "I can't make decisions now on things if I'm already committed in the future. Take the ring, hide it away. I'll let you know when I'm ready. Right now I'm busy finishing up school. I'm getting a job. I'll work for a while, and decide what comes next later. Don't be offended. I want a chance to live life for a while."

"I'm not offended. I figure you wouldn't take it. It was only to let you know I love you, and I'm calling dibs." Paul said.

"Dibs?"

"Yes. You know, like 'seat saved,' or 'I call it!' 'Dibs.' I call dibs on you." He kissed her to drive the point home.

His sister Carla was hosting an NYE party out at her place in Connecticut and figured Paul wouldn't come, he never did. This year he replied he was coming with a guest. They weren't aware Paul was seeing someone. "He's probably got some snotty bitch," Carla said.

"Yeah, some kind of 'corporate executive Barbie.'" Melly said. Melanie and her husband, Kevin came early to help Carla get organized. Kevin was a successful divorce lawyer and they had a very nice house in Connecticut as well. Rumor had it Martha Stewart was their close neighbor. Carla never married. She was a psychiatrist with more than enough clients to keep her busy. She worked a lot with children who had adult problems placed on their thin shoulders. Memories of Paul as a young child might have had something to do with it.

Paul rented a car and they drove up. "Are you nervous meeting my family?"

"Kind of. You accepting an invitation you normally would pass on, and bringing a date makes me a little nervous. Have you told them anything about me? Anything at all?"

"Nope. You're flying blind here. I've not mentioned you at all." Paul laughed.

"Yes you did. You told them you were bringing a date."

"I didn't say what kind of date. You could be my squash partner."

"I don't believe you. And for the record, I'd kick your ass in squash."

Paul looked at her, a slight smile pulling at the corners of his mouth. "I bet you could, too. I've never played squash."

They arrived early at Carla's to give Leslie a chance to meet his family without a crush of people. Leslie didn't know what to make of his family and their friends. Doctors, lawyers, estates, Money with a capital M. She was a little intimidated, something she wasn't used to feeling. Paul could sense her reluctance and sought to calm her.

"Les, don't psych yourself out over this. You'll be fine."

"I know, I know. I've never felt like this before. Nervous." She grabbed his hand.

"You will be a breath of fresh air in a room full of windbags and blowhards." She smiled and relaxed a bit.

Paul went up to the front door and rang the bell. A darker, heavier female version of Paul answered the door. "It's Paulie! Paul's here." She threw out her arms and smothered him in an embrace so large all Leslie could see were his feet. She released him and grabbed Leslie in the same embrace. "Oh, Paulie, she's lovely! Lovely!"

Paul helped Leslie out from her ample bosom. "Come on, Carla, let go!" Leslie's head appeared. "Leslie Phelps, my sister. Carla."

"Melly! Come meet Leslie! Paulie's date!"

A woman who looked a lot like Paul walked over. *She looks just like Paul, all smooth with no rough edges,* Leslie thought. The name Melly did not fit her. It was too bougie for her. The name Cheris or Bianca were more her style. "Leslie, it's so nice to meet you. My husband Kevin. Kevin, this is Paul's date, Leslie."

Leslie smiled and looked at her directly in the eyes. "Hi. Nice to meet you, Melly. You should change your name. Melly doesn't do you justice."

How quickly this young girl turned the tables. Now, we all going to talk about is Me. Not that I mind, but still... "Another name? What?" Melly said, startled Leslie didn't slink off somewhere like a corner and try to blend into the wallpaper.

"I can't say, I haven't known you long enough. Him either." She waved her hand at Paul. Kevin, who didn't have any interest in his wife's family whatsoever, suddenly found an interest in Paul. He shouldn't be surprised at Paul, he was the ultimate great catch. Rich, attractive, and available. He knew Paul's ex-wife and thought Paul dodged a bullet there. Paul caught her with the dishwasher repairman. The repairman said she came on to him, saying she was divorced.

All Paul said was, 'she will be,' and went directly to a divorce lawyer, Kevin Leibman. Melly's husband. As to the future ex-Mrs. Paul Nelson, she was never seen again.

Kevin watched Leslie without anyone noticing. She was a looker. Paul never dated homely girls. They were expensively dressed, manicured, stiletto-wearing sharks, all on the hunt for a guy like Paul. It never had an effect on him, they were interchangeable women as far Paul was concerned. Except now Kevin could tell Paul liked this girl. His body language tilted towards her. Paul had a satisfied look on his face as if he had chosen well.

Kevin couldn't help noting the age gap. She looked so new, so *young. Paul's fishing in the kiddie pool.*

He joined the rest of the guests. Kevin found it curious how Leslie managed to detect his wife's weak point and go right for it. She hated the name Melly. It was her childhood nickname, and those days were gone. It's Melanie now. *MELANIE. Bitch, more like it,* Kevin thought.

There were cocktails, appetizers, and a full bar. They had a love/hate relationship with alcohol. Their parents split them into two groups: half of them drank rarely, Paul and Carla, and Melly was the one who decided it was their parent's problem, not hers. Melanie and Kevin held no restraint and drank. Leslie fell on Paul's side. She usually had wine with dinner but no cocktail hours. Paul, the same. He was good with just one. If it wasn't for his sisters Paul could have gone in either direction, but his opinion was booze made his dad a monster. Rarely he had more than two, almost never.

There were about thirty couples. If you walked over the hill you could see fireworks at midnight. After dinner some left to wish the New Year in at home with the kids. The people that stayed were those that wanted to party. They'd seen enough fireworks to know they didn't need to see them again. Paul and Leslie were the only ones going. As they walked along, he grabbed her hand. They went over the hill and sat in the cold, damp grass. Paul kissed Leslie and asked her what she thought about this family.

"Your family? Very nice. They have nice friends, too." He kissed her again. "Will you stop, please? I'm trying to talk. What do you think they thought of me?"

"First off, you made a good impression. They were surprised you're so young. That's why we left, to give them time to talk about you."

"Is that bad? You're ten years older. Maybe they think you are too old for me.." She let the sentence trail off.

"You are the perfect age for me. I made all the dating milestones mistakes before I met you. My sisters were not going let an uncivilized, rude, ill-mannered snot loose on the world. I make nice arm candy. I can cook and am a very good kisser. You want to get a head start on the fireworks?" he said and pulled her over onto him.

They walked back. Most of the guests had left by then. The company picked rooms as they got there and Paul, being last was stuck with the room with bunk beds. At least it had its own bathroom. They decided to both stay on one. After a lot of flopping and flipping around Paul went to sleep in the upper bunk.

His sisters were concerned with his choice. Leslie wasn't a bad choice, but. She was a darling. Leslie had much to learn, and while everyone dressed for the evening, she barely got it. A simple black dress fancied up with some vintage rhinestone jewelry. Leslie was a very attractive woman and her flare with antique jewelry lit her up so people didn't look at the Birkenstocks she wore.

The verdict was she was a sweet lovely girl. Paul was hooked. They liked and welcomed her.

"I think your family liked me, don't you?" Leslie asked Paul as they drove home. "I tried to use my manners. I wasn't a huge embarrassment, was I?"

"Fishing for compliments, Leslie?"

"No. I'm trying to make you say I was a hit, everyone loved me, and you are one lucky guy."

"I don't need anybody to tell me how lucky I am to have you, but you were a hit and everyone loved you."

"I'm tired from all this social interaction. I need to be quiet now."

"You just relax. Leave it all up to me."

Leslie moved in and made Paul's apartment their home. Furniture Leslie thought must be some designer's dream was sleek and modern. It looked like it was staged for sale. Not a blanket or throw pillow in sight. No vases, no family pictures, catalogs, or junk mail. Everything hidden away. The trash in a cupboard, and even the salt and pepper were stowed somewhere. It fit his life as a bachelor but Leslie worried she was encroaching on his space and asked him about it. "Paul, am I going cramp your style moving in? It's a bachelor pad. It doesn't feel very homey. Will it bother you if I decorate a bit?"

Paul came up behind her and put his arms around her. He gave her a squeeze. "Leslie, darling, tear it all down and make it look like a barn I don't care. But the goats can't sleep in bed with us."

"How long have you lived here?"

"Oh, eight or nine years. Since I work so much, I can't say I've ever really lived here but it's all yours. It used to be my grand parents. Knock yourself out." Leslie threw an afghan over the sofa and a few pillows around. It was too sterile an environment to make it comfy.

***

They had a lot of fun together. He worked alot, she now had a commute, so the weekends were theirs. It was sleep-in/fool-around until noon on Saturday and do fun things in the city. Even though Leslie lived in NYC for a couple of years, she was a poor student and had no funds to enjoy it. With Paul, anything and everything was on the table.

After hanging around Central Park one afternoon she asked him over dinner about his budget.

"Budget? I don't have a budget." He laughed at her and then realized she was serious. "Or, I don't need a budget. I make a lot of money for a lot of people, and an accountant to keep track of it all. If there's something special you want, use the card I gave you. Buy anything your heart desires."

"The only thing my heart desires is you." Paul smiled when she said that. "I'm a business major with an accounting background. I used to help in my Dad's office. I'm not some ninny who can't get out of her own way."

"I would never underestimate you. Never."

***

When she graduated, her father hosted a party at a rooftop bar. It was such a trendy spot everyone was wowed the hick from upstate picked it out. The reality was a man he golfed with had a daughter who lived in Brooklyn, and Bill Phelps hired her to plan the event. It had an ambiance native New Yorkers had yet to experience, the next Uber place to be. It was a splendid evening enjoyed by all.

Leslie liked a good party and it was, but she was exhausted. Paul told Bill she was exhausted and needed to leave. They made an arrangement for brunch the next day and Leslie was there, no problem. Bill Phelps went to pay the bill and was told, "It was taken of by Paul Nelson."

48

Bill Phelps took it as the sign of a young man who either wanted to show off how much loved his daughter or display how much money he had. Paul could take care of Leslie as good or better than he could. Bill decided Paul did love Leslie, so he should butt out.

***

Leslie and Paul settled in. He did work a lot, and Leslie worked for a temp agency until she found something she liked. Business B.A.'s littered every corner, searching for a bite of the Big Apple. Leslie was lucky. The apartment was in mid-town Manhattan. Leslie could walk twenty minutes in any direction and have an opportunity. She worked a few different positions and was hired as office staff at a large food broker. She was in the health and beauty category. After a few months they promoted her to buyer.

Leslie had her own office and met with reps all day. She had no idea what she was supposed be doing as a buyer of Vitamins and Supplements, and nobody trained her. Leslie figured they'd tell her when she screwed up. She never dreamed there were so many kinds and types of expensive over-the-counter health aids, vitamins, pills, supplements, teas, and so on. That was just scraping the surface. Companies fought like gladiators over shelf space.

Leslie had an assistant hired through a temp agency who did a lot of the grunt work, but Leslie always helped her negotiate the mock-up of a company's display. Kelsie was her name, young and hungry to make her mark. Leslie was more than willing to show her the ropes. A lot of the senior people guarded their jobs like they were nuclear codes, afraid of young and hungry new hires who could accomplish by lunch what took them all day. Leslie was happy to teach people, but Kelsie liked working for her and wanted to learn all she could so she elbowed out any challengers.

Leslie left for work at 7:30 and walked to be there by eight. Paul was just getting out of the shower when she called out "Goodbye. I'm leaving now." Paul came out dripping wet. "Where are you going so early?"

"Work? Remember? I have a job."

49

"Yes, but it's early. Call for a car."

"With traffic I'll get there faster if I walk. Besides, I like it."

"Say that next year."

"If I walk there and back I don't need to use the gym. You take a car and have to stop at the gym."

"There's no need for you to walk, but if you want to that's fine. Promise me you'll take a car if it's raining."

"There's no reason. I won't melt."

"Promise me."

"I have to go, but yes. If it's raining I won't walk."

He walked over to her, dripping wet and wearing just a towel. "Call in sick and go back to bed. I think you have a fever."

Leslie laughed. "I don't have a fever. I can't call and say I won't be in today because my boyfriend has a raging hard-on." She kissed him and left. He went to finish getting ready for work but his mouth curled in a smile. Paul loved that girl, he really did.

Much like she did when she interned she got to know the neighborhood, except there wasn't much designed to cater to the professionals that worked among the tall buildings. She made friends with the man who ran the newsstand.

His name was Manny. There weren't many places around to eat, except if she wanted a hot dog. They were pretty much a cart on every corner. Many of the offices among the skyscrapers had their own in-house caterers. They didn't want the staff to leave the building lest they keep right on going. Leslie usually brown bagged it, a peanut butter sandwich and a piece of fruit.

She was talking to Manny one day, a hot dog in her hand. As she took her first bite, she heard someone calling her name. It was Paul, hanging out of the window of a cab. He paid the cabbie and got out.

"Leslie, what are you doing?"

She held out the hand holding the hot dog. "Eating lunch. Want a bite?"

The idea of eating one of those he found revolting, yet he was starving. "Just one." Paul was surprised at how good it tasted. He almost got one for himself but he was going to a luncheon downtown. She introduced him to Manny.

"Your wife is very pretty, Mr. Paul. Very pretty."

"That's right. I saw her first so don't get any ideas." He kissed Leslie, told her he'd see her at home, and hailed a cab.

She finished her hot dog and went back to her office, smiling at Paul's very short visit.

***

When Leslie moved in, she looked around the kitchen. It was a bachelor's paradise. It lacked things like bread and peanut butter, or regular butter. She opened the stainless steel fridge and found a couple of beers but not much else. "Paul. What gives? Don't you eat? There's no food in this place."

Paul came into the kitchen, looking at Leslie with her head in the refrigerator. "What are you looking for?"

"Food. Something to eat. What do you live on?"

"I have coffee and a bagel when I get to work. For lunch we order out, usually sandwiches. I have a small refrigerator at work with water or soda. Depending on what the evening looks like, dinner with clients. If not, I order two sandwiches at lunch and eat the other one for dinner. I never bring leftovers home. Why?"

"Because I can't live with no food in the house. What if I want to make a sandwich?"

"Order one."

51

"No. I want normal food. You said you were a good cook. Let's plan to have dinner here on Sundays."

"I lied, the part about being a good cook. I lied."

"You *lied?* What else have you lied about?"

"Nothing. It was a spur-of-the-moment untruth. I wanted to impress you, so I lied."

"Well, I know how to cook. I'll teach you. Where's the grocery store?"

He walked to a drawer and pulled out some flyers. "Here. Order whatever you want. They deliver. What shall we cook on Sunday? I'm looking forward to you teaching me everything you know. You might want to look in the cabinets. You may have to order some pots and pans, too."

"Men," Leslie said, a crease appearing between her eyebrows. "Roast Chicken and vegetables."

"Sounds delicious, but I know where we could order one."

"Food, Paul. Eating together, preparing a meal. It's a bonding experience. It's what makes a family a family."

"Family? You think we're a family?"

"The start of one, anyway."

Paul went into the bedroom and came back with his hand in his pocket. "What's the rest of one?"

"Marriage, kids, soccer games, stuff like that."

He took his hand out of his pocket, holding a blue box. "Leslie, I love you. I always have. Do you want to take the next step? Will you marry me?"

"Paul," she smiled, " I think I'm ready to take the next step. Let's get married!" She threw her arms over his shoulders and kissed him. "Let's!"

He picked her up, tossed her over his shoulder, and headed towards the bedroom.

"Paul!" Leslie screamed. "What are you doing?"

He threw her on the bed and jumped next to her. "I'm ruining your reputation. Putting a stain on your good name. Now, no other man will want you."

Paul looked down at Leslie. She was so beautiful with her hair a mess and her dark eyes flashing. Down deep, somewhere in his gut, the thought he didn't deserve her crossed his mind.

"Hurry up and tarnish my reputation!" She reached up and pulled him down on top of her. They loved each other all afternoon and ordered dinner in.

***

Leslie had been out of college a few years, she and Paul lived together the entire time. They hardly ever fought except over money, and it was more a heated discussion than anything else. He had a very casual attitude about it, Leslie was much more cautious. Her family never needed more than they had, and they lived very comfortably, but Bill Phelps knew what it was like to grow up poor. He didn't believe in wasting money. Yes, he gave her mom a Tiffany necklace for Christmas. He wasn't one to throw money around, but he wasn't a total cheapskate. He gave her a luxurious gift and her mother was too self-conscious to wear it. Perhaps her father taught her about money, reinforcing her frugal nature. "It's short trip from the penthouse to the outhouse," he was fond of saying.

Leslie was twenty-five when Paul proposed. The ring was large diamond surrounded by more diamonds. Leslie was like her mother in the way ostentatious displays of wealth made her nervous. She was slowly getting used to living like the cosmopolitan urbanite. Here, her father's lessons and concerns about money seemed archaic and old-fashioned. Leslie was getting comfortable with the Cartier watch and Tiffany engagement ring.

When Leslie was younger, she used to spend time haunting house and garage sales with her mom. Denise Phelps had a stall at the farmer's market. She used to take her second-hand treasures and restore or repurpose them by making them into décor items. Paint, glue, magazines, old books, anything Denise thought she could use they bought it. Leslie created jewelry out of junk and had a successful side hustle. She did that all during high school and vacations. She had her own philosophy about money, partly due to her father's views and the experience of running her own business. It cost money to make money. Return on investment, as it were, and it helped her with her career.

***

Leslie wanted to drive home and immediately show her parents, but Paul said to wait until the weekend. The last time he saw her parents, Paul approached Bill about proposing to Leslie.

They've been together a few years, and Paul wanted to get the 'father's permission' part over with, regardless of when he proposed. Paul dreaded this conversation. They were on the patio enjoying a fine Cuban.

"Bill, how traditional are you?"

"I'm not a traditionalist, and if you want to ask me about marrying Leslie, I've no problem with it. It's *her* you have to convince. If she says yes, have her call her mother to work out the details."

"I'm not sure, it'll be any time soon, but if it's the right moment, I'd like to be ready." Paul said and held his cigar out to look at the burning ash.

"Well, welcome almost to the family, son."

"It's an honor, Dad to be," Paul said.

The two men looked at each other and laughed.

***

Paul had to rent a car since he didn't own one in the city. Since he drove so infrequently, he wanted a car worth driving. He chose a loaded black Audi, unsure if it would be understated enough for his future father-in-law. If he drove up in a Mercedes he was sure Bill would think he was showing off.

An Audi might fly below the radar. It's like Bill did not want to be perceived as a rich man. Paul looked into Bill Phelps's financial history and was more than surprised. He was a man involved in many business ventures and did extremely well. Paul looked through the public records of William Phelps. He could have poked further but felt it wasn't necessary.

Bill Phelps appeared to be an honest man who used his wits and intelligence to accumulate quite a portfolio. A long-term prospect. He wasn't marrying Leslie because he was a ruthless fortune hunter. Paul loved Leslie. Her father's assets were merely side benefit as a rich man didn't hurt.

✱✱✱

Leslie, her Mom, her sister Jenny, and Billy's wife Stephanie all crowded around the kitchen table, Oohing and Ahhing over her ring.

"I can't believe it's so big!" Steffi said.

"It's so bright! Look at sparkle!" Jenny said.

"It's so big, Leslie," her Mom said. "Isn't it a bit much?"

"Not really. It's the same size of most of the other wives. Paul said it's all about the presentation. If I don't look on par with his clients' wives it will cast doubt on his ability to be successful. I thought it was a bit much in the beginning, but I've gotten used to it."

They decided on a late summer date. All the women talked and decided they needed to go dress shopping as soon as possible. Jenny would reconnoiter the dresses and locations, and Steffi the cakes and flowers. Leslie had to check with Paul if he wanted either of his sisters involved and to what extent. Leslie and Paul needed to get back to the city but made plans to return in two weeks. With many kisses and hugs they said goodbye and headed back for home.

"That was quite a visit, wasn't it?" Leslie asked once the ride got underway.

"I wish you told me you wanted to get married up there. I thought we'd do it in the city. It's centrally located."

"But I don't know anybody there. I want to get married at home."

"Leslie, you haven't lived there in years."

"I grew up there. My friends and family live there. It's more than a house I grew up in. It's my *home*. Whenever ever we have a fight and I say, 'I'm going home to Mother!' that's where I'd go. You're a guy. Guys don't get sentimental."

Paul looked at her. Her dark brown eyes were focused straight ahead, a tell she had when she was not willing to discuss the subject anymore. The sunlight glinted off her hair. The wispy hair she had as a child appeared in little strands here and there. He thought she looked angelic. "Baby, we're only getting married once, so have it be everything your heart desires."

Leslie turned and looked at him. "So, it's ok it's out in the sticks? You don't mind?"

How could I disappoint a face like that? He thought. "It's all up to you. Tell me what time to show up."

"Oh, Paul! Thank you!" Leslie said a huge smile on her face. *When she looks at me like that, how could I deny her anything?*

✳✳✳

Paul still exerted a soft pressure regarding where they were getting married. He wanted a huge celebration in the swankiest place they could find. If he was honest with himself, he wanted a wedding that would be talked about for years. He knew Leslie wouldn't be the sweetheart she was if she grew up anyplace else, so he tried to keep his opinion to himself.

His sisters had different ideas. Paul had his family over and they made their announcement. His sister Melanie had one daughter a teenage girl named

56

Grace. She was going through her goth phase. She had no interest in being a bridesmaid much to Melanie's dismay. Melly felt she was too old to wear the same dress as a bunch of other women. She wanted Grace to pinch-hit for her and Grace was having none of it.

"Why, Grace, why? Why can't you cooperate this one time? It's for Uncle Paul and.... Leslie." Melly was so unimpressed with his choice of a bride she almost forgot her name. "Why do you have to be so difficult all the time? I swear it's just to make me look bad." Melanie took a hunk of her processed blond hair and tucked it behind her ear.

"It's always about you, Mother, isn't it?" Grace snarled.

Leslie couldn't believe how difficult two people could be. Melanie was not someone who was used to people saying No to her, and Grace was not in the habit of saying Yes. Neither side would give in, and Leslie thought the tension would ruin her wedding and felt the need to intervene. "Melanie, I understand if you've been in so many weddings the thought of being in another one causes you to break out in hives, and Grace, I want you to enjoy our wedding. If wearing a dorky dress will ruin your good time, that's not fair to you. Could we just talk about what you *would* like to wear?"

Grace gave her mother the stink eye and remained silent. Leslie waded in again. "Grace, would you wear a dress? One *you* pick out?"

"Can it be black?"

"Absolutely not!" Melly said.

Since she wasn't helping any Leslie ignored her. "Yes. I don't care if it's black. What about shoes? Is a one-inch heel doable?"

Grace said no. Leslie pointed at her Doc Marten's. "Those?"

"Yes."

"You've got to be kidding me! There's no way you're wearing those." Melly snarled, sounding a lot like her daughter.

Leslie ignored Melly again. "Would you polish them up?"

"I can do that."

"Since you're getting your choice of dress and footwear, would you not wear fishnet stockings?"

"What about tights? Black tights?"

"They would work. OK, last one. Nail polish or make-up? Do you want black fingernails or goth makeup?"

"What color nails would I have to have?"

"Pink."

"No thanks. I'll take the black nail polish."

"Fine, I think we have all the details worked out. I'm being very vain, I know," Leslie tried to sound kind, "but I just don't want people looking at you and your torn-up fishnets. I want people looking at me, saying, 'She's the most beautiful bride I've ever seen.' Have we reached a compromise?"

Grace looked at Leslie. Initially, she thought she was one of Uncle Paul's bimbos, but this girl was smart. She knew how to get Grace to agree to things she swore she would never do.

"OK. I can work with that," Grace agreed.

"Thank you, Grace, I really appreciate it. With Carla doing a reading, Paul's side is represented. I hope having it where I grew up isn't too big an inconvenience."

Without realizing it, Grace walked over and hugged Leslie. "I've never been there. It should be fun."

Melanie's face got red. Her reticent, mono-syllabic-speaking daughter having a conversation and physical contact with this woman went too far. Melanie thought her child's behavior was on par with other teenagers, but it must not be because Leslie didn't have any trouble relating to her. *Was that woman trying to show her up? Just wait until she has a couple of brats,* Melanie thought.

***

Paul had a plan. He wanted her wedding dress to be one for the record books, but he doubted she'd find it upstate. He asked Melanie and Carla to take her around the city to some exclusive bridal shops and have her try on a few dresses, so they didn't feel left out. Their mission was to find the dress of her dreams and decide that style looked perfect. After they found the dress, took a few pictures of her in it for reference and go out to lunch.

Melanie should send Paul all the specifics, and they would ship it to a bridal shop in Leslie's hometown. Paul would pay whatever it cost to buy the dress and ship it upstate to a shop the owner recommended. He told the owner she could keep any profit; he just wanted her in on the ruse. If Leslie got the idea she was being set up, she might call the whole thing off. Leslie was an honest person and expected the same in others. If she thought Paul was pulling a fast one, she'd be furious. Paul told the owner of the upstate bridal shop if asked to say she got it from a going-out-of-business sale, and it was just part of the inventory she purchased.

"I'm not sure, you guys. I'm going out with my mom and sister." Leslie said when they offered. "There's no reason for you to waste your time."

"Oh, don't be like that," Carla, the nicer or more understanding sister said. "We won't be there when you pick it out, and we'd like to be as involved as you'll let us. After all, it is Paulie. We can just go to a few places and check them out. That way, when you're shopping, you'll at least know what you're looking for. Oh, please, Leslie, let us be involved."

Leslie caved. "Yes, I'd love to have you feel included. Do you have any time on Saturday?" They planned on late Saturday morning.

"Thank you, Leslie, for including us just this little bit."

Melanie made appointments at two shops. If Leslie didn't find a suitable one, she'd have to get something from her hick hometown. She was ticked off she had to do this, but what really wound her up was Grace. Grace wanted to go. She liked Paul's future wife better than she liked her own mother. Carla could see Melly's pinched lips and that crease between her eyebrows try to form but had been botoxed into extinction. "Melanie, could you give me a hand in the kitchen? I'm not tall enough to get to the cupboard."

"I suppose so," and glared at her daughter as she left the room. "What, Carla?"

"This cupboard over here." Melanie went over to her sister. Carla put her finger to her lips miming hush.

"You know Grace is doing this to get under your skin. She knows you're mad and she's trying to provoke you into blowing up. Don't give her the satisfaction. Ignore her. Go outside and have a cigarette."

"Cigarette? I quit years ago."

"Yes, and I was Brooke Shield's body double. Do what you have to do but don't take the bait." She spoke louder and said, "There was a punch bowl of Mom's I want. I thought Paulie had it."

"Why the hell would Paul have Mom's punch bowl?"

Carla shook her head. "I don't know. I thought it was here," and ushered her sister into the living room.

"Speaking of Paul, where is he?"

The door opened and Paul and Leslie walked in. "Sorry, we're a little late. Hey, how did you get in here?"

"You gave me a key," Carla answered. "All set, Leslie? This is going to be so much fun! I've never gone shopping for a wedding gown. Mel here eloped in Vegas."

"You did, Mom? I never knew that. How come you never told me?"

"I figured you wouldn't care."

"You figured wrong." Grace narrowed her eyes and looked like she was going to let loose.

Paul stepped in. "Ladies, ladies, please. We don't want the bride to back out. The town car is out front waiting for you." He kissed Leslie and wished her good luck.

***

There was tension between the two men in her life. Her father, a well-to-do property owner, did not do business with family. Not even when his son-in-law offered his services as a financial guru could guarantee double-digit growth and move his money into a more profitable portfolio. Her father told him the first time they met he would never mix the two so don't even try, but over the years Paul exerted pressure to do business with him.

Paul thought her dad would get old and feeble over time and not have the faculties or stamina to challenge him, and Leslie would be so grateful he could step in ease this burden for her. In the meantime, the old man was a shrewd businessman, and his money made money, so it was safe to leave it in his care for the time being and not push until things were further along. He was going to be an exemplary husband to Leslie, support her when her father's health started to fail, be her hero and help manage his father-in-law's finances, and finally get his hands on his considerable wealth.

***

Leslie did find the perfect dress and took down the information. If she didn't find anything she liked better, she'd be back. They went through the motions of having the dress set aside, and Paul's plan worked perfectly.

***

Leslie shopped with her sisters. There was no dress that competed with the one she fell in love with, the one the city. They tried the second shop. Leslie and her family had no success up to that point. neither shop seemed to have it. Leslie and Jenny were gathering their things when the shop owner, her name was Carol, asked them to sit.

"I have an idea. I just got some in from a sample sale. I think I have the perfect one! I'll be right back!"

She skittered across the store to the supply room, rooted around a bit and skittered right back a little slower, weighed down by the dress. Carol made a grand charade out of unzipping the garment bag. Carol was quite the salesperson or show woman and with a practiced swish she pulled the dress out. The bag slid to the floor and Voilà! The dress came to rest with unseen air fluffing it out.

"Oh my God, Mom, this is the dress. The exact dress! Wait until you see it!" she ran off to the dressing room, the owner following behind. A few minutes later Leslie floated out of the dressing room and went out into the salon to show her mother and sister. She gave a little twirl and showed off the dress.

"Isn't it beautiful?" Leslie asked. It had a sweetheart bodice but was covered in lace. The lace went past her chest and gathered atop her shoulders. It was two lace triangles with a deep vee in the middle, her neck and chest exposed. It nipped in at the waist with an underskirt of satin with an overlay of lace that fluttered when she moved. She could tell it was the right dress because her mother started to tear up.

"Leslie. You look positively angelic." Jenny said.

"I might cry myself." Steffi agreed.

"Okay. Now we know what I'm wearing, let's pick out yours. Paul's teenage niece is in the wedding, and she's wearing black." Leslie turned toward the owner and asked about black satin suits with long skirts.

"Not in the shop, but I have something similar on the floor. I believe I can order it in black. I think it's over here." She located it and brought it over. It was a champagne-colored fitted tuxedo jacket with a slim skirt.

"Steffi, you'll have to try it on." Jenny said. "There's no way my fat ass will fit in that dress."

She went to the fitting room with Carol and came out looking fabulous.

"Stef, that dress was made for you." Leslie said. "It looks great."

Steffi laughed. "There's no way my fat ass will fit into it either. It's not zipped in the back."

Carol asked if Leslie was committed to black. "This champagne color flatters these two ladies. What if we order it in black for the young girl, and these two can wear this color? We can get a camisole in this color for the black, and it will somewhat tie it all together."

"That works, and you two wear black shoes. We'll paint your nails black, too."

"Leslie, you are giving this girl way too much control. Black? At a wedding? The pictures will look awful."

"Yes, it does look that way, but somebody needs to represent his side. So, it's his emo niece. If the pictures look like crap, so what? In twenty years when she's a suburban soccer mom, let her kids rag on her that she once looked like that. Carol, could you check if it comes in black? If it does, I'd like the item number."

"Leslie, I can do you one better. Here's the website, and it's pictured in black." Carol said.

The three women crowded around her computer decided she could wear black if she wanted to, but Jenny and Steffi wanted the champagne one. Carol took their measurements and said it would take four to six weeks to get them in and would call them for the final fitting. She would email Leslie the measurements needed for Grace's. Their party left and went to lunch, happy to get that out of the way.

✳✳✳

"So, tell me," Jenny said, "He's got an emo niece. What's the rest of his family like?"

"His oldest sister, Carla, is an unmarried psychiatrist. Melanie, Grace's mom, is the rich wife married to a divorce lawyer. A rather successful one,

63

from what I understand. There's an age gap between Paul and his sisters. Paul came along later.

"I guess his parents split up, reconciled for a brief time, and Paul was born. They divorced shortly thereafter. He didn't have that great a childhood. Both his parents were terrible alcoholics. His sisters and his grandparents helped raise him. His mom died when he was young. She fell down the stairs and broke her neck. He was a very angry kid. Paul hated having a drunk for a mother. She'd forget stuff, like his lunch money, or show up half in the bag to school functions. I think he hated his dad abandoning him, but they always fought when they were together, so at least he didn't have to grow up with that kind of continual stress. He found out later that the reason his dad left was sobriety. He hit rock bottom, and his mom didn't. That's what they always fought about. She wouldn't quit drinking, and unless he left, he wouldn't be able to either. When Paul was old enough, he went away to boarding school. His father remarried an everyday kind of woman. She wore jeans and sweats. Her name was Rose, never married or had kids, and never drank.

"From what Paul said, he was awful mean to her. She just let it slide. No matter how mean he was, she never held it against him. I think after his rage was exhausted, he realized what a kind woman she was. Once he was older, they became quite close. His sisters went on and created their own lives, Rose was there to offer him a home and stability.

"I think it's one of those steps, but his father apologized to him for not being a good father and Paul forgave him. When he was in college his dad died. Cancer, I think. Rose came to see him graduate from college and then law school. She died from breast cancer not much later. He told me that the only time in his adult life he ever cried was when she died. He said he sobbed like a baby and almost didn't attend the service, but Rose deserved better. She was the only adult who never failed him. So that's Paul's origin story."

"So, the emo girl is whose daughter again?" Jenny asked.

"Paul's sister Melanie. Boy, you should see those two go at it. Grace will one day be a beautiful woman, but right now she's out to embarrass her mom any chance she gets."

"And you're endorsing her bad behavior."

"No, I'm not. I'm compromising. When Grace outgrows her emo phase, her mother will really have a fit. She'll be a ten and even though Melly has her plastic surgeon on speed dial, time marches on. I want everybody at my wedding to be happy. So, what if Grace looks like she got her dress at Hot Topic? I think, though, if she stands between you two it will look just fine."

"We need a final head count for the ballroom."

"My assistant at work mailed them out, so Jenny will start getting the responses."

Leslie, for being as sweet as she was, had very few invites of her own. Her best friend from high school, Tracy, and from college, Annie and KaSu. They kept in touch by email, and Leslie picked the date they both were available. Annie and Tracy were married, and KaSu married to medicine. They never did get together after they graduated so Leslie was looking forward to seeing them. She even invited Kelsie from work.

Paul laughed, surprised she didn't invite Al and the bodega cat.

"Do you think I should?" Leslie asked in all seriousness. "I'd have to invite Manny and every hotdog vendor in midtown."

Paul laughed again. "We could save a lot of money if they catered it."

"I think my dad is excited about this. It's at the Grand Ballroom in the historic hotel downtown."

"What's the budget?"

"What's that supposed to mean?" Leslie was annoyed at the remark.

"Your Dad. He keeps a tight grip on his wallet."

"That's true." Leslie had to admit. "I'm sure he'll let us know if we get close."

Paul grabbed her by the waist and pretended to drag her off to the bedroom. "Let's have a rehearsal for the honeymoon."

"Where is our honeymoon, anyway?"

"Top secret."

"If you don't tell me, what's under my top is secret. You'll have to wait for the honeymoon."

"You drive a hard bargain, future Mrs. Nelson. What's the most romantic city in the world?"

Leslie's jaw dropped open. *"Paris? You're taking me to Paris?"*

"Yes, but it doesn't matter. We won't be leaving our suite."

"You deserve a little sugar for that. Race you." And she took off for the bedroom.

He caught her on the bed and started to kiss her. Paul loved kissing her. There was something innate about their lovemaking. Each knew what the other was going to do and either met it or danced around it, but it ended up the same.

Both sated and basking in the afterglow. Leslie loved how it felt when he circled her in his arms. He made her feel like she never had before, safe and cocooned in his love.

***

The morning of her wedding, the sun showed through high thin clouds. *No chance of rain today,* Leslie thought excitedly. She was glad the ceremony was later in the day. Paul threw one hell of a rehearsal dinner and many of the guests needed time to recover. He rented out a local winery, the four corners of the room offered food from a specific region: Italy, France, the US, and China. All of the food was served in large martini glasses.

The US offered mashed potatoes, gravy, and a chicken nugget. Italy, mini meatballs, and bowtie pasta browned in sage butter. China wontons and egg rolls, and France crepes, with tables scattered about for seating, and a DJ.

It was a spectacular party. Leslie and her father stood side by side watching. Their idea was a sedate party not a rave. "I never saw this kind of party for a rehearsal dinner, Les. You've got to go. They can show up tomorrow all hung over, but you can't."

"Yeah, I think that's wise. Goodnight Dad."

"Wait up, Les. I think I'll go with you." Her mom said, and they went back to the hotel. Bill Phelps couldn't help but feel obligated to meddle this last time. "Billy, catch up with the groom. See what he's doing."

Billy looked around at the miscellaneous groups but didn't see Paul. He found him in the back settling the bill. He caught Billy walking by and yelled, "Hey Billy, wait for me! I gotta hit the hay. I'm getting married tomorrow!" Billy walked with him to a waiting limo and sent him on to the hotel.

He returned to his father to report back. "Paul was paying the bill and seemed happy he was getting married. I put him in a limo and he's on his way back to the hotel."

Bill Phelps looked at the stragglers left behind. They still wanted to party but had to buy their own drinks and the dance floor was silent. He didn't care for these people; they were Paul's guests. Bill was pleased Paul didn't feel obligated to stay and entertain them. As much as Paul seemed like a slick lawyer, and he hated slick lawyers, Paul's priorities were what made Leslie happy. "Let's go, Billy. Tomorrow's a big day."

✳✳✳

All the women crowded around the bridal suite. Mimosas were offered, but very few people took one.

Melanie was furious at Grace. She was tall and slender, something Melly used to be. Melanie in her youth looked like a Ralph Lauren model, only now she looked like Ralph Lauren's mother.

Grace's black dress bothered her. It bothered her because it worked. Standing between Stephanie and Jenny she didn't look out of place.

All the women wore black nail polish, even Leslie. Grace did wear her boots and the ladies' black pumps.

An old friend of Bill Phelps, Judge Delvecchio married them. The ceremony was held at the hotel the aisle lit with candles of assorted sizes and baskets of flowers. The men looked smashing in their tuxedos, everyone joked maybe Grace should stand on that side. Melanie was still fuming, Grace had to push it by styling her hair with gel so parts of it stuck straight out and the front plastered across her forehead. Leslie didn't care. She was on cloud nine.

The music started and Leslie stood next to her dad. "Last chance. I can drop you off at the bus station."

"No, Dad, I'm good."

"Leslie, you are the most beautiful bride I ever saw. Don't tell your sister I said so, but you are."

"Thanks, Dad." The music started. "That's our cue." They started off. Leslie had her eyes on Paul, and he put his hands over his heart like he was going to have a heart attack. Bill delivered his daughter, and when he turned to join his wife, he brushed his hands together like he was washing his hands of the whole thing. The crowd laughed, and before Leslie knew it, she was Mrs. Paul Nelson. As he slid the ring down her finger he stopped when he noticed the black nail polish. "Oh, you wicked woman," he said under his breath. Sealed with a kiss, they walked together down the aisle to much applause.

The hotel had a central courtyard with a stone fountain. It was perfect for pictures. The guests wandered around and had champagne and appetizers. When the pictures were finished Paul stood on a stone bench and called everyone back. He wanted a special toast. "To my beautiful bride, Leslie, who's made me the happiest man on earth."

Leslie was so happy she wanted to cry. She didn't know it was possible to be this happy.

***

Paul took Leslie to Paris. Just like the Leslie who marveled over the Medivac helicopter, she was in awe of the most everyday things. The babies were left out in their prams while the mothers drank coffee at café tables. The Champs-Élysées. The Louvre. The Notre Dame Cathedral. Leslie made Paul get up early and attend Mass. The little side streets each with their own character fascinated her. At night, after a full day of exploring, they explored each other. Cuddling up next to Paul, Leslie fell asleep with a sense of contentment she never felt in her whole life.

Paul looked down as his wife slept. To be honest, he'd been married before, but he couldn't remember the emotion of it. It was like his ex-wife had a blueprint of the whole day and Paul was directed where to stand and when to smile. He also did as he was told when in Italy. That was when he realized he shouldn't have wasted this girl's time. It was destined for divorce. Paul did not like to be told what to do by anybody. He tried hard to make his marriage work and to accommodate her needs which only led to more needs.

The way she pouted drove him nuts. He finally asked her when she was going to grow up. She called him mean. "I've got to tell you I don't think we are compatible. You're right. I am mean, and I don't want to be. I really think my personality is abrupt. It's been developed because of the work I do. I have to project a strong convincing business persona. I swim with the sharks, and unfortunately, I can't be tender and soft. It's just not me and I think there is a man out there who can treat you the way you should be treated. The way you want, no, the way you *need* to be treated. I think we should divorce. You deserve a better man."

"You think so?" She moved towards him. Samantha got up right under his chin. "That's what you think, huh? We should divorce. Well, I Don't Think So!"

Paul was stunned. He didn't think she'd go off like this. "You're happy here? With me? Am I giving you what you deserve?"

"No, but we should try. A lot of history between us." She waved her hands back and forth. "I think we should try. See a counselor?" The pain in her eyes made him say yes.

"Okay. Let's try. Could you find one tomorrow?"

"Yes. I'll find a good one."

Paul went with her without complaint. He often behaved like a real prick. Enough that it might not be a coincidence, but after the first few weeks the counselor looked at Sam. "You're fighting for this? For *him?* Lose this dick immediately."

He bore Sam no ill will, but they weren't right for each other. Sooner or later, they would divorce, and he didn't want to prolong the inevitable or God forbid, put children in that situation. He paid her more than she wanted. He did love her once. Paul felt bad putting her through the dissolution of their marriage. Samantha walked away with enough money to brag about. It was worth it to Paul to not be perceived as that 'cheap asshole.'

***

They came home from their honeymoon and settled in like an old married couple, but not much changed. Paul and Leslie lived together a long time before the wedding, so the paper meant nothing. She went back to her job at the broker, and he to the office. He deliberately tried to be home more than he used to, but it was hard on him. He had a million things circulating around his brain and hoped he was a good husband. Paul was faithful and kind. He loved bringing Leslie to a business dinner. He was proud of her and liked to show her off. She started to look like a stylish New Yorker. Leslie was still so good with people. He often found her in a one-on-one conversation with a new wife, unsure of her role and Leslie would give her pointers on what was expected of a corporate spouse. Most of the other wives were snotty bitches and wouldn't tell you if your hair was on fire.

Paul also found her engaging with the staff, listening to their everyday problems. He did not like her mixing with the help or how it would reflect on him, but he knew of Leslie's innate approachability. Everyone felt comfortable around her. That was one of the reasons he was initially attracted to her. Being married didn't change her much. She was still the Leslie Phelps who liked slushies and went out of her way to make sure his reputation stayed intact.

***

Leslie was twenty-eight when she got pregnant. They didn't plan on having children, but they didn't plan on not having them either. Pregnancy was hard on Leslie. She continued to work and came home with swollen feet and ankles. "What's beyond cankles?" She asked him. "Thankles?" referring to her thighs. Paul rubbed her feet every night. Being on her feet all day didn't get any easier the closer she got to her due date. She had been training Kelsie and she was proficient enough to handle the upcoming workload. Paul made Leslie take the last month off and rest up for the delivery.

She felt like a beached whale. Moving around with her changed center of gravity was almost impossible, but Leslie made Paul walk around the block with her. Being on baby watch made her nervous. What was going to happen when labor started? Fear of the unknown scared her. She never before had she doubt about her competence in any area of life. She'd learn and carry on. But a baby? She'd learn and carry on but what if she dropped it?

Paul was very kind to her. He made sure he was home to take care of dinner and be her rock. He sensed her floundering, her doubt of being able to be a good mother was something he needed to keep reassuring her she'd be fine. Two days before her due date she went into labor. Not a twinge, like was that a contraction, as in a question, except was more like, 'holy shit, I think I got hit by a train,' her water broke, and it was game on!

Leslie insisted on leaving immediately for the hospital. Paul knew from LaMaze class first-time moms had no idea what lay ahead. Hours of labor could be done in the comfort of their own home, yet they showed up at two centimeters positive the baby was minutes from being born. Leslie's OB said because her water broke it would be better if she went to the hospital, but she should start practicing her breathing and calm down. She had a long road ahead of her and it was too soon to panic. The doctor was already at the hospital and would meet her there.

Before they left, Paul had Leslie practice the breathing. She couldn't focus because her water broke, and she was afraid the baby was subject to germs now it lost the protection of its amniotic sac. Paul never saw her like this before Leslie was out of mind, frantic at the loss of her ability to control her own body. He needed to talk her down before they left for the hospital.

"Leslie! Look at me!"

"I don't have time. The baby's coming! We have to leave now!"

"No. We have to get the breathing down. Remember in class? They told us we need to do this."

"I don't think I can! I have to go NOW!"

Paul decided to take control. "Leslie. Look at me. Focus now. When you feel the next one coming, get out in front of it. Now breathe," he said firmly. "Breathe, just like they taught us. Start. Keep going. Focus on the breathing, not the baby."

"But Paul-"

"No. Focus, Leslie. Let's get this down now. The sooner we get a grip, the sooner we can leave. Feel it coming? Breathe, Leslie! Breathe! Good girl, Les, you're getting it now. Stay in front of it. Breath. That's it! Just like that."

Paul was able to coach Leslie through a few more, and she started to calm down.

"I'm going to call the car around, but keep breathing, just like that. In the lobby, in the car, in the street. Ignore everything else. You breathe and I'll take care of the rest."

They got to the lobby, and Ed, the doorman, held the door open while Paul helped her get seated in the car.

"Good Luck!" Ed wished them as he shut the door.

Leslie was still the same old Leslie and thanked him as he shut the door.

"That was nice of you, Les, but you have to pay attention to you, nobody else."

"Paul...."

"Breathe. Breathe right through it. That's my girl. We're almost there."

Paul was so good with Leslie. Whenever she felt panic, he talked her through it. They got through admitting, and they put her in a wheelchair to bring upstairs to labor and delivery.

"I don't think I can sit. I'm sitting on a soccer ball."

"We better get you upstairs. You don't want to have this baby in the elevator."

"Paul?"

"I'm here. You just breathe like you did before. You can do it. Focus. Breathe." Paul ordered, feeling Leslie needed him to act strong and be strong. "You got this, Les. You got this."

She changed into the hospital gown and got on the bed, stopping once for a contraction. When they got set to examine her, she barked at them. "Hurry up! I'm having a baby!"

The nurse quickly checked her and said, "You most certainly are! You're at eight centimeters. Good job! I'll have the doctor come in as soon as she finishes up. She's down the hall, so it shouldn't be too long."

"What about the epidural? Can you send that guy in here?"

"I'm sorry, Mrs. Nelson, but you're past the point of no return. We don't give them after seven centimeters." She smiled and left the room.

Leslie looked at Paul. *Fuck this place. Fuck that nurse,* she thought. "Paul, this is bull..ow! Ow!"

You've been doing great Leslie. Just keep breathing." He coached her through the next contraction. She had a fetal monitor on, and Paul could see the spike when she had one. It gave him time to coach her to be ready. They were coming fast, but Leslie had found a resolve deep down that burst through the pain. By now, she was capable of running the show.

She was totally focused inward, doing the breathing without Paul's help. He told her what the fetal monitor said, and kept telling her how great she was doing, but he wasn't sure she heard him.

The nurse came back and told her the doctor was coming in. The nurse wanted to do another internal, but Leslie refused. "The doctor's coming, right? She'll do one, right?" She distracted Leslie out of her zone. She didn't prepare for the next contraction. She felt like a freight train was coming and wasn't ready. Leslie suffered through that one. "Look. If you're just gonna stand there and watch, get the FUCK out of here!" Leslie yelled, disappearing into the zone and started breathing.

"OK, Les, get ready. Here it comes."

The doctor entered the room mid-contraction. She observed Leslie and waited for her finish. "You're certainly working hard. Hi Leslie, Paul. I'm going check you now. Try to relax." She took her position between Leslie's legs and did the internal. "Good news. You're at nine point five centimeters. A little bit longer, Leslie, and you'll be ready to push."

"That's just great," Leslie said through gritted teeth. "It better be soon. I'm getting tired and I don't think I'll be able to hang on much longer. Here comes another one." She felt different. It was no longer a contraction; it was an undeniable urge to push. "Doctor, it's coming. *It's coming.*"

The doctor told her she was going to check again and sat between Leslie's legs. Leslie said, "If you stick your hand up there and don't pull the baby out, I'm suing this place."

"Sorry, Leslie, but the baby has to decide when it's ready, and I think we're ready to start pushing."

"*We're* ready? You mean I'm...Oh, I have to push!"

"OK, Leslie, next one you're going to push. Ready, go!" Leslie pushed as hard as she could. "What is it?"

"Leslie, it's not out yet. You need to push more than once."

"What? Oh, no! Here's another one. Paul where are you?" she groaned as she pushed. "Paul? Paul, where are you?"

"I'm right here, Leslie. Over your shoulder."

"Help me, Paul. Help me, here comes another one," she moaned.

"Paul," the doctor said, "get behind her and push her forward. Leslie, you're doing great. Not too much longer. OK, now push! Bare down like you're taking the biggest shit of your life!"

Leslie went to her internal well of resolve one last time. She bore down and pushed as hard as she could, thinking it better be soon because she was running out of gas.

"Great job, Leslie. The head's free, that's the hard part. Next push, and little baby Nelson will join us."

Leslie pushed the last time, and the shoulders were free. The baby wailed as the doctor placed it on Leslie's bare chest. "It's a boy, Paul. It's a boy." Leslie burst out in tears and couldn't stop crying. She did it. They did it, and here he was. They were now a family. They took the baby to clean him up and check him out while Paul held Leslie.

"You did it, Les. That was the most incredible experience of my life. You *did* it."

She continued to cry and clung to Paul. "We did it. A little boy."

They brought him back swaddled like a football. "Here you go. He's absolutely perfect. Leslie, I need to sew up a small tear. After that, you can go to your room and get acquainted."

***

Leslie didn't know it, but Paul made a very generous donation to ensure his wife and child had a private room, a room they could share to acclimate the two of them who were now three. His name was Charles Russell after Paul's grandfather, the grandfather who lived in the Hamptons. The sanctuary of Paul's summers.

His parents visited twice, once to drop him off, and again to pick him up.

His summers were spent with his grandfather. Every morning, they went to breakfast and met Charles's friends, a bunch of old men, at the East Street diner, even though it was located on Main. All the other old men said, 'well, hello there, minnow,' and that was all they said to Paul for the rest of the summer. His Grandmother cooked old-style food, meatloaf, and roast chicken with gravy. Macaroni and Cheese, the orange kind. On rainy days, they played cards or watched movies. Paul loved the shore and went there each summer until eighth grade when his grandmother had a stroke, and his grandfather needed to tend to her.

His parents sent him to Boy Scout Camp for a few weeks instead. Paul enjoyed any place that wasn't home. He loved the outdoors. He loved the seashore. Paul used to think he wanted to grow up and be a Forest Ranger until he went to boarding school. There, Paul became conscious of money. The value of money. An off-the-rack blazer from Macy's or custom Brooks Brothers.

He liked the Brooks Brothers crowd better. He was a decent lacrosse player and ran cross-country, loving the air among the trees. Paul gravitated to the upper-crust crowd. He gradually became seduced by money, and what it got him. The kids from the ultra-rich families did the same things, just leveled

76

up. For spring break he'd go to Florida, and the rich kids went to the south of France. His parents threw money at whatever he wanted. Money was good. Money was very good.

He originally planned on hiring a nurse to meet them at the apartment right when they got home, but Leslie wanted to wait a week. She thought it should be the three of them, getting to know each other. Private. No outside interference. Paul was taking the rest of the week off to care for his family. Some of the older guys lived for the job and let the wife and her friends handle things. Paul took it off anyway.

All the women thought it was about time men learned the ropes of running a household. They thought Paul was right progressive in his family life. He smiled smugly at them for noticing how he stepped so easily into domestic bliss, and just as easily back into the boardroom.

The second bedroom they used as an office had to be converted into a nursery. There was a daybed as well as a crib, so if the baby was fussy Leslie could just sleep there and not bother Paul. She nursed baby Charlie but wasn't really a fan. It took him a bit to latch on, but once he got the hang of it that's all he wanted to do. Leslie thought once she delivered the baby, the hard part was over, but it was just the beginning. She still didn't know where pieces of her were. She would dream she was searching for something but all she found were babies.

Paul watched his wife with their son. He worried about Leslie's mental health. She seemed too tired to care if she was depressed. Charlie was a good baby as far as babies went, but he was still pretty demanding. Paul brought home a breast pump. "A gift for you, my darling wife."

"Um, thanks? What do I need this for? His head would be in the way."

"What if you wanted to take a shower but couldn't because he'd be hungry? What if I took a turn?"

"Are you telling me I smell? Because I probably do."

"I'm telling you quit hogging the baby. I want a turn."

Leslie smiled. "You really haven't had a chance to bond, have you?"

"If I were Charlie, I wouldn't want to give up your boobs, either. You have the most gorgeous tits."

"Let's see what you think when he's weaned. They'll probably be down to my knees." Leslie peeked into the crib and at her sleeping baby. "I'm going in the bathroom and figure this thing out. Wish me luck."

It wasn't too hard to figure out, and Leslie pumped enough to cover his next meal. "Here. I'm taking a shower. Tag you're it!"

Leslie found pumping breast milk and having a bottle on hand let her relax a bit. She had a four-month Maternity Leave and help in the morning from eight until two. Leslie found with each passing day she was getting the hang of motherhood. Right around three months, he pushed her breast away and preferred the bottle.

Pumping was a pain, and if he didn't want to nurse, it might be a good time to try formula. Once her milk dried up Leslie felt like her old self. Now, she fell head over heels in love with her little boy. He was a happy, smiley baby. Paul moved his desk into their bedroom. They were all settled. Just in time for Leslie to go back to work.

***

Leslie moved her schedule up an hour. She started at seven, and Paul left after the nanny came. The earlier start gave her an hour to get on top of the paperwork. Leslie was back to managing her department solo. She came in at seven to be home at four. Charlie and Leslie had a couple of hours to themselves until Paul came home around six-thirty. Helen, the nanny, prepped dinner for her.

While she cooked, Paul fed Charlie and got him ready for bed. He sat in his highchair while they ate. Paul cleaned up while she put Charlie to bed. Paul's idea of cleaning up meant leaving it piled high in the sink for Helen. Leslie was too tired to care.

78

One Thursday night, they were lying in bed. By Thursday, the weekly grind usually had her running on fumes. She loved her husband and her son. She loved her job, too. Her life seemed like an unending game of Twister or Whack-a-Mole.

Paul rested his head in his hand as he leaned on his elbow. "Leslie, I'm worried about you."

"Worried about me? Why?"

He pushed the stray lock of hair off her face. "You're doing too much. You're thin. Tired. I don't think you are enjoying life very much these days."

"It's so hard to manage it all." She gave a little laugh. "I've got a nanny who takes wonderful care of our son, and she gets dinner ready. I've got a wonderful husband who doesn't have to be asked to help. Working is hard, and I sense an undercurrent of resentment. Everyone thinks I'm slacking off because I leave early, but they aren't there when I start an hour early."

"Has management brought it up?"

"No."

He pulled her over. "I know exactly what you need."

"What's that?"

"Me. You need a good dose of me." Paul said as he pulled the covers over their heads.

Charlie seemed to grow daily. One day, gums. The next day, teeth. Creeping, then crawling. He started walking. Then running. Charlie loved to be chased, his absolute favorite activity. Poor Helen. She didn't even chase her own grandchildren.

He turned one. One Saturday, Leslie put him down for his nap and went into the bathroom. She covered her face with a towel and sobbed.

It was a Saturday morning. Paul had gotten into the habit of going into the office on Saturday mornings. He wasn't able to get any work done at home. He came home and found her in the bathroom, crying into a towel.

Paul knelt next to her and gently rubbed her back. "Les? What's wrong? Let me help."

She pulled the snot-covered towel off her face. "Help? You want to help me? You've done enough."

"What did I do?"

Leslie let out a wail. "I'm pregnant, Paul. Pregnant!"

"That's wonderful, Leslie. We'll have two close together, and I'll get a vasectomy."

"You promise?"

"On my honor." He held his palm up.

"I'm scared, Paul. I had a hard time being pregnant with Charlie. I don't know how I'll manage chasing him around."

"Leslie, you are one of the strongest people I know. If we need a nanny for each kid, that's what we'll do."

"Do you think we have enough room?"

"For a while. Don't get too far ahead of yourself."

Paul took her in his arms. "I love you, Leslie. We'll do it together."

For the most part, once she got through the first trimester, Leslie felt better. The experience wasn't so foreign to her mentally and physically, and she had an easier time overall. As she started to show Charlie like to pat her belly and say, "Ball!"

Whenever Charlie stopped moving enough to get a good look at him Leslie thought he looked just like Paul must have as a child. He was a happy, busy little boy.

Unfortunately, things started to fall apart. Helen's husband was diagnosed with cancer, and she needed to care for him. Leslie took vacation time while she vetted a replacement. The agency sent a woman younger than Helen who seemed to have the energy to keep up with Charlie. When she returned to work, the undercurrent of tension she felt earlier seemed stronger. Her manager called her into his office with a "Leslie, we need to talk.

I don't know how to say this, Leslie, but we have a problem."

"'We' do?"

"It seems a number of people take issue with the flexibility you have. They feel you've had preferential treatment because of your pregnancy."

"You mean last week? That was vacation time. My vacation time."

"You also leave early."

"That's a load of horseshit and you know it. I come in early. I don't believe I've ever had a less-than-excellent performance review. I'm surprised at you, Jim. You are letting a bunch of subordinates dictate how you run your division."

"It's not that simple."

"Oh yes, it is. You'd rather push one pregnant woman out than tell a floor full of adult men to grow up."

"Leslie, don't be like that."

"You have no idea what I can be like. You forget I'm married to a lawyer. I'm taking my break now."

"Leslie-"

"On my break." She left and went to talk to the head of HR. Leslie described the situation from her side. "Judy. I want to ask you something, and it's a big ask. Would you be willing to give me a copy of my personnel file? I'm afraid if I get legal involved, they'll fudge my file, and I want the most recent records." Leslie stood up. "Judy, do what's in your best interest. This isn't your fight, so don't risk your job over it."

"Leslie, no promises, but let me see what I can do."

As she exited the department, one of the administration assistants stopped her. She and Leslie were both pregnant at the same time when she had Charlie. They formed that bond women get when they shared organic, womanly experiences.

"Hi, Leslie. Enjoying motherhood so much you're up for round two?" Meghan asked her.

"Oh, hi, Meg. This one sort of slipped past the goalie. How's your little girl, Cassandra? Keeping you busy?"

"And how. I thought little girls were supposed to be sweet and nice, but if Cass wants something, get out of her way."

"That's a good trait to have if she ever ends up working with a bunch of old men." Leslie paused. "Meg, would you mind doing me a favor? It's a little out there, so if you're not into it, that's OK."

"No problem. What do you need?"

"I'd like you to start a rumor."

"A rumor? Like what?"

"Find the biggest gossip in the place and start a rumor that my husband is a real shark, that his law firm handles workplace violations like discrimination, the American Disability Act, OSHA claims. They're one of the largest Labor Law firms in the city."

"Sure. I know exactly who will give that rumor legs. I didn't know that's what your husband does."

"It's not. He's a tax attorney, but I need to rattle a few cages here."

"Good as done, Leslie. Good luck with number two."

"Thanks, Meg. It seems a lot easier the second time around. Let your little girl know it's OK not to let the big boys push her around." Leslie left and went back to her office but left the door open.

Things were very chilly that afternoon. Nobody got within ten feet of Leslie. Nobody spoke to Leslie. She left for the day and said goodbye to the receptionist. "See you tomorrow, Jessica."

"Oh, Mrs. Nelson, this came for you," Jessica said and slid a large plain Manila envelope across the desk.

"Oh, thank you Jess. Have a nice weekend," Leslie said as she slid the envelope into her bag and called a car service to pick her up.

After dinner, they sat at the table watching Charlie play with his woodblocks while she shared the details of her day. Leslie tossed the plain envelope on the table.

Paul picked it up. "This is?"

"My entire personnel file, and if anybody asks, you're with the largest Labor Law firm in the city."

He looked at her with admiration. "You still got it, Les."

"Mrs. Nelson." She smiled.

***

Leslie went to work the rest of the week with no further mention of her personnel issues, but she knew it was only a matter of time before the objections were raised again. She spent the weekend with her boys. Sunday night after Charlie went to bed, they turned in early. Leslie was reading a dime store novel, something Paul hadn't seen her do since the return flight from Paris. Paul had papers he was going through, but he set them aside. "What's going on, Les? You're awfully quiet."

"I'm turning a few things over in my mind. I think I'm walking into a trap tomorrow. Things have settled down and I bet they think springing

83

something on me first thing Monday morning, I'll be caught off guard. I do need to talk to you about a few things, but I don't want to disappoint you."

"Disappoint me?"

"Yeah. I don't know how essential my salary is to our bottom line, but I need to know how much risk I can afford to take tomorrow."

"How much risk? How much do you want to risk?"

"All of it. If I don't get what I want, I want to be able to walk away. Say fuck you to those corporate assholes." Leslie was trying to work up a sustainable nerve. She needed a slow burn but wasn't sure how much time she had. "I'd like to take care of the kids for a while. I'm tired, Paul. I can't do it anymore. I *don't* want to."

"Then you walk."

"Good. I don't think I could work there anymore. If we need the money, I can look around, but right now, let's work up a severance package. A very *generous* severance package."

"Mrs. Nelson. You drive a hard bargain." Paul whispered. "Can I come watch?"

"Better yet. You can be my legal counsel. Represent me." She laughed.

Leslie's intuition proved correct. At 8:30 am she was called into the conference room. She walked in and saw her manager, Jim, Judy from HR, and two other division managers. Right across from her was the VP of Employee Relations. They all sat around the table. Everyone was drinking coffee, but nobody offered her any. *This looks a lot like I'm going to get fired,* Leslie thought. *I hope they're prepared for the blowback and pray the rumor mill made it all the way up the rank.* She sat silently and waited for them to start. It was her manager, Jim, who drew the short straw and had to initiate the conversation. He was a short, balding man who kept rubbing his temples.

"Leslie, ah, do you remember the conversation we had in my office?"

She nodded her head but said nothing.

"We talked a bit about the perception of you getting preferential treatment, and we need to resolve it. It's created a situation that's affecting employee morale and performance."

"Who created this situation, and if it was me, a PIP would have been written. I didn't get a copy. May I see it?" Leslie asked, her voice calm and non-threatening.

"I don't have one," Jim admitted.

"What's the point of this meeting? I was given no notice of my required attendance."

"I'm afraid the situation has grown out of control."

"Let me see if I can recall the gist of our conversation. You said there was a problem with me taking a week off. I used my own benefit time, my vacation. I come in an hour early, but there was a problem with me leaving an hour early. The *perception* of me not putting in the same amount of work as other people. Is that correct, Jim?"

"Yes, Leslie. That was the conversation." He wasn't sure she how she would handle it.

Leslie pulled out the white envelope. "Here is my personnel file. Pay attention to the number of excellent performance reviews." She shuffled the papers. "It's all of them. Look at my performance metrics. Once again, I have not missed any. Not one. Here is a copy of my computer logins for the last three months. I have signed on between 6:45 and 7:00 every day. My performance isn't the problem, it's the *perception* of others, correct? My performance has less value than the perception of others."

Jim looked at Leslie's file. "Where did you get those?"

"I've copied every piece of paper that crossed my desk if it pertained to me. Yet that's your concern?"

"Um, no," Jim said. "You aren't supposed to have a copy of those."

Leslie looked around the room. Judy's face remained blank, and the VP, Andrew Weiss, was the only person who met her eyes. Leslie stared back at him, and he blinked. He shifted uncomfortably in his chair, and Leslie decided to go in for the kill.

"In my opinion, all these issues are because I'm pregnant. I'm a better performer than anybody else, the only difference is I'm pregnant. Because I'm pregnant, you don't have any confidence in my ability to do my job. I've already had a baby and none of these 'problems' were of concern. Now you think being pregnant is an impediment to me delivering the bottom line. This looks like discrimination. It's not fair, and it's a bunch of horseshit because I have documentation that says otherwise. You are discriminating against me because I'm a woman, and I'm pregnant."

"Don't be like that, Leslie."

"That's the second time you said that to me, Jim. Don't worry about my position here. I'm not going to, but you sure are."

"Leslie, now, we are just having a discussion here."

"You have the head of HR and Mr. Weiss. They are here because you want to can me. You want to create a hostile work environment, so I'll quit. You want me gone to satisfy all those grumpy old men out there. To tell you the truth you have deeply offended me and treated me like a less-than-valuable employee. Any loyalty I have to this place is equal to the loyalty you have shown me. Absolutely none.

"I wouldn't work here if you paid me, but that's exactly what's going to happen. This company is going to give me a six-month maternity leave at full pay effective immediately, and when that's up you are going to give me a month's pay for each year I worked here. That's seven years, Jim. Six plus seven is thirteen months."

"You're out of your mind, Leslie." Jim scoffed.

"Am I? Either you give me what want, or I sue the shit out of you in a very public way, and I will notify all my accounts to take their business elsewhere.

Their loyalty is to me, not you. Not to anybody else who works here. Do you remember my husband, Paul? He's an attorney with the largest labor law firm in the city. I've already discussed this with him, and he thinks I have a very viable discrimination case. Either give me what I ask in a severance package, or you'll hear from my lawyer. You tell me what direction you want to go."

Leslie looked at Jim, who looked at Mr. Weiss. He gave an imperceptible nod. "Leslie, don't be like that." Jim repeated.

"You have worked here for so long. I hate to part under such harsh circumstances."

"I don't know about that. You told me to be here at 8:30 with no notice the VP of Employee Relations and the head of HR would be present. I can't believe you would actually take a pregnant woman and push her out for no reason other than to massage a couple of old guys' egos. That isn't fair, and you know it, yet you expect me to walk out of here with my tail between my legs. How dare you. I loved this place, my job, the people. Not anymore. Give me what I want or prepare for a very long, drawn-out, and expensive public lawsuit."

Jim looked again at Mr. Weiss.

"OK, Leslie, you win. Meet with Judy Friday morning and sign the papers."

Leslie took her mini cassette player out and held it up. "If you try to pull a fast one and deny me what I ask, think again. I've taped the entire meeting."

"Clean out your desk. I'll have someone from security escort you off the premises."

Jim looked positively green at the discussion he knew he'd be having with Mr. Weiss. He rose first, and thanked Leslie for her years of dedication, and asked Jim to follow him out. Judy walked out with Leslie.

"Leslie. You were on fire. Well done. Friday at ten work for you?"

"Thanks, Judy. I couldn't have done it without you." Leslie headed to her desk. Someone had thoughtfully left her a box for her things. She filled the box and showed the contents to the security guard.

"Would you mind carrying this out for me? I think it will be too hard with a belly like this." She passed the receptionist and said goodbye to Jessica.

She smiled at him. "Thank you for carrying it." He walked her out and hailed a cab. He put the box in the backseat and helped Leslie in.

"You take care now, Mrs. Nelson. Congratulations on the new baby." He shut the door and went back into the building, and she headed home.

***

Leslie thought about going home and if it would upset the nanny's routine. She decided to call Paul and see if he had time for an early lunch. He did and would meet her downstairs. Paul met her cab and helped her out, grabbing the box. Paul held the box and lifted it up and down. "What's in here? It's not very heavy. There's not a lot in the box for the time you worked there."

"I know. I kept my desk as devoid of personal items as possible. There's a baby picture of Charlie, and of the three of us when we went to the Christmas Tree farm last year. I also kept my work computer separate from any personal communications. The only thing I have is my account list backed up in my phone."

"Let's leave it in here and walk to the coffee shop on the corner. Be right back." Paul went back inside, dropped the box off, and came out. He put his hand on the small of her back and ushered her to the café, held open the door for her, and followed her inside. Paul found a booth in the back. They sat down on the old fake leather seats, cracked with seams from years of use. The Formica tabletop was dated but clean. The table rocked a bit from not being totally level. He went up front and placed their order. Paul returned and slid into the booth.

"They'll call when our order is ready. I take it from the box you are no longer employed. The question is, were you fired, or did you walk out?"

88

"I wasn't terminated, I wasn't let go. It was a mutual agreement to part ways. On Friday I go in and sign the papers. I negotiated thirteen months at full pay." Leslie was finally able to relax. She still couldn't believe she pulled it off. "I'm shocked. They folded like a cheap suit. I should have asked for more."

"Leslie, you're a shark. It's too bad you didn't go to law school. We could use someone like you. You can drop a hammer, and nobody sees it coming." His phone beeped. "I'll go get our order."

Leslie was shaking as the tension left her body. Paul came back with their order. "You OK, Les? You look kind of pale."

"Yes, I am now. I didn't think about what if it went in the opposite direction. I can't believe I had the balls to pull it off." She smiled as she slipped her coffee.

Paul gave her half of the sandwich. "This sandwich tastes wonderful. Maybe I should bitch slap some old men more often."

"How about me? It sounds exciting."

"Maybe after the baby's born. My center of gravity's off. What am I going to do now? Let go of the nanny and take care of Charlie?"

"No," said Paul, a sly grin on his face. "You let her stay until number two gets here. I don't want you to have any more stress. Let Heather chase Charlie around. You rest up so you can take care of your husband when he gets home."

"I think I can manage that." Leslie said, answering his sly grin with one of her own.

Leslie had a much easier time with her second son and named him after her father, William Phelps Nelson. When she brought him home, Charlie was all over her. She sat on the couch, and Charlie climbed up.

"Here, Charlie, look. You have a little brother." He climbed on his mother. "Gently, Charlie, gently. Look."

She pulled the blanket back and said, "Look, you have a little brother." Charlie frowned.

"No!"

"What? He's a nice baby," Leslie said. "Don't you like the baby?"

"No baby! Dog!" Charlie said and climbed down.

"I think he wanted a dog," Paul said as he watched his son climb back-up. "Maybe next time."

"I don't think so, Paul. No Dog. Vasectomy."

"That's right. I did say that. I'll ask around and find a doctor."

***

Heather stayed the length of Leslie's package. She left when William was six months old. Charlie only had interest in his brother when nobody was looking. He put stuffed toys in the stroller and buried him with cars in his crib. Charlie took the bed Leslie used to sleep in and William the crib. It was crowded in the second bedroom, and it seemed there was no way to make it through the day without stepping on a toy. Paul usually was the unlucky one who bore the brunt of this.

William was too much of a name for such a little boy. Her father was Bill, Leslie's brother Billy. "I think we should call him Willy," Paul said.

"Willy Nelson? Very funny."

"Oh. How about Will?"

"Will Nelson? That works."

The apartment was very unfriendly for two little boys, with its decorative moldings and angled furniture. Leslie tried to make it 'homey' but unless she completely renovated it still wouldn't solve the problem of not having enough room. Paul was stressed out in his home because Leslie was always rescuing one of the boys from harm. She never sat down. He wanted his wife

90

back. After nailing his shin on the coffee table again he broke and he said "Leslie, we've got to do something. This isn't enough space for four people of which two are children."

"Like what? Move? Where? Upstate? Like the Maloffs did?"

"I think that's the best option, to be honest. You and the boys live there full-time and I'll commute. Stay here during the week and come up on the weekends. It would help so much to have my office back. These boys need some room to run. I know families who've done it and it worked out fine."

"I agree about the boys. They need to climb trees and build forts. Ride bikes. I'm not totally sold on the idea, though, of us being apart. Look around and see if you find anything reasonable." As if to validate Paul's position a loud crash came from the living room. Leslie ran in there and found a lamp in pieces on the floor.

"Sorry, Mommy," Charlie said. "The ball bounced too high."

"What's Mommy say? No balls in the house."

The boys grew so fast. Will was walking, doing his best to keep up with his brother. For every broken lamp, there were fifty 'I love you, Mommy.' Charlie taught Will how to climb out of his crib. Leslie would find them sleeping together in Charlie's bed. Climbing out of the crib was more like pole vaulting. Will would pull himself up and throw himself out. Occasionally they would hear a thud during the night and find the two of them the next morning sleeping together.

Paul came home with a lead on a house. One of the partners was divorcing, and he had his wife and kids living in a house upstate. An anonymous note came to her about the woman he was seeing while he stayed in the city. "She hired a P.I., and it only took a few days to gain enough evidence to divorce him into the poor house and that's exactly what she's doing. If we like it, we have to be prepared to buy it."

"You mean we buy it today?

"Yes. Today."

"Not even one night to sleep about it?"

"We don't have to buy it, but if you do like it, we have to move quickly, that's all. If you need one night to think about it, it's not the house." Paul assured her.

"You promise?" the Bill Phelps in her would never proceed without doing due diligence, but the wife in her wanted her husband to take over, puffed up with responsibility. "Okay. I'll keep an open mind."

The house was part of a horse farm, the farm part leased to the Ulster County Riding Academy. It was a four-bedroom cedar shake-shingled colonial painted green with white trim and a wrap-around porch. The yard was a wide expanse of lawn with a wooden swing set. It was far enough outside the city but commutable. They drove up to a look. It was about an hour north, and they had to rent a car. The boys climbed out and ran up on the porch yelling, 'Look at me, Mom!' 'Look at me, Dad!'

"Let's go look inside," Paul said, and they walked up the stairs. He used the key and opened the door. Sunlight poured through the windows and left the pattern of the lace curtains on the floor. A front parlor on one side, a living room that led into the dining room which opened into a big, new kitchen. Off the kitchen was an add-on master suite. The boys ran through the rooms, connecting into big circle around the center hall staircase.

"Jim says it's fully furnished. The Ex, Mrs. Jim, is only interested in money, so it's only value to her is what they can get for it. Jim, however, wants to give her as little as possible, so it's a bargain. Let's go upstairs and check out the bedrooms." The bedrooms were good-sized, and a full bathroom. Leslie could sleep upstairs with the boys if needed. "Jim said the schools are excellent, and it's a short ride to the town center. We can take a drive and check out the scenery."

The drive was pretty, the town quaint. Leslie asked him to park so they could walk a bit. They went in the library. There was a table with flyers for the upcoming programs. A little park with a statue of the town's mayor from back in the day was right there in what was called Beaumont Park. Iron benches were scattered around the perimeter, perfect for people-watching while eating ice cream.

"It's cute, Paul. I like it." The boys were running in circles around the statue. "Come on, boys."

They ran over and wanted ice cream. Paul went. Leslie sat between them, but it only put her in the middle of pokes and laughter. Tears sprang up from nowhere and flooded her eyes. *Her boys.*

Paul came back, gave two cones to the boys, and went back for theirs. Everyone got the chocolate and vanilla twist. If Leslie or Paul got something more exotic, like Rocky Road, one of the boys would want that, and then the other boy would decide he wanted it too. Pushing and shoving started, somebody would drop their cone, crying would occur, and blaming would happen next. Paul would take all four cones and pitch them out with no explanation. "Mommy! Daddy's being mean." Charlie said.

"Yeah. Mean!"

"Sorry, boys. Daddy took mine, too. Next time we need to use our manners," and Leslie would take a wet nap out of her bag and clean them up. "Next time. Manners."

Leslie decided to make the move, and Paul made the offer and closed the deal. They bought Leslie a car. Paul wanted to buy the best car he could find, but Leslie was able to dial him back. She wanted a station wagon and Paul laughed at her. "Leslie, they haven't made station wagons since 1979."

"Volvo makes one."

"Volvo *did* make one, but not recently. What else?"

Leslie thought about her dad driving a Jeep, and she liked it. "How about a Jeep?"

"You know, that's a perfect choice for you. Among all those wives driving high-end cars, a Jeep would perfect. You're not like those women, why drive a vehicle like them? A Jeep is perfect."

He asked her what color she wanted, and she said Army Green. One day she came out, and there it was.

Before she knew it, Paul hired a moving crew, and all their things were packed up to go. He took a Friday and made a long weekend of getting them settled. The first night they grilled hamburgers and hot dogs, watching the boys climb on the swing set. Swing Set didn't do it justice. It had a rope bridge, a climbing wall, and a covered platform. They had a year until Charlie started school, Will the year after. They took Paul to the train station and saw him off.

Next Friday, Paul was there by four. He leased a Mercedes. Leslie was surprised he got there early. She hadn't planned dinner, so they went to a place in town. It was nice to see Paul in a totally different light. She didn't know where he got such aged—in clothes. His Levis looked naturally faded in the right spots. He had a whole closet full of golf and tee shirts. Clothes that looked worn in, and he looked comfortable. His hair got a little curly.

Leslie wondered why he never dressed like this before. Maybe he did, and she didn't notice. Maybe it was the fresh breeze, but Leslie looked relaxed and comfortable.

She watched him with his boys. He was a wonderful father. The boys were tired that night, and it only took the promise of pancakes in the morning to get them asleep. Leslie jumped on Paul as he lay on the couch.

"You look wonderful, Paul. I've missed you. Let's get it on."

"Let's get it on? I'll race you!" he rolled her off him onto the floor and took off to the bedroom. She sat there and laughed. Leslie got to her feet and ran after him. That was the general pattern to their weeks. Then years.

***

Leslie worked at the school as a substitute teacher. Her math background was highly valued. She could sub in if a teacher left or went out on maternity leave. She stayed after school, and some parents paid her a lot of money to tutor their student-athletes to get them ready for college. Leslie opened a bank account and had her checks direct deposited. She also had them deduct money and put it in the Teacher's Retirement Fund. It wasn't enough to bother Paul with, and after she left, she forgot about it.

Things changed when the boys reached high school. Both moved on from interests like Little League or sports. Charlie found an old movie camera and became totally engrossed in movie making. Will, of course, worked in front of the camera as Charlie's lead. The summer before eleventh grade, Charlie wrote a feature film and cast their friends as players. It was a horror movie about some haunted woods. Rumor had it there was a family nobody had ever seen living deep in the woods. Anybody that ever tried to find them disappeared or turned up dead.

Will spent the spring at the library investigating techniques for horror makeup, beyond ketchup substituting for blood. He was also in charge of props. Leslie watched that summer as kids came in and out of her house in various stages of decomposition. A girl sweet on Charlie acted as his right-hand doing makeup and anything else he needed. Another girl who liked Will was the female lead. She got killed, but Will made it out alive.

Being in front of the camera was a good place for Will. He very handsome and taller than Charlie, with curly dark hair. He reminded Leslie of Carla, who was darker and thicker than Paul. Will had movie star good looks, and she could not recall him ever having a pimple. He melted hearts for sure.

They were brothers bordering on twins. Charlie told everybody they were twins, but Will flunked second grade. They were best friends. Charlie was the idea man, and Will was the executor. Being so close meant each knew the other's business. Charlie had a temper, and Will exactly where to poke him to get him riled. He'd explode, and they'd come to blows. *I think Charlie may look like Paul, but I think he got him temper from my side,* Leslie thought. She remembered her brother getting into fights.

Charlie worked on his film on rainy days and weekends. His dedication came as no surprise. Will would get bored and go play video games, but Charlie poured his all into the project. It was premiering Halloween night.

He obsessed over the weather the whole week before and was as jumpy as a cat. Leslie and Paul watched out the window as they hung a sheet in front of the garage door. Charlie had a rough cut on tape. He rode his bike into town and talked to a photographer. The guy helped him clean it up and transfer it to super 8mm film and loaned him a projector.

Showtime was at 8 p.m. Leslie and Paul sat at a card table to collect donations to the food bank, the price of admission. Pretty much every kid in town showed up carrying camping chairs and food. Leslie was surprised at the generosity of their friends; they filled two clothes baskets with canned food. Five minutes before showtime, a man came up the drive. He introduced himself as Dave Daniels, the owner of the photography shop who helped Charlie. He brought a bag of canned goods.

"I hope you don't mind, but Charlie invited me. He did a really good job."

Charlie started the projector and crossed his fingers. It opened with a shot of a manual typewriter introducing the movie "The Legend of Backwood Falls." It dissolved into a close-up of a bicycle wheel spinning by itself as it lay on side among the leaves, some loose leaves carried by the wind behind the spinning wheel. Charlie must have been on his belly filming it. A group of kids came into view, looking for the owner of the bike. They found his bike but not him. They start all talking at once about where the friend could be when the female lead said, "Oh, no. Look!" Charlie followed her hand as she pointed to something: the missing boy's crushed glasses. All the kids started talking at once, faster and in a higher register. The next shot was a wall phone ringing and ringing. Finally, Will answers: Hello? He listens. End scene.

"Wow, Paul. It was like Hitchcock or something." Leslie whispered.

"I know. I started getting really tense with that ringing phone, and Will finally picked it up. We still don't know who it was. Let's watch."

"I especially liked the opening scene where the wheel kept going around with the dry fall leaves lifted by the wind," said Dave Daniels. They forgot he was there. "You should reward the kid. He worked really hard, and it showed."

Leslie and Paul were so happy Charlie found his passion. As a surprise, Paul hired the Ice Cream Truck and threw a wrap party.

They were in awe of Charlie's movie. It was good. When he went to NYU Film School, they weren't surprised. Will followed after as a Theater major. They both moved to Hollywood. Paul and Leslie saw them a couple times a year. It was easier if they visited California. Paul asked Leslie to move home and said it was time to sell the house to the next generation of families looking for a place in the country.

They talked about selling the upstate property. Over the years, it had increased in value, and Paul wanted to cash in the investment, but to Lesli it was home. She planned on them getting out of the city and retiring there. The property was in his name, and he sold out from under her. Leslie moved back into their place in the city, not happy about it, but she trusted Paul's judgment. Paul was a financial wizard, so she didn't pay attention to the money. She was financially sound with him managing her retirement fund and other investments. Until one day the shit hit the fan, and everything changed.

PART THREE

Leslie woke, not knowing where she was. It took a minute to get her bearings, and she realized she was still at the hotel. She got up and saw her father with a room service cart. "Hi, Dad. I thought you were leaving."

"Morning, honey. I'm on my way out. I wanted to say goodbye and make sure Jenny was coming. Her flight got off on time so expect her about eleven. Here's Don's card. Call if you have any questions." He walked over, gave her a hug, and kissed the top of her head. "It'll be OK, Les. Your family will help. It's too bad nobody knows where Paul is, your brother Billy would love to come up and beat the shit out of him. I have to go now. Stay here as long as you need to. I'll call later to check in."

"Call Jenny's phone. The police still have mine."

"Will do. The coffee's still hot. Grab a cup and wait for Jenny. Goodbye, Les. Try not to worry."

"Easier said than done."

He left. She grabbed a coffee and the remote. The TV turned on, and the crimes of Paul Nelson was on every channel. People who lost money were interviewed. Poor widows and autoworkers, comfortable one day, suddenly destitute. Accountants and CPA's dealt with the financial things picking off what's left of the carcass that was once their lives. Leslie saw a clip of herself getting out of the police car and quickly turned it off. She went back to bed and read a travel magazine, but her eyes got heavy, and she was soon asleep.

Her sister Jenny woke her by jumping on the bed. Jenny was the youngest. She hadn't lost the sweetness that made her Homecoming Queen and Head Cheerleader. She had thick, shoulder-length light brown hair, a smattering of freckles and dimples that bracketed her million-dollar smile. Under her cute, perky, outward appearance lay the heart of a cutthroat dealmaker able to close any sale.

"Wake up, you little jail bird! Wake up!"

Leslie woke up with a start. "What the? Who? Jenny! Stop that! Who let you in here anyway?"

"Dad left a key for me. What do you want to do now?"

"Do? Nothing. I can't leave this place." Leslie said and stuck out her leg and showed Jenny her shackled ankle.

"Sweet! Doesn't Tiffany make ankle bracelets?" Jenny bounced and lay down. "Is there a spa here? A salon? Let's spend the day getting all dolled up and charge it to Dad. Just because we're adults doesn't make us mature, y'know. Let me call the desk." Jenny reached across Leslie and elbowed her in the gut, trying to grab the phone.

"Oof!"

"Sorry." She spoke to the desk and made arrangements. "Thank you. OK. Goodbye." She rolled back over to her sister.

"Oof! Stop that, Jenny!"

"Sorry. We have an appointment at two for a massage, and 3:30 for blowouts and Mani-Pedis. Sound good?"

"I guess so," Leslie said. "I'm not in the mood for fun. I have this axe hanging over my neck. I won't be able to enjoy myself."

Jenny laid next to her. "Ooh, this bed is comfy. I may sleep in here with you. We're going this afternoon to pass the time until you're out on parole."

"Thanks. I can't really go anywhere. All I have is my pajamas, and these jail sweats."

"Dad warned me you didn't have clothes, so I brought some." Jenny opened a bag and threw her some track pants and a couple shirts with the tags still on. "I'll give the bill to Dad. You can wear my hoodie. You're too shiny without it, and here's some underwear." She tossed them to her sister.

"You take a shower. I need to make a few calls." She exited the room, leaving Leslie was alone with her choices.

They were all good options, and she took the one that looked the most comfortable. The heat from the water kneaded her muscles, loosening her tight neck and shoulders. They got the couple's massage package so they could talk to each other. It was too hard. Somebody would say something but trail off, overcome by the pleasure of someone peeling the muscle off their ribs. They spent the afternoon luxuriating in the spa. When they got back to the room, Jenny looked at the menu.

"Are you hungry? Let's order room service and eat in our pajamas. You can tell me all about it."

"Sounds great. Order me whatever you have. I'm gonna take a quick shower." when Leslie got out, she saw housekeeping washed her jail sweats. She could search around for something else but didn't. She put her jail sweat suit on and went in the center room, meeting Jenny as she came from her shower, towel-drying her hair.

"That feels wonderful. I hate feeling all greasy from a massage. Nice outfit. Do you have to return it?"

Leslie looked down at her clothes. "Someone sent them out to be washed. At least they're clean. After all the shit they put me through,

I'm keeping them. I'll get it." Leslie walked over to answer the door. It was Room Service with their dinner. Jenny ordered a bottle of wine, conveniently opened and on ice. Leslie picked up the bottle and looked at the label. "This any good?"

"I have no idea. The restaurant suggested it. It's on Dad, so it's probably the most expensive they had. I'm not a wine snob."

"I don't drink very much. Paul doesn't either."

"That's no longer an issue, is it?"

"Jenny-"

"Let's sit at the table and eat. You can tell me all about it over a glass of wine."

They sat at the table with their dishes and a glass of wine. Leslie looked at their identical chicken salads. "I guess this looks OK."

"It looks fine. You don't want to pollute your body after our cleansing day at the spa."

Leslie looked at her sister. "You didn't get one of those high colonics, did you?"

"They weren't on the menu. Eat up and tell me your tale of woe." Jenny took a sip.

Leslie took a few bites of her salad to get her thoughts together. "You know about as much as I do about what happened. You've seen the news. The nut of it is Paul stole a whole bunch of money from a lot of people and left for parts unknown. The bastard even took my retirement and savings, but people are really angry at me, and I lost everything, too. There was a crowd around the apartment hoping to run into me. That was on the news." Leslie sipped her wine. "I know the cops tore the place apart. I don't know what shape it's in now."

"Do you have any ideas how long it's been going on?"

"No clue. I keep going over things in my head and can't really pinpoint any one thing. I know once the boys were at college, he met them in the city for dinner on Fridays. He got here early Saturday morning. Did you have any money invested with him?"

"No. Christoper's brother's a financial planner, so we always went through him. I do have to say he mentioned it every time we saw him, though. He could 'put our money to work' and make us a double-digit return."

"I know Dad's philosophy about doing business with family. Paul pressed him a couple of times but stopped when Dad got wound up. I hope Billy stayed clear of him."

Jenny sipped her wine. "I think Billy stuck with Dad and our family's financially sound, but it doesn't seem you came out unscathed."

"No, I did not. I'm broke. I can't even buy dog food," Leslie said, spearing some lettuce.

"Good thing you don't have a dog."

"Paul was allergic, or that's what he said. He was probably lying about that, too. I can't believe I was such a sheep, following him blindly all these years. I never questioned anything."

"That's always been your M.O., trusting people. You think you'd learn by now."

"I can't help it. I'm not built to be suspicious. I believe everyone has the capacity to be good. Otherwise, it's just too much negative energy."

"That's you, bringing home stray dogs and cats. Your boyfriends weren't much better. Always hoping for the best, and even if it was bad, you never wised up."

"Look at me now. Paul, that fucker. I can't believe I fell for his bullshit. I still can't get my head around that it was all fake. The last thirty years was just a sham." Leslie frowned at the truth and took a gulp of wine. "My boys. Who was their dad? How can you walk out on your family like that? Sneak out and leave?"

"Maybe he didn't. He loved you, Leslie. I swear to God, he loved you, and his sons, too. Maybe he got caught up in the money aspect of it all and lost his head."

"Now, who's wearing the rose-colored glasses, Jenny? Paul loved money and all that came with it. He loved money more than he loved me. When I first met him, he gave me a Cartier watch. He thought wearing a twenty-dollar Timex was beneath me. I was some broke college kid. Why did I need to upgrade my watch? They both kept time."

"He gave you a Cartier watch. Wow. What did you do?"

"I gave it back to him. Walking around campus in thrift store clothes wearing a watch like that. Ridiculous."

"Wasn't he insulted?"

"No. He said he'd give it to me as a graduation gift. That's the thing. I'd say no, and he would think a way to postpone whatever it was and bring it up later. The one thing he did was sell the upstate house after the boys left. He said the real estate market was hot, and we needed to capitalize on it. I thought we could retire up there, but he sold it. I wasn't ready to leave. It's like it was his apartment, and that was my house. He probably stole that money, too.

"I keep thinking there's something I missed. But I don't see any red flags. Maybe when I moved back, he continued to go into the office on Saturday mornings, but that's about it. It doesn't matter anyway. I'm stuck, and I have to wait it out."

"Can you get in the apartment?"

"Not yet. I'll call the lawyer in the morning. I'm beat, Jen. I have to go to bed. I'll see you in the morning," Leslie said as she headed off to her bedroom.

"Goodnight, Les. Don't think about it anymore."

***

Leslie got up before Jenny made coffee with the in-room coffee maker and looked for her lawyer's card. She found it and dialed his number. He answered on the second ring.

"Hello, Don, it's me, Leslie Nelson, I mean Phelps. Have you heard anything?"

"Leslie, how are you holding up? I was going to give you a call in a bit. We need to be the precinct at eleven. Do you want me to come and get you?"

"No. My sister is here, and we can take a cab. It's OK if I bring her, isn't it?"

104

"There shouldn't be a problem, and if there is start crying and throw yourself into my arms. I'll be ready for you. We'll meet at eleven. Call me if you can think of anything. Goodbye." Leslie replaced the receiver. Her sister walked in.

"Hi, Les. How'd you sleep?"

"Not great. You?"

"Like a baby. I heard you on the phone. What's on the agenda for today?" Jenny made herself a cup of coffee and sat down. Leslie looked at her little sister, who looked so much like their mom, with her bright eyes and dimples. Leslie had the same, amber-colored eyes. They sucked in the light and bounced it back tenfold. Jenny had coppery freckles across her nose that matched the coppery freckles in her eyes, her complexion rosier, Leslie paler-like their dad.

"Are you changing?" Jenny said, pointing at her jail uniform.

"No. You're going to escort me through the front door. It's the perp walk. A once-in-a-lifetime experience."

"Copy that."

"Will you stop quoting Chicago P.D.? Just follow my lead."

"Jay Halstead is such a hunk."

"Whatever. Do not engage." Leslie used her shoulder to exit, pushing the door open, the bright daylight blanched their eyeballs for a minute. They heard the crowd while the door opened. Ed rushed them right down the steps into a waiting cab. People yelled and pounded on the car as they pulled out.

Jenny turned and looked at the crowd. She turned back and looked at Leslie. "Wow. That's incredible."

"You have no idea. Nobody's meeting us outside at the station, so we run the gauntlet alone. Remember. Do not engage."

The traffic wasn't so bad during the late morning, and they arrived downtown quickly. They got out of the cab. Either nobody expected her to show up at the front door or wearing the jail sweats with a skully pulled low over her ears, but they sailed right into the building. They heard people yelling once they were inside, realizing they missed their opportunity, and angry about it.

Don met them by the sergeant's desk. Leslie introduced him to her sister. A man appeared at her elbow and ushered her into a conference room, one with windows, so Leslie detected a different vibe since her last visit. Their usher was an FBI officer she remembered from the initial visit when they tore through the apartment.

"Jenny, this is," Leslie couldn't remember his name or recall if she ever learned it. "This is Mr...Spook. He's a G-man. This is my sister, Jenny Phelps, a Tops Sales Associate with Greater Charlotte Properties, a member of the Greater Charlotte Local Chamber of Commerce Business Association, and a notable small woman-owned business."

Jenny stood back in awe of Leslie's impersonation of her regurgitating her elevator pitch. "Yes, that's me," Jenny smiled and leaned in to shake hands. "You did such a good job I should hire you," she said to Leslie.

"I'm Mr. Jassen, Jenny, nice to meet you." He turned to Leslie. "I'm with the FBI, Leslie. A spook is the CIA."

"I'll try to remember that the next time somebody breaks down my door." They turned at the sound of the door opening. An ancient pair of Venetian blinds clattered against the glass. Leslie looked at them, broken and bent, a more than a few missing. *So much for privacy,* she thought. It was her lawyer and another man who looked just like Mr. Jassen. *The Feds must recruit on college campuses for unassuming, blockheaded, interchangeable types.*

Her lawyer made their introductions and suggested they sit.

"Leslie, we have good news. Judging from the findings so far, you appear to be innocent of the fraud your husband was perpetrating against his investment clients."

"No shit. Are we finished?" Leslie stood. "Come on, Jenny. Do you have a back exit? The crowd outside is getting restless."

"Hold on, Leslie. You appear to be uninvolved, but there are number of things left to clear up."

She sat back down. "Like what?"

"The forensic audit is ongoing, and until that's finished you still are under house arrest. We still need you to clarify a few details." Don said.

"Like what?"

"Like *this*," Mr. Jassen #2 said with a smile on his face. He had about enough of the confrontational Ms. Nelson. *These rich assholes are all the same,* he thought, and spread out a number of banking documents in front of Leslie. "How did this money end up in your name in these two local banks outside of the city?"

Leslie glanced down, puzzled. She stared at them and nodded. "I don't know how deep you looked into *my* background, but I lived in Senecaville when my kids were little. My husband lived here, and my kids and I lived there to raise our sons outside of the city. We went back and forth. I taught math there as needed and also did college prep classes. This money is from that, and this other account here is an IRA with funds deposited from my salary." Leslie looked up at the agents. "But you already know this, if you were any good at your jobs. Did I give the right answer?"

"Yes, Leslie, that is correct. Why were you hiding it? Were you deliberately keeping it from your husband because you had some idea what he was doing, and you were hiding it from him? Or were you helping him hide it?"

"You probably won't believe me, but I forgot about it. When I was married, everybody raved about my husband's business acumen. He was a genius who everything he touched turned to gold. I had no reason to doubt him. Maybe I should have paid closer attention to our finances, but I didn't. Shame on me. I bet these accounts weren't big enough for him. At least I have some money to start over with."

"Not so fast, Leslie," Don said. "All accounts are frozen until the audit's finished."

"Am I able to at least get into my apartment? If you looked into it further, you'd see I'm flat-busted. I'm living in a hotel I can't afford. I had to bring my sister because I didn't even have enough for cab fare."

The first Mr. Jassen pulled the keys from his pocket and slid them across the table. "Here are your keys. You may return to your apartment but still under house arrest. If you want to leave, call here first for an escort. Ask to speak to the desk sergeant, and they'll assign someone."

"We done?"

"Yes. Temporarily."

Don looked at Leslie. "I'm parked outside in the back. I'll take you home." They exited with no problem. Don was going back to Paul's apartment.

"No, Don. The hotel. We haven't checked out yet. We'll take a cab."

By now, Leslie was done with the whole circus. Angry people could jump down from the eaves for all she cared but she had her hand ready to hit the panic button on her key chain. Once again, she escaped detection. "I don't think they even know what I look like." Leslie said to Jenny as they entered.

Leslie and Jenny returned to the apartment. Leslie said hello to Ed, the doorman. He looked down at his shoes and mumbled something. She stopped and looked him. "You, Ed? You too? Did Paul steal money from you?"

He looked at her, his eyes watering. "Yes, ma'am."

"All of it?"

"Yes."

"I'm so sorry, Ed. I know it won't help, but if it helps to make you feel better, he fucked me too. I got nothing, he stole everything. I'm his wife, and he took my money right out from under me." She fished around in her purse and found one of Don's cards. "Here. This is my lawyer. Call him and have a judgement filed against Paul Nelson, and against his firm. Immediately. If he was playing fast and loose with their client's money, they had an obligation to enforce their fiduciary responsibilities. Do it now, get your claim filed as soon as possible. I imagine the apartment will have to be sold as well as anything else of value. Good luck, Ed."

Leslie and Jenny rode the elevator up to the apartment. "Paul was an equal opportunity fucker." Jenny observed. "To take the doorman's money."

The elevator opened to the apartment. Leslie slowly looked around. "Jesus. They trashed the place."

All the cushions were on the floor, a few sliced open with the stuffing escaping the wound. All the drawers emptied on the floor. Everything torn off the hangers and left in a heap. Leslie got her phone out and took photos of the damage and sent them to Don. "I don't know if it matters, but I just want the damage documented."

"Jeez," Jenny said. "What shall we do first?"

Leslie put a few cushions back on the sofa and flopped down. "I imagine this place plus any other assets will be sold to pay off outstanding debts, but that's just a spit in the ocean. I didn't make this mess, and I'm not cleaning it up. Anything belonging to Paul just throw it in his closet. We'll sort the stuff in my closet. There is a lot of high-end designer items in there that must have some value, again, a spit in the ocean." Leslie sat up and placed her face in her hands and started to cry. This was too much loss to bear. Jenny came over and hugged her sister.

"It will be okay, Les, I'll help you."

"Where am I supposed to go? I can't stay here. What am I supposed to do? I'm too old to start over."

"Don't get too far ahead of yourself. Let's get dinner and figure it out."

"There used to be a drawer full of menus in the kitchen."

Jenny found some and placed an order using her card. A while later, Ed called and said their order was downstairs, ready for pick up. "Things have changed. Usually, Ed called and brought it up. Now we have to go get it."

"I'll run and get it."

Jenny came upstairs with a bag and a bottle. She got her sister a glass of wine and served her a burger and fries.

"What's this? A burger and fries?"

"Yes. You look very thin. Eat the burger. The restaurant said Pinot noir pairs nicely with hamburgers."

"Jenny. Do you drink like this every night?" Leslie said as chewed her burger. It tasted heavenly.

"No. Only when I'm out. Besides, a little fruit of the vine helps improve your outlook."

"I rarely drank. Paul didn't like it."

Jenny looked at her sister and frowned. "You know, Leslie, fuck Paul. That life is over. Your marriage is over. Your husband shat all over it, and you on his way out of the country. It's time for you to think for yourself. What's your plan for the next six months?"

Leslie sat there and thought about it. "This has to be cleared up," she said, shaking her foot, "and I need to leave. This place is toxic. Maybe I come stay with you for a month, and we go out west and see the boys. Act in their movie. Make a second career as bit players, playing women at the grocery store like pigeons on a wire in front of the dairy section. Make it a diversity thing with two old people who tick a couple of boxes one of whom is confined to a wheelchair. After a couple of months, you go home and have a nice suburban life. I'll head back to Dad's and figure out how you divorce someone whose whereabouts is unknown, how to make a living and support myself. I'll figure it out." She shrugged her shoulders. "But it would be great fun. Think about it."

"Who gets to sit in the wheelchair?"

"You can have it."

"No. You're older. You should be in it."

***

The next morning, they started cleaning up the mess left from the police. Anything that belonged to Paul they shoved in his walk-in closet, also torn apart by the cops. Leslie looked at the pile of high-end labels and custom clothes. *What a waste. I'll send it to Goodwill, and some people are going to be dressed to the teeth out there, panhandling in his Armani.*

"Hey, Leslie! Come over here," Jenny called from her closet. Leslie went over to see what was so fascinating. She had all of Leslie's designer bags and shoes sorted and lined up. "What are you doing with all this stuff?"

"Give it away. If I wear it, I'm afraid I'll get mugged on my way to the soup kitchen."

"Do you care if I take any? You've got some really nice stuff."

"No, take whatever you want," Leslie said and sat down. "Let's go through it."

Jenny sorted through the clothes, and Leslie took the handbags and shoes. She dragged a suitcase from the back of the closet. "Here, Jenny. Put what you want in here." Jenny pulled it closer to the hanging garments.

"Can you check the wheels? It doesn't seem to move right."

Leslie moved it back and forth. She looked inside the bag to see if the wheel was hung up on something inside. The base where the wheels were wasn't lying flat, so Leslie pried it up with her fingers. "Holy shit, Jenny! Look at this!" Underneath the false bottom were bundles of hundreds.

"Wow! How much do you think it is?"

Leslie counted the bundles. "Jenny. It's fifty thousand dollars. Cash." Leslie sat back on her heels. "The FBI went through this place for days. How did they miss this?"

"Maybe because it's your closet. All the bags were open, so they were looking for something. The coats are on the floor, so they went through them. It's odd they overlooked your suitcase."

"I'm not sure they did. All the suitcases were opened. Maybe they thought I wouldn't have anything, so they didn't go through them all that thoroughly. They tore Paul's closet to shreds, ripping out the linings of his suits and coats. This bag was just tossed in the back."

"Oh my God, Leslie, do you think Paul forgot about it?"

"No," Leslie said. "I think he left it for me. It's in my suitcase in my closet."

"No, Les. Don't go down this road. He wasn't thinking about you. He hasn't thought about you in a long time. Paul Nelson is an asshole who thinks only of himself. If he was thinking of you, he would have brought you with him. You have to get over him starting now." Jenny put her arms around her sister, but Leslie didn't cry. She removed herself from her's sister embrace.

"You're right, Jen. For most of my adult life I was married to someone who didn't exist. It's hard to accept but I can't mourn a stranger. I'll be glad to get out of this city. I wasn't kidding about coming for an extended visit."

"What do we do with the money?" Jenny asked.

"Leave it. Pack whatever you want in it and take it home when you go."

"You mean not telling anybody? Don't tell the FBI?"

"Yes. Remain totally ignorant of anything other than the clothes you pack. If anyone was looking for it, they would have found it. It's not like it's in a safe. If it turns up at TSA, play dumb. I loaned you a suitcase, that's all. You know nothing. When I come for my visit, we can figure it out what to do with it."

They kept sorting, Jenny taking a number of designer bags and outfits. After a while, they ordered dinner and ate in front of TV, watching 'the Batchelor.' Jenny had to give Leslie a run-down on who was who. Leslie didn't care what they did she as long as she wasn't alone. They went to bed, but Leslie could not sleep.

Paul was everywhere, his scent on the clothes they sorted. His favorite ties. Leslie sat on the edge of the bed and fingered one of the ties, her heart breaking in little pieces when a wave of emotion so strong she wished he was right there so she could take this tie and strangle him with it.

Leslie's eye caught the glint off a silver frame. She stood and walked over to it. It was a picture of them on their wedding day. She looked so happy her whole life wide open in front of her. Leslie looked in disgust at the stupid girl she used to be and threw the picture as hard as she could at the wall, the glass splintering like her marriage.

The next morning, they were enjoying their first cup of coffee when the phone rang. It was Ed calling to tell her Paul's sisters were on the way up.

"Do you want to change?" Jenny asked, pointing out her Department of Corrections sweats.

"No. I have no idea what they want, but I think the visual will help them get some idea of my point of view."

They heard the elevator open.

Carla and Melly came into the kitchen, fretting and tut-tutting the condition the apartment was left by the police. Leslie and Jenny were working on Leslie's things and didn't worry about the rest of the place. Leslie offered them a cup of coffee and re-introduced Jenny to them. They declined the coffee and sat down.

"Oh, Leslie, we feel so bad for you, Paul taking off like this and leaving you in the lurch. This is not something my Paul would do." Carla said.

An idea popped into Leslie's head. "Yes, Paul left me with nothing. How about you two? How big a hit did you take?"

Paul's sisters looked at each other. "It didn't affect us at all. All the income is tied up in a trust, and we draw an allowance from there."

"Really," Leslie said and leaned back in her chair. She looked at her sisters-in-law through slitted eyes. "What is the purpose of your visit?"

The two women looked at each other. Carla spoke. "We imagined you wouldn't want to stay here in light of the circumstances."

"What's the hurry? It's not like I have somewhere to go and if I did, I have no money to get there. This used to be my home, but it feels like I'm being evicted. Is that why you came? I figured you'd need to sell the apartment. I imagine it will take some time."

"See, that's the problem. This apartment and its contents are part of the trust our parents set up. The trust was not affected by Paul's actions."

"So, Paul and his family skate away unharmed, yet I'm being investigated by the SEC and the FBI for wire fraud and money laundering? He left me broke, with nothing, yet you two show up like vultures circling a carcass wanting to know when I'm planning to vacate the premises. I thought we were family. I guess not. I never was, was I? You don't have to answer that. I already know."

"Don't be like that, Leslie," Carla said. Melanie fidgeted in her seat but said nothing.

Leslie stuck out her leg, showing them her ankle. "I can't go anywhere. I'm still under house arrest. When this is remedied, I will be on the first train out of here and where I go will be none of your business. I'll leave my key with Ed. I'm taking very little from here. I thought there would be an appraisal and an estate sale, but I'll leave all that up to you. Your brother is a real bastard, you know. He walked out on his wife and kids. He walked out on me, sticking me with cleaning up this mess. I'd leave right now and tell you both to fuck off, but I don't have any money for a hotel." Leslie got up and searched her bag for another one of Don's cards.

"I am under house arrest until this is over, so don't plan on moving in here any time soon. Here is my lawyer's card. Please don't contact me again. Any questions or communication, please go through him. I'll be out as soon as possible. Now I think you need to leave." Leslie walked over and called the elevator. It opened and with a flourish like game-show spokes model she showed them the exit. "Here you go. Goodbye."

Melly was in a hurry to leave and headed to the elevator. "Leslie, don't be like that." Carla said again.

"I expected more from you, Carla. I thought after thirty years I'd be considered family. Apparently not."

She got on and the doors closed. "But Leslie.." she heard as the doors closed.

Leslie walked back to her coffee. "Well, that's that. Do you care if I come stay with you when I'm released?"

"Of course not, Les. I'm not sure how much longer I can stay. Do you care if I leave in a few days?"

"You can leave whenever you need to. Will you take the suitcase with the money? If you get busted just play dumb. Say you borrowed it from me. Otherwise, let's go through my closet and gut it. If Paul's family isn't concerned about the people he screwed over, why should I care?"

Jenny stayed until the weekend, clearing out what she wanted, and left. Leslie called a high-end reseller who took the rest. There was her open jewelry chest, plenty of things tossed about but it looked like nothing had been taken. She sold those items, too. They were fakes. The real ones were located in a safe deposit at the Senecaville Community Bank. Leslie had Don drive up there with her and clean out the safe deposit box. He took it all and said he knew how to dispose of them if she wasn't in a hurry. He would funnel the money back to her dad. Leslie also told him her dad would be giving him money from the suitcase Jenny took.

Just pay attention to it, she thought. It looked like a couple of different small accounts would add up to a modestly significant one, or at least one enough to cover the costs for the next month or two. As soon as she was released, she was taking a flight to Charlotte to stay with Jenny.

Leslie was stuck in that apartment for six months. She secretly thought by keeping her on ice she'd contact Paul to help her. If that was their strategy, they were dead wrong. Leslie never wanted to see him again. He took a young woman with a pure heart who believed, perhaps naively, there was more good than bad in the world and blew up that delusion.

Yes, the world at large was a horrible place to so many innocent people. Leslie stopped watching the news because she'd cry at the evil advanced by certain agendas. The commercials of animals, so many animals who suffered at the hands of ignorant or abusive people would send her running for the tissues.

She always tried to be the light when people considered her. Leslie spent her whole life trying to help others, to be a bright spot in an otherwise dismal world. All it took was a smile, a smile that said I see you and you matter. Her husband almost destroyed that part of her. Paul had taken everything from Leslie, and she vowed he was not taking anything else. The part that made her *her* she hung onto with all she had. *Maybe I'll be older, smarter, and a lot less gullible,* she thought, *but I'll still be me.*

She met Don down at the precinct. She was taken to the room with windows, so they didn't plan on things getting confrontational. "We almost done here, Don?" Leslie asked as they sat down. Before he could answer the door squeaked open and two men in suits entered. Leslie wasn't familiar with them; she did not recognize their names as they introduced themselves. She looked at their feet and only one of them wore wingtips. She decided she liked him better than the other guy.

"Hello, Mrs. Nelson. How are you today?" The man not the wearing wing-tip shoes asked her.

"Just peachy. And it's Ms. Phelps. Leslie. Find my husband yet?"

"We have not. Have you?"

"No. If I did, you'd be arresting me for murder."

"I know, Ms. Phelps, how hard the last six months have been for you. We have completed all we need to as far as the missing money, and we are sure you were not complicit and are as big a victim as anybody else. We are releasing you." Wingtip came over and removed the ankle bracelet.

She took her free foot and moved it in circles. "Thank you. I'm afraid I'm going to miss it," Leslie said sarcastically.

"Please try not to leave the state in the near future." The first man said.

"I'm afraid that's not possible. I have no place to live and no money for a hotel. I have what's left of my things in Don's car. I've returned the keys to the doorman. How the Nelsons get them is their problem. I've severed all relationships I had with them. I'm going to my sister's place in Charlotte for a while and then out west to see my sons."

"I'm afraid-" the second man started, but the other guy cut him off.

"Ms. Phelps, I can understand your need to leave, and I don't blame you. You have been kind and generous with us and I thank you. As long as Mr. Fraiser knows your location, that's fine. You are free to go, and again I thank you."

Leslie couldn't help it, but she smiled at him. Her smile reached the corners of her eyes and sparkled at him. *Whoa,* he thought, *a smile like that could do a man in.*

"Like I said, I'm going to visit my sister. Don has my number should you need to reach me." They all shook hands and let them go.

"Shall we go to the airport, Leslie?"

"My flight isn't until seven. I feel bad asking, but I'd like to get a new phone. New number. I need a fresh start, and I'm starting there. You'll be one of maybe five people who will have my new number. You can bill my dad. I'll pay him back."

"I'm not worried, Leslie." After she took care of her errand, he dropped her off at the airport. "You've held up well, Leslie. Get as far away from here as you can. You've been so stressed out; you deserve a long rest."

"Thanks, Don. It's been a real trip; I'll tell you that." He helped her get her bags out of the car.

"You going to be, ok? Do you want some help with your bags?"

Leslie smiled at him. "No, I'm good," and gave him a hug. "Bye, Don."

She got to the gate with plenty of time and used it to switch her phone contacts over. Leslie boarded the plane and took her seat in first class. It was the only seat left, and she hoped her dad would understand. She looked out of the window, the city lights below her fading away. Leslie said a silent goodbye to the place she'd never call home again. The part that hurt Leslie the most was Paul ran off with his partner, who was a probably a beautiful younger woman, or maybe it was the part where he managed her retirement funds into oblivion. She wasn't sure. Leslie trusted him and gave him access to all her accounts, which were now zeros with no hope of double-digit returns.

∗∗∗

It was so hot at Jenny's. Leslie could not believe Jenny, as the sole seller real estate agent met with strange people alone in empty houses. Leslie went on real estate appointments with her as a safeguard, so Jenny never went alone. Leslie saw something on Dateline about how female realtors were sitting ducks for serial killers. Jenny left and went with Leslie to see the boys for two months after which her husband requested her return. Leslie was right. It was great fun.

Leslie stayed a few extra months in California; she lived in the guest house of a famous celebrity who was on location. Will was staying there but moved in with Charlie, so she had the place to herself. Charlie needed an older woman for some scenes and rather that put out a casting call she volunteered. The scene called for her to be a sweet old lady on a bus sitting next to a gorgeous girl, knitting. When the bus stopped, a wild-eyed girl possessed by demons got on. She went right for the beautiful girl, but the sweet old lady stuck out her foot, tripped the demon and stuck a knitting needle in its eye right through to its brain.

He used her for background in another scene. She sat and had lunch with a stranger. They had to do it five times. She worked enough to get SAG card. It was great fun, but she was tired. Leslie was looking forward to heading back to her dad's house.

Leslie returned to her father's house while he was away. The first thing she did was dye her hair the darkest brown, and the second was watch TikTok videos on how to cut your own hair. She cut it into chunks like the shaggiest shag. If the groomer cut her dog's hair like this, she'd want her money back, but she kind of liked it.

PART FOUR

Michael Caldwell offered to watch his neighbor's place while he was away on business, but as soon as he left, Michael saw signs of life. Bill didn't mention anybody staying there, but he saw lights on upstairs and heard a car pulling in and out. It was an attached garage, so Michael could never get a good look at this mysterious house guest. He considered calling Bill and ask him or have the cops stop by and check the place out.

Michael walked over and knocked on the front door. He heard the car pull in, so he knew somebody was there, but nobody answered. Michael tried again with the same results. Initially, he wasn't too worried about the resident hiding out at Bill Phelps's but refusing to answer the door made him suspicious. Michael was going try one more time, and if nobody came to the door, he was calling Bill to see if he knew anything about having company when an answer presented itself.

It started with the mailman mistakenly delivering an envelope to Michael's house. It was addressed to Leslie Nelson c/o Bill Phelps but his house number. The name Leslie Nelson sounded familiar. He thought Bill had a daughter named Leslie who'd been in the papers. Bill never discussed why, and Michael didn't care enough to ask. He lived in this small town all his life, retiring as a high school science teacher. Unless it happened locally, Michael never paid much attention to it. The envelope gave him a reason to uncover the mystery next door.

He sat on his porch reading, using the envelope as a bookmark. He was ready to run over when he saw Bill's Jeep pull in, but he didn't get there before the garage door shut. The next time he made it. A young girl got out, saw him, and shrieked. She dropped the bags from her arms and looked scared at the sight of him. She was white as chalk and backing away.

"Hello," he said. "I didn't mean to give you such a fright. My name is Michael Caldwell. I lived next door and told Bill I'd keep an eye on the place for him, and he didn't mention any company."

"Oh," was all she said.

Michael bent over. "Here. I'll get those." He packed the groceries, stood up and extended the bags to her. He hoped he didn't groan. She tentatively took them. Her hair looked like she cut it herself; it was short and spiked with no identifiable style. It also looked like she dyed it black. Once he got closer, he saw she wasn't a young girl; she was a woman who had lines on her face and hollows under her large, dark brown eyes. She remained quiet as she stood there.

"Oh, yes. The mailman left this in my box. Bill has a P.O. Box, so I thought this might be for you." He held the envelope out to her, but she did not attempt to take it.

"I don't think so," she said.

"Your name isn't Leslie Nelson?"

Her eyes opened wide. "No, that's my sister. I'm Jenny Phelps."

"Oh," he said, his hand still holding the envelope.

"Why don't you keep it until my dad returns? I'll probably lose it."

Michael sensed something was going on he wasn't aware of, so he kept the letter. "It was nice to meet you, Jenny. I'm next door if you need anything."

"Thanks, Michael, but I think I'm all set."

"Goodbye. See you around," Michael said and headed back home, listening to the garage door gears cranking down, securing her inside. He entered his house got out his laptop and typed her name in the space bar, cyber-searching the woman next door.

✳✳✳

122

The name Jenny Phelps cast a wide net and many appeared. A Jennifer Rose Phelps popped up; she sold real estate down south. He remembered the name Phelps was well established here. Bill had been a factor in local politics and ran the volunteer Food Bank at St. Elias Church. Michael moved back here twenty-five years ago to take the open position for a high school science teacher. *For being a teacher, I'm not very bright,* he thought as he called up the high school yearbooks and entered the name Phelps. Jennifer Rose Phelps appeared. It was her senior picture and not the woman next door. Jennifer was the Homecoming Queen, head cheerleader, and senior class president. She looked shorter than the woman next door, with deep dimples and a wide smile. Jennifer also was a blonde, but it wasn't unheard of for girls to change hairstyles or color.

He typed Leslie Nelson, but no one of that name ever attended. Michael shook his head at his error and typed Phelps. Up came the woman next store. *That's her!* She was a beautiful girl. Her hair was ash blonde with highlights contrasted by her big dark eyes. She was active in Mathletes, Chess Club, and Drama Club. She graduated two years before her sister and ten years before he arrived.

Michael sat back in his chair. *Leslie Jean Phelps.* He typed in the Google search bar Leslie Nelson, and his computer screen blew up with images of her and headlines. The FBI was investigating her husband, Paul Nelson, and another associate at his firm for operating one of the biggest Ponzi schemes in history. Paul Nelson and his partner fled the country the night before the Feds busted in, his whereabouts unknown. The part that hurt Leslie the most was his partner was a beautiful younger woman, or maybe the part where he managed her retirement funds into oblivion. She wasn't sure. Leslie trusted him and gave him access to all her accounts, which were now double digit goose eggs.

***

Michael knew the woman next door was in hiding, claiming to be somebody else. He didn't bother to call Bill. He was fascinated by this woman. All the intrigue and subterfuge were kind of exciting, the most exciting thing that's happened to him since his wife died.

His wife died some eight years ago from ovarian cancer. It happened suddenly. His wife Emily dropped a lot of weight in a short time. After she had their two daughters she put on weight and Emily was not comfortable with her post-pregnancy body. She dieted and exercise constantly. It was the same ten pounds that came and went. Michael didn't mind her being a little on the heavy side he was getting a little thick in the middle himself. Emily was still as beautiful as the day he met her, but he couldn't convince her so. He wished she'd accept herself the way she was. It was exhausting to watch her read labels and count calories. When the weight finally slid off she was overjoyed.

It didn't last. She was tired and had trouble eating, feeling generally unwell. A trip to the Doctor's lead to another doctor's appointment, followed by a biopsy and the diagnosis of ovarian cancer. They were reeling from the news, and his daughters wanted to move her across the country to a world-renowned Cancer Center. Michael thought she was too sick to travel. As they processed the cancer diagnosis and argued about the best place for her, she rapidly declined and passed away six months later.

Right in front of my eyes. She wasted away while we argued. My poor Emily, Michael thought, *the fact that she had to listen to that as her last words. She didn't have the luxury of time.* He always felt he let her down. There should have been something he could have done to save her, but there was nothing.

His sister told him to get over himself. Quit making it about you, she said, his daughters needed him to man up. Michael took a deep breath, centered himself and went to his girls who were worried about him. They shared an equal amount of grief and leaned on each other. No drama, just catharsis.

His daughter Rebecca left first, her husband was lonely, and she wished to return. Her sister Julie was reluctant to leave him; she wasn't sure how he would get on without her.

"Julie. Please go. I'd like to grieve your mom alone. It was good having you girls close; it helped a lot, but I need to do this by myself. Please call me and make sure I haven't stalled. If I'm spinning my wheels, you get your sister and intervene. You have my permission." Michael said as he walked her to the car, carrying her bags.

"But Dad, you'll be alone in a house full of memories."

Michael kissed her cheek. "There are more good memories than bad, and I want to remember all of them." He seated her in the driver's seat, and before she drove off, he assured her again he'd be OK. He closed the door, watched her drive away and went inside. He sat on the couch and bawled like a baby.

Every time he saw something that had a connection to Emily he'd break down and sob. After a few months his grief no longer manifested itself as tears. It was now an ache in his chest. That faded, too, after a while. His girls worried about him once he retired, afraid he'd be lonely. He dated a few women, nice women, but his heart wasn't in it and nothing ever became of them. He created a workshop in his garage and made things out of wood. Michael made unique, one-of-a-kind tables hand rubbed to a deep finish. If asked, he'd say he was content being a bachelor. It was fine. The guy next door was a bachelor, so if he needed male companionship, there it was.

***

Leslie felt like she finally woke up from a bad dream, a bad dream that lasted almost thirty years. Here she was, in her old bedroom of her childhood home. Her dad usually left after Thanksgiving returning mid-March, but this fall he was leaving early, stopping at Jenny's for a while. He asked Leslie if she wanted to come, he didn't want to leave her alone, but she wanted to stop and think for a while what her next move should be.

Being out of sorts since Paul effectively fucked her left her searching for a place in the world. Since she left New York, she hadn't been back, busy with Jenny and her boys. Now back, she needed a new plan, but she had no idea in what direction. The easiest thing was to blanket the schools for substitute teaching jobs, but she couldn't muster up the desire. The college prep courses left her free to pursue other options, and the parents rabid for their spawn to seek the upper echelons of academia paid good money. Very good money.

One call to the athletic director at the high school and she had three seniors whose scholarships were in jeopardy. The school gave her a conference room, and she was there Tuesday and Thursday afternoons would meet with students at the local library on Saturday morning. She was cobjobbing a career together, enough of one to cover expenses for now.

Leslie thought about her dad, how he was too old to get mixed up in his kid's drama, but it did give him a purpose. He was still sharp mentally, and while Leslie's troubles were dire, they weren't life-threatening. Bill would give his girl time to figure it all out. Bill took an instant dislike to her choice in husbands and thirty years later he would swear he was wrong, except he wasn't.

When Leslie got married, her dad put aside some money in a trust fund for her. He also put the house in the trust. Back then, it was only to help her should things between her and Paul go south, but now it gave her some time to think about her future. Bill didn't tell her, he didn't want her to think he had no faith in her judgment, but it was an emergency fund should she find herself in a bad way. Now Leslie was too grateful to be angry about his actions. Bill was happy to see her every morning and she could stay as long as she wanted.

He thought about cutting back on his business travel. After years of it, he was tired. He only traveled so much because he didn't want to live in an empty house. Maybe Billy could pick up his slack. He did have to leave earlier than usual this time and hoped Leslie wasn't making herself crazy wondering what she did to drive Paul away. *Don't waste the time, Les,* he thought. *I had his number the day I met him. Smarmy.*

✳✳✳

Michael had his wood shop in his garage. When he retired, he wanted a hobby, and woodworking was something he pursued. Michael was partial to staying home. He was not despondent or depressed. He always was a homebody. Leslie would hear his power equipment but didn't want to appear interested in his activities, so she acted indifferent. They hummed and scraped loudly. Leslie hoped he wore ear protection.

126

After a few weeks she started waving to him when she went out, then waving upon her return. He returned the wave but nothing more. Michael decided his neighbor was out of his league. Leslie was too pretty for him, too young, and she had this cosmopolitan sheen that left him feeling like a country bumpkin.

She was hiding from something. *Oh,* he thought, *her husband. That's some pretty big baggage. She probably wants to be anonymous.* He couldn't fathom being in the public like that, people watching your every move. Any headline he generated would be *boring man lives boring life.* He was content to admire her from afar. He doubted she'd be around more than a couple of months, life there *was* pretty boring.

Michael didn't hear her over his circular saw when she entered his garage; it was a casual look up when he saw her. He was lucky he didn't cut off his thumb. "What's up? Jenny?" She didn't blink. He tried louder. "Jenny!"

Leslie blinked a few times and refocused. "Oh. Yes. Hello?"

"Need something, Jenny?"

"I'm kind of bored, I guess. I took a ride to apple country and think I overdid it. I made an apple pie, but I don't even eat apple pie, so I was hoping you'd liked it. I'll bring it over if you want."

"It's your lucky day, Jenny. There's nothing I like more than apple pie. I'll take it, but I insist you stay for a slice. I'll put the coffee on." He looked down at hands as he removed his gloves. Michael looked up at her. "Deal?"

"Deal. I'll be right over."

He saw Jenny with her hands full and went to get the door. "I'll hold the door. You can just put the pie on the table and take a seat." Michael cut two slices of pie and put the coffee on the table. He sat and watched her bring the sweet to her lips, put it in her mouth, smile and say, "Yum."

"Wait a minute. You said you don't like apple pie."

"That's kind of a fib. I'm only good for one slice." Leslie reached in her pocket and pulled out a can of Reddi-Wip. She filled her mouth and passed it over. The fact that in front of him she sprayed cream into her mouth he found shocking, with a little tingle on the back of his neck. He took the can and did the same. They both laughed.

"I think it's supposed to go on the pie before you eat it, but that way works just as well," Michael said.

Leslie smiled. He was struck by how her whole face lit up. "The boys used to do that when they were young."

"You have sons?"

"Yes, Charlie and Will. They live in California. Charlie makes films, and Will acts."

"Are they surviving on the Boulevard of Broken Dreams?"

"Yes. Charlie is the idea man. He'd be happy making small indie films. Will is the one with the stars in his eyes."

"Anything I'd recognize?"

"A McDonald's commercial, and a reoccurring part in a soap."

"McDonald's. Not bad. I confess I don't watch the soaps."

"That McDonald's gig has been the gift that keeps on giving. It plays a lot overseas, so he always has an income stream. Before I came here, I was out there. Charlie put me in a few things. I didn't get discovered, but I did work enough to get a SAG card."

"Wow. A movie star."

"Not really. It was more like the third old lady on the left. I did have a speaking part."

"Really? What was it?"

"I was sitting on a bus knitting when a demon got on and attacked the girl next to me. I stuck a knitting needle through its eye and said: you're lucky I'm not crocheting. I'd make a tea cosy out of your brain."

Michael took another bite of his pie. "Impressive."

"Not really."

"I was referring to the pie."

"I'm glad. I'm leaving it here."

"I'm not going to give it back. Did you make a lot of pies? I imagine you didn't have any leftovers. Growing boys eat a lot."

"Their friends do, too." Leslie looked at him. Was he trustworthy? She decided there was no harm in talking about her boys. "When they were young, we lived in Senecaville. I didn't want to raise them in the city. I grew up with grass, fresh air and had a wonderful childhood. I thought the boys needed room to be boys. They both went to NYU and ended up in the city anyway. We sold it not too long after. I loved that place. I was sad when I had to move back to the city full-time." Leslie paused and looked off in the distance.

"How about you? Do you have kids?"

"Two daughters. One's a nurse, the other one has a house flipping business with her husband. Neither of them lives close. After my wife died, they wanted me to move closer to them, but I passed. I'm happy here."

"Your wife died? I'm sorry."

"Yes, about eight years ago. Ovarian cancer. At least it went quick."

Leslie felt like she should offer something equally emotional. "My husband left me. I never saw it coming."

"He was a fool."

"What?" Leslie wasn't sure she heard him correctly.

"Your husband. To walk out on you: a fool."

"Yes. Absolutely. A fool. And an asshole."

"That too." Michael smiled at her. *Gosh, she's pretty.* Their pie plates were empty.

"Well, okay. We can talk later. Sure." Leslie rose and put her mug in the sink, said goodbye bye and left.

Michael watched her as she went out of the door. *Poor girl.* He was crushed when his wife died. That wasn't supposed to happen. They were supposed to retire in Florida and learn how to play Pickleball. The grandkids were to come down on their breaks.

Suddenly, she was gone. All their plans gone. What was once a future of fun and possibilities was now a dark endless chasm of nothing. He made his peace with his circumstances, and if he was honest with himself, he hated Florida. He knew his affection for Leslie Nelson was based on how many times he ran to the window when he heard her car. Apparently, he was quite fond of her.

***

Michael had just finished in the garage and was standing at the kitchen sink. He heard his phone ringing. He wiped his hands on his jeans reached for his phone. The caller ID said Bill Phelps so he answered it.

"Hi, Bill. How's your trip going?"

"I hate to admit it, but I must be getting old. I can't keep pace like I used to. I thought consolidating a few meetings would make it easier. The only thing it did was make for more time in the air. I'm going have to let Billy take this over, and I'll manage the office."

"Do it. I'll even take up golf to keep you company."

"Speaking of company, have you met my daughter yet?"

"Jenny? She's a sweetheart."

130

"That's not Jenny. That's her sister Leslie."

"I know. She told me she was Jenny. I figured she must have a good reason to go by an alias."

"She does. The last year has been hell for her, what with that business about her husband."

"I confess I googled her. I knew she had some trouble and boy, did she have some trouble."

"That's my Leslie. I had a different opinion of her husband, but I kept it to myself. She loved him, so I didn't want to burst her bubble. It took him thirty years, but he proved me right. Unfortunately, he's off somewhere and left her holding the bag. That asshole even stole from her, took her retirement, and left her with nothing."

"If it counts any, she has two sons she absolutely adores."

"That's true. They're good boys, too. I'm not sure how they feel about having a crook for a father."

"I know she's holed up over there. Is there anything you need me to do?"

"I just wanted to check on Leslie and be sure she's okay."

"She's okay. I'll keep my eye out and call you if anything looks amiss." He said and ended the call.

Michael grabbed her pie plate and headed next door. He knew she'd come to the back door to see who was there, the front was there but she never answered. He peeked in the window and saw her sitting at the table, bathed in sunlight. It reminded him of Vermeer, it could be titled 'Woman in Kitchen Paying Bills.' He rapped on the window lest she look up and see him watching her. Leslie raised her head and motioned for him to come in.

"Hey, Jenny. I wanted to return your pie plate. It was a delicious pie."

"I'm glad you liked it. Have time for a cup of coffee? Take a seat."

Leslie took the plate and placed it on the counter while she got the coffee. She placed in front of him a cup of coffee, steam wafting above it in little circles. "Careful. It's hot." She sat opposite him and blew on her mug. "What's new? Anything good?"

He would risk burning his lips rather than answer. He noticed a bag on the counter and decided to talk about it instead. "You went out to Steele's Orchard?"

"Yes. Why?"

"It's only the most expensive place there is."

"Really? Why was it so crowded?"

"Caters to families. They have the petting zoo and a corn maze, with apples twice as expensive as the place down the road. If you want to go again, I'll show you a much better place."

"What about pumpkins? Is there any place in particular I should go?"

"For baking?"

"No. Apple is as far as I go. Purely decorative."

Michael smiled at her. He couldn't help it. He wanted to act cool and aloof, maybe impress her a little with his local knowledge, but instead acted like a drooling idiot. He took a sip of his coffee. "It's supposed to be nice next week. Let me know what day."

"It's wide open. Wednesday?" Leslie smiled.

Michael nodded. "It's a plan, yes?"

"Yes. A plan."

"Oh, by the way, I talked to your dad." He said and watched her body language. She definitely tensed up.

"My Dad? What did he want?"

"Just checking in. Wanted to see if I met his daughter. I told him I did, that you were doing fine."

"Did he ask for me? Did he mention me by name? Jenny?"

"He just said his daughter."

"He'll always worry about me like I worry about mine. And you worry about yours." Leslie said.

"Comes with the territory, I suppose."

Leslie leaned up against counter but remained quiet. He spoke. "Thanks for the pie. And the coffee. Let's get some pumpkins on Wednesday. Talk to you soon. Bye, Jenny." He showed himself out. She spent the afternoon sorting and choosing carving tools, laid them out, and waited for Wednesday.

✳✳✳

Monday morning was bright and sunny, the whole week was predicted to be perfectly fall-like. He thought about asking Leslie if she wanted to take a drive to check out the foliage. One big rainstorm with gusty winds, and they'll be clogging gutters and storm sewers alike but right now, it was as crisp as a fresh red apple and when the wind blew the landscape looked like a kaleidoscope in full bloom. Michael decided to neaten up his yard.

He took a rake and started to clean up by the curb. Michael was so focused he didn't hear the van that pulled up next to him. Its logo as a news station was large and boldly painted on its side. It was a local affiliate but judging by the reporter's presentation she had network news aspirations. Her blonde hair was coiffed into a helmet unruffled by the wind. "Oh, sir," she said as she exited the van, "Do you have a minute?" and shoved the microphone in his face.

Micheal used his hand to push the mic away. "Lady, I don't know what you're looking for, but it ain't here. This is the dullest street in town. Nothing ever happens here."

She took the opportunity to shove the mic back in his face. "I'm Lindsey Willock with WSPO, the local channel for NBC and local 7news. Hello sir, do you mind telling me your name?"

Michael noticed the mic and the cameraman trying to come from the rear to tape their exchange. Michael pointed at him. "You, no tape, so get back in the van. You," he pointed at Lindsey, "I'll talk off the record whatever it is. What's your question?"

Lindsey pointed with her mic at his neighbor's house. "Is that the home of Bill Phelps?"

"Yes, but you could have just asked the mailman. He's not home. He's away on business."

"What's your relationship with Mr. Phelps?"

"Next-door neighbors. I keep an eye on the place when he's gone."

"So, you've been in the house, I take it?"

"Your interest?" Michael asked.

"Have you noticed a strange woman living there?"

"No. If he had someone staying there, he wouldn't ask me to water the plants."

Michael put on his grizzled cantankerous old goat face. "Lady, you've got two minutes to leave or else I get you a rake and you finish this with me."

Lindsey, a credit to her profession, held fast. "Are you familiar with Mr. Phelps's daughter? Leslie Nelson?"

"I know he has two."

"You may remember Mr. Phelps's daughter was caught up in her husband's financial Ponzi scheme. His location is unknown, and I was hoping she might be here."

"If she's involved why ain't she in jail?" he scratched his beard with his thumb.

"She was cleared of any charges."

"Try her parole officer."

"She wasn't arrested or charged. As I said, she was cleared."

Michael wanted to ratchet it up higher. He took a bandana out of his back pocket and let loose with the snot, noisy and viscous. That last part might have done the trick she was backing away. "There are lights on at night. Why do you suppose that is?"

"Timers. You want to know anymore grab a rake." Michael said and went back to work. He watched the news van pull away and turned back to raking. He didn't notice Leslie peeking between the lace curtains. He finished raking and returned his mind to the issue of dinner.

That was the worst part of losing your spouse, there was always somebody there to help or care or even fake interest in the subject. Dinner. Michael hated dining alone. He preferred to get lunch at the Union Diner where he could sit at the counter and flirt with the waitresses. Michael ordered a big meal so later if he got hungry a sandwich would suffice.

He piled some tree limbs and brush in his fire pit. *That's full, I better burn it soon,* he thought, and an idea popped into his head. He walked to Leslie's back door and rapped on the glass. It took a second time to bring her to the door. "Oh, hey, Michael. What's going on?"

"I was wondering if you had plans for dinner."

She shook her head. "Why? *What do you mean, why?* I just topped off the fire pit and was gonna burn it tonight. I figured have hot dogs on a stick cooked over the fire. It's not much; it's more of an impulse, but I've got a nice red that might make it more palatable."

"A weenie roast? I'd love to. What do you want me to bring?"

"Wine glasses. See you around dusk." He waved as he walked away. He went inside, cleaned up, and had a sudden anxiety attack. It felt like his scalp shrank. Michael sat at the table and put his head in his hands. He breathed through it. *What am I doing? She'd never be interested in an old Chevy. She's more of a Mustang kind of girl.* He remembered why he was interested in her. Boredom. Maybe she was bored, too, and they could be bored together.

As evening faded away, Leslie walked over to his backyard fire pit. He was adjusting the pile, so the underlying wood got enough oxygen.

"Hey there, Boy Scout. Good job there."

Michael looked up at her. "You could say I'm a perfectionist. If I start something I'm driven to finish it. Like your pie. By the time I was done with it there wasn't a crumb left. What do you have there?"

"Just some cheese and crackers. And the wine glasses."

"I'm not ready. The hot dogs are in the house."

"Go get them and a corkscrew. We can have a glass of wine with our appetizers." She looked at the cheese and crackers. "These barely count as an appetizer."

"Take a seat. Use the big stump as a table. I'll be right back." He left to go in the house and came back and sat in the chair on the other side of the stump. Michael opened the wine, and she passed him the glasses.

Michael looked at the finely cut crystal glasses. "These are kind of fancy. Don't you have any paper cups?"

"Maybe," Leslie said. "These are the first ones I found. Besides, it elevates the hot dogs to an entree. Do you have any sticks? For the hot dogs?"

"Yes. Anything kebab is an entrée." He leaned over and picked up stick with a perfectly pointed end. He opened the cooler and placed a package of hotdogs on the stump with the condiments. There was room for everything on it. Leslie remarked about it. "A very big tree once stood here."

"Yes, this was a very good tree to my family. She had branches low enough to climb. Every kid I ever knew wanted to climb that tree. It was getting pretty old, and the year we had those horrendous storms she broke in half and split down the middle. It could have gone in fifty different directions and cause thousands of dollars in damages, but it landed right across our driveway. I was sad when she was gone, but they shaved the stump flush like this."

"Why are these holes here?"

He went in the garage and came out with some tea lights that set inside, and when he lit them, it looked pretty. The light fractured from the crystal and danced around them.

"Wow. That elevates this from a weenie roast to a picnic."

"I like them. They're pretty." Michael said.

A man who appreciates beauty in everyday things, Leslie thought. "They are. Very pretty. Could you hand me my stick? I'm ready to roast."

He passed her over the stick and loaded his too. "I think I'll join you."

They didn't talk too much while they ate. "Do you want another one?" He nodded yes.

Leslie fixed him another hot dog while he ate the first. While he ate, she stood and picked up the trash.

"Look. If you want to pick up my trash, come back tomorrow. Right now, sit down and enjoy the wine."

She did as he asked. They sat in silence for a while. Leslie asked him why he became a science teacher.

"Truthfully, science club in school got to launch rockets and blow things up. It appealed to the teenage boy in me. I didn't particularly like kids. I could take them or leave them, but at the high school level, a lot of teenage boys like to blow things up. Girls, too. I enjoyed my career as a teacher."

"That's what I ended up doing. When we lived in Senecaville, I subbed as needed. Since I had a business degree and a background in math, I turned down a lot of work. I could have worked full-time if I wanted to, but I started teaching college prep classes. I could make a week's salary in a few afternoons. So that's what I've been doing. For now."

"Do you miss it? The city?"

"Not at all."

"Those crowds were really something. You could barely leave your building."

"It was awful." Leslie paused. "You know, don't you? You know I'm not Jenny."

"Yup."

"For how long?"

"Since I met you. I was making sure your dad had two daughters, so I googled it. You were front page news for a while."

"That wasn't very nice to keep it a secret like that."

"Why? You were the one keeping it a secret. I just honored it." Michael stood up and took a stick to poke the fire and get more oxygen near the bottom. The embers shot up with the wind, twinkling like little stars that flew into space. Satisfied, Michael sat back down. "That's a nice fire right there."

"Yes, very nice. How come you never said anything?"

"Why? You said your name was Jenny. You lied. When those news people came, they asked all these questions I couldn't answer. I told her I watched the house and watered the plants while your dad traveled. They asked about a woman, Leslie Nelson. I said I never met her."

"Thanks. I'm done saying I'm sorry. It was a sequence of events that occurred in a way that had very little to do with me, but someone has to pay. I'm the closest the thing to Paul they're gonna get." Her shoulders sagged with the realization it would always be linked to her. *I'm tainted,* she thought. *Tainted? Oh, geez! Quit being so melodramatic.* She smiled at the thought.

Michael reached out and touched her shoulder. "You'll be alright. It'll take time, but things will settle down. It's already stale. The people at Paul's firm are now on the hot seat. Some other scandal will become front-page news. In a year, nobody will have any idea what you've been through. Do you want to open your mail now?" Michael stood up and took the envelope from his back pocket and sat back down. He passed the well-worn and folded envelope to her, but she didn't take it. "You really should open it. What if it's important? I've been hanging on to it for a while."

"If you're so curious you open it."

"No. I think you need to do it. It's probably something stupid like a sales flyer or a Chinese menu."

Leslie took the envelope. She looked at the front and noticed the reason she got it because it was sent to Michael's address. Whoever sent it knew her dad was away, and his mail was held at the Post Office, so mailing it to Michael made sure she'd get it. Or maybe it was just a mistake. It was typewritten and postmarked from Miami. She slid her finger under the flap and gingerly opened it. Leslie pulled out a copy of newsprint that had the picture of her in the back of the police car. Someone took a red marker and drew a heart around her. "What the fuck is this? Do I have a stalker now? How did they find me?" Leslie's voice had a tremor in it, a tremor of fear. The hand holding the letter shook.

Michael put his hand her shoulder when what he wanted to do was encircle her in his arms and tell her she was safe. He wanted her to know she wasn't alone; he would help her in any way she needed. Leslie was hurting in a big way, but unless there were tears, Michael respected her personal space. He left his hand on her shoulder, gave it a gentle squeeze, and took it back. He watched her, trying to get a bead on her mood, but she sat there in silence.

Leslie snapped out of her reverie. She unfolded the clipping and looked at it again. It didn't seem like a random event, it felt like it was some kind of message. It was probably the local news trying to generate a response.

She thought the people Paul screwed over stopped looking for her; she had nothing of value they could take. It was now a feeding frenzy among the lawyers, and Don was there as her counsel. He kept her updated, but there was no news.

"Well," Leslie said, "the postmark is Miami. Whoever's doing this is playing mind games with me. I refuse to play." She leaned in toward the fire, shoved the letter between the burning branches, and watched as the paper caught in a sudden burst of flames. It burned bright and died, the ashes fell and joined the others.

"That's the end of that," Leslie said. "Anything left in the bottle? I'm dry." She extended her fancy glass over to him. He filled her glass and topped his off, emptying the bottle.

"That's the end of that unless you have any at your house."

Leslie took a sip and swirled the liquid in her glass. When she looked at him, the fire danced in the darkness of her eyes.

"No, I'm good," she said and smiled. Michael felt his heart lurch in his chest and looked down to see if she could see it through his shirt.

*∗∗

The letter confused her. It was front-page news on a number of nationwide news outlets for a while, so somebody in Miami could grab a paper at a newsstand and end up with one of her on the front page. But why? What did the heart mean? A stalker? At her age? *Yeah, right.*

She thought maybe it was fan mail, maybe there was another woman who was as disgruntled as she was somewhere else on this planet. Some mad deranged housewife chasing her husband with a meat cleaver. Now, to her, Leslie could relate.

Leslie did everything she was supposed to do like it was preplanned. Don't ask too many questions. Look pretty. Go to college, get a career, get married, become a mother. Buy a place in the suburbs. *Good god, that sounds dreadful!* Leslie thought, *but that was her life's trajectory.*

Wednesday was bright and sunny. The big storm needed to clear the leaves from the trees had yet to occur. The leaves were past peak and were now

140

dull yellow and rust, still clinging but soon to fall, losing the energy to hang on any longer.

Michael went over around ten-thirty. She was in the kitchen and let him in. "Want a cup before we get on the road?" Leslie offered. He wanted one, so she prepared one for herself. They both sat at the table. "Looks like a beautiful day for pumpkin picking."

"Yes, it is." Michael agreed. Leslie started laughing. "What's so funny?"

"You. Me. We match." Leslie had on jeans, work boots, a tee shirt covered by a flannel shirt. He did, too.

"We do. You have to go change. I'm not walking around a pumpkin patch with some girl dressed like me. They'll think we're a couple of goofballs. Like those leaf peepers who came up from the city to 'experience' a real farm."

"Yeah, we do sort of match, but I'm not changing. If anybody asks, we're part of a cult."

"You know of a cult around here?"

"It's a secret cult. Nobody knows about it." He laughed when she said that. "OK. Our name is the Secret Society of the Orange Orb."

They finished their coffee. Leslie had to run and go pee before they left. Michael laughed her. "Why do all women pee so much? My wife was always in the bathroom." He mentioned his wife without feeling guilty or sad. He bet Emily would've like Leslie. Everybody liked Leslie. She had a nice, welcoming way about her and could talk to anybody and make them feel special. Michael was surprised he could think about his wife and Leslie in the same sentence without feeling a sense of betrayal; that was progress. To be honest, he never found a woman who compared to Emily.

He wasn't that much older than Leslie, and a relationship wasn't inconceivable, except she had so much happened over the last year. The reality of her life turning over and straightening things out could take years. The one thing she needed was a friend. He liked her enough to be her friend. Michael wasn't sure he wanted to get involved with a woman anyway. He'd be happy stay on the sidelines and lust after Leslie. It was nice to know he was still capable of having a woman smile at him and get hard.

Leslie came back laughing. "Maybe it has something to do with having a couple of kids sitting on our bladders for nine months."

"Fair enough. Take my truck?" He asked. She got in, and he headed out to the country. It was a beautiful day. Leslie rolled down the window, but it blew her hair all crazy, so she rolled it back up. Michael looked at her as she tried to settle it back into place.

He was surprised she could still be considered pretty. Usually after 50, women start to look like grandmas. Creepy skin, moles and skin tags, unfortunately, came along with your Medicare card, but Leslie seemed immune to them. Yes, she had crow's feet and lines on her face, but when she smiled, it all blurred, and she looked ageless.

"Here we are," he said, and turned up a gravel drive and headed to the barn when his right tire went bam! As it went into a pothole. The resulting bounce out of the hole caused them to almost hit their heads on the roof. The glove box popped open. "Are you alright? Did you hurt your head?" Michael asked before he parked the truck and got out to check his tire.

"No, I'm good. Seatbelt did its job."

He stuck his head in the driver's side door. "It looks ok. We'll see if it's flat when we're done."

"What will we do if it is?"

"Worry about it then." He looked at her, puzzled. "What?"

Leslie held up a ziplock bag containing three rolled joints. "These fell out of the glove compartment."

"Oh," he said and got in the truck. He closed the door and looked at her. "Poker Night. Twice a month. Does that offend you?"

"No. I haven't got high since my wedding. We had this goth girl at the wedding, Grace. Paul's niece. She made it a point to go opposite the status quo. There was an outdoor patio with a cigar bar, and Grace and I wandered off and lit a blunt. Then these two guys come over. I couldn't be caught out there with a bunch of stoners. I kept laughing at everything and left. Later when I ran into Grace we just cracked up."

"If you want, we can fire it up now."

"Now?"

"Now. Here's the lighter."

Leslie lit it and smoked like a teenage boy at the skate park. She passed it over and he smoked it like, *this is an interesting turn of events.* They each took another hit, and he stubbed it out. He took it with him. "I hope it wasn't too much. We go on a hayride in a little while out to the pumpkin patch. I'd hate it if you fell off."

They walked around the general store for a bit, waiting for the tractor to return. Michael looked at the gemstones. Leslie looked around and wandered away. It took Michael a few minutes to realize she was gone and few more to find her. She was sitting on a bench outside, her eyes closed, her face tilted towards the sun. Michael sat next to her and said, "What're you doing? I thought I lost you for a minute."

"Sorry. It felt so good to just sit here and absorb nature. I didn't want to lose my seat looking for you. I figured you'd be by." She blinked and opened her eyes. "I was just thinking about the boys going pumpkin picking. They could have any pumpkin as long as they carried it. What a fiasco. The old farmer came over with a wheelbarrow and took the pumpkins up to the checkout. He gave them rides in the wheelbarrow while I paid.

He helped load everything and waved goodbye. "I just had a moment of clarity. Paul wasn't there. I thought we shared everything, including memories, but I guess not." Leslie stood. "Come on," she said as she pulled on his hand. "I hear the tractor."

Wednesday wasn't the busiest day at the Pumpkin Patch. It was just them and a kindergarten class. They climbed and sat atop the hay bales. It took the two teachers a while to get all the kids corralled and on the flatbed. One little girl got on crying and sat near them. Leslie asked the teacher if the child was okay, and the woman said, "That's what she always does. She's very slow adapting to to new environments. Once she's used to it, she won't leave. She'll be crying all the way home."

"Poor thing," Leslie said to Michael. "Kids are so different. Not everyone learns the same way. Why am I telling you that? You're a teacher."

"Yes. God help the kid that's a square peg trying to fit in a round hole. I had one class of misfits. Behavioral problems, ADD, and troubles at home. It was a step-down class. The curriculum was watered down, anything to get them to graduate."

"Wow. How hard was it teaching those kids?"

"Great. I loved those kids. They liked to blow things up as much as any other kids, maybe more." Michael tapped the crying girl on the shoulder. She turned around, still weeping. "Psst. I have something for you. Is it hard to go to new places?"

She stopped crying, slowing to hiccups. Snot ran down her face. Leslie whipped out a tissue and cleaned her face before she could protest. Michael took a small crystal out of his pocket. "Is your name Rose?"

"No," the little girl said. "It's Emma."

"I only asked because that's the name of this crystal, Rose. Rose quartz. How funny would it be if you both had the same name?"

The little girl laughed. "I'm glad we don't. I don't think Rose is a pretty name."

Michael jerked his head toward Leslie. "Don't say that too loud. That's her name. This rose quartz is special. It helps you be brave. It can't be brave for you, but if you're brave, it can help you stay brave if you rub the crystal. You have a lot of bravery inside you, this will just help you get it out.

"Now, it's a very special crystal, and I only have one. I'd like to give it to you, but I shouldn't because I don't have one for everyone. I think you need it the most, so here's what we'll do. I'll give it to you and you carry it when you need to be brave. Keep it in your pocket. If anybody asks, tell them a magician gave it to you. Now put it in your pocket so it's right there when you need it. Keep it there so you don't lose it."

Emma stared at him. "You're not a magician."

"Oh, yeah? You don't think I'm a magician? You should be there when I saw Rose in half. If you don't think I'm a magician, I guess you don't need the crystal." Michael put his hand out.

Emma shoved her hand back in the pocket with the crystal. "I think I want to keep it. Just in case."

"That's fine. Go sit with your class and keep the crystal safe."

Michael turned and looked at Leslie, who was stifling a laugh as Michael talked to the little girl. "What?"

"That was very sweet. Do you always carry magic crystals with you?"

"I bought it in the gift shop for five bucks. It spoke to me. I was going to give it to you. Sorry. She needed it more than you do."

The tractor hit a bump, and Leslie fell back against Michael. She started laughing again. It was a beautiful sound. Michael wondered when the last time she laughed like that, and the tractor hit another bump. She rolled in the other direction, and he grabbed her to keep her upright. "Leslie cut it out! You're gonna fall off. Stop laughing. What's so funny?" He looked at her with her eyes shut and a wide smile. *Oh.* He laughed along with her.

The tractor stopped and all the kids screamed and took off in all directions, except the kid who got his head stepped on. The teachers were outmanned and overwhelmed at once, but the field, strewn with pre-picked pumpkins, the greenery flattened under so much foot traffic they could always see the kids. Outside, the fall air is just what pumpkin ordered.

They watched the kids jump off and run. Michael and Leslie laughed again and headed in the opposite direction. "That was a trip," Leslie said.

"And how," he said, shaking his head.

They surveyed the field in front of them. Pre-picked pumpkins lay in front of them.

"I feel like we got ripped off. It's supposed to be a patch. A pumpkin patch."

"Maybe it's late in the season. Which ones do you want?" Michael asked. "Remember, you only get one if you can carry it."

"Good thing I was a shot putter in high school." Leslie said.

"You were?" Michael said, impressed.

Leslie grabbed a pumpkin by the stem. "Hell, no." She laughed, and the pumpkin she had by the stem broke. She fell backwards, still laughing.

"What is *wrong* with you?" Michael stepped over to help her, caught his toe on a root, and fell next to her. He started laughing because she was laughing. They could hear the tractor. Michael got up and ran to meet it, close enough to hear the farmer yell he had to get the kids to their school bus and he'd be back for them. He trotted back to Leslie who was sitting in the dirt. Michael asked if she wants to finish the rest of the joint. She did, they did and were laughing about the fact they were sitting in the dirt, laughing their heads off.

"This has been a really fun day, Michael. I think I finally fell off the radar. There are bigger fish to fry than me. You were right. Something else is front page news. It helped the Feds announced I was no longer a person of interest."

Maybe it was the joint, but Michael opened his mouth, unsure of what would come out. "I think you're a person of interest. I've never been friends with a felon before."

"Alleged felon. Exonerated felon. Felony adjacent." She clarified. Leslie laid down in the dirt. She pointed to the sky and said, "That cloud there looks like a felon." Michael lay down next to her.

"It does not. It looks like a dog." Leslie started to laugh again.

"Will you stop laughing? Somebody's going to say something."

Leslie sat up, shook the leaves and dirt out of her hair. She said, "who? The Scarecrow? I haven't laughed like this in a long time. It feels good not to worry about being happy when somebody could be watching."

Michael sat up, too. His lack of hair required a swish or two of his hands. Michael didn't care about his lack of hair all, the Caldwell men were bald and he was used to it. Emily never minded his lack of hair. She used to rub his head for luck. An inside joke they shared. Being here with Leslie felt like he was cheating on her.

"What's up? Why are you so quiet?" Leslie asked, sensing Michael's uneasiness.

He wasn't sure how to answer her when he heard the tractor. "We better get out there or we'll miss our ride. Grab your pumpkin, Leslie."

"I want two. Will you carry the other one for me, please?"

"No. When we get back, they have them down where you pay."

"I guess so." Leslie didn't sound convinced and picked hers up. "Uh. This is heavy."

"Here, let's switch. Mine's smaller." They swapped pumpkins with each other, laughing made it harder than it needed to be. They got situated in the back of the flatbed with their feet hanging down and the tractor lurched forward. Michael put his arm out in front to catch her, but it wasn't needed when the tractor hit a bump. Leslie fell his way, a pumpkin rolled off and smashed to bits. They both laughed and laughed some more. They arrived back at the lot and were only ones left. The farmer waved and drove off.

They went into the barn and into the neo-homey old country store, inside plenty of gingham and barn wood. Live~Laugh~Love signs were everywhere, painted on everything. Mrs. Farmer waited on them. "You two got lucky today. Those are two fine pumpkins you have there."

"Oh. Can you add on two more?" Michael said and grabbed two from the display. "We lost a couple on the way back."

"Yes. The road is kind of bumpy. Occupational hazard, I guess." The woman took their money and gave Michael the change. "Take the wheelbarrow and load it up so you don't lose anymore." Michael ran and got it.

"You know, I could have paid for my own." Leslie said. "You didn't have to."

"I know. I figured it was easiest for her to do them all at once. Let's put them in the truck." They loaded his truck with the pumpkins. "Would you sit in the wheelbarrow for a minute?" He asked her.

"Why?"

"Humor me. I paid for your pumpkin."

Maybe because she was still a little stoned, she did as he asked. "Now what?"

He picked up the handles and started off. "You're going for a little ride!" Leslie screamed. She wasn't sure if it would pitch to the side and dump her out, but her screams turned to laughter, and he joined in. He went faster and pretended to tip her over. "Watch out! Oh, oh!" He yelled as he pushed her. They were back in the gravel rocks parking area. The farmer and his wife stood by the register and watched. Michael and Leslie didn't notice until he tipped it over, and she fell out. He leaned over and helped her up. They were dusting themselves off when the farmer spoke.

"You're lucky those kids left, or you'd be giving them rides, too."

"I don't think my back could take it. She's heavy enough," he laughed.

"Hey!"

"You two seem to be having an awful lot of fun," Mrs. Farmer said.

"It's your fault," Leslie said. "There's too much to do here."

"There isn't that much," Mr. Farmer said. "I think he's sweet on you."

"Her? I'd be crazy to get involved with her. She's a bad influence." Michael said. "Thank you. We had a wonderful time but have to run. She's out on a day pass from the halfway house, and if she's late getting back, she'll be on lockdown until spring."

"Goodbye!" They said as he hustled back on the road and drove off, beeping to the Farmers as they left.

Leslie leaned back and stretched. She looked at him out of her side eye, but he was looking straight ahead, his eyes on the road. Leslie wasn't sure she liked him not looking at her. *Think about it. If he was looking at you, it would only make you angry,* Leslie thought. It was true. Michael's voice pierced the quiet.

"You too tired to grab something to eat? We didn't have lunch."

"No, we didn't, and yes, I am."

"Oh, good. There's a BBQ place up here. Does that work for you?"

Leslie nodded. "Are you sure it's this way? Doesn't look like there's anything here."

Michael turned down a road that only qualified as one because it was bigger than a path. Hidden in the brush was a rusted sign, visible only when you were driving by it. "Piggies Bonafide Bar-be-que. Best East of the the Mississippi," Leslie read. "When were you last here?"

"It's been a while, but it looks the same as it did last time I was here." He continued on down the road until it opened to a wide parking lot crowded with cars. "See? Lots of cars." He pulled into a spot. Michael got out and went over to help her out, but she was on the ground before he got close. *It seems like chivalry is dead, after all,* he thought.

They walked over to the door, and Leslie let Michael hold it open for her. "Thank you, kind sir," she said and smiled at him.

Gulp.

✳✳✳

It wasn't crowded, most of the cars must have belonged to the bar patrons. The hostess took them to a table furthest away from the bar. "Is this table, okay? I tried to get you away from the bar. A ball game is on, at least here, you can hear each other talk."

Michael looked at Leslie to see if it was acceptable, and she nodded. "Looks great," Michael said. "We have a window." They sat down, and the server took their drink order and walked away, promising to be NASCAR fast.

"Is it good? To be that fast?" Michael asked.

"Yes, it's very fast. But you know that," Leslie answered.

"Busted. I just said that to buy some time figuring how to approach you."

"Why don't just say hi?"

The hostess came back with their drinks, dropped the menus off and left.

"If I say hi and you tell me 'no thanks' I'd be crushed, so I'd rather live with a possibility than a definite no."

"What if I said I have no idea what you're talking about?" Leslie took a sip of her lemonade.

"Well, it's like this. My wife has been dead for a number of years, and I finally thought I was ready to rejoin the human race. Locally, pickings are slim. I never worry about it, and I keep myself busy. I see your dad and drink a beer. Then I spend an afternoon with you, and it's the most fun I've had in ages. My eyes opened to the possibility of having a partner."

"Me?" Leslie squeaked.

"You? No. I'm too old for you. But somebody. I'd like to have a girl I could call up and say, 'you want to come up to the lake tomorrow?'"

"I think that sounds nice. It's hard being alone. That's not anything new to you, but my life got chewed up from the inside out. I don't know where

150

I belong. My old life- I don't miss it at all. My husband? Him, I miss. But that's because I have a bunch of questions. Exactly who was my husband? When he said I love you, I believed it. I trusted him to take care of us, his family. I was wrong. The last thirty years were based on a foundation of sand. So, who am I if he's not here to define me?" Leslie said, looking out of the window as if searching the horizon for answers.

"Leslie, I haven't known you that long, but I do know this: your life has not been a figment of husband's imagination. You have two wonderful sons, and your dad and siblings adore you." Michael searched her face to see if he was getting through. "You have been a source of joy for those that have had the pleasure to know you. You are more than capable of defining yourself. Don't let your husband rob you of one more second."

Leslie sat and digested what he said. She finally spoke. "Michael, you're right. Maybe what got me here was bullshit, but I'm here. Here isn't so bad. I have a great family. I'm healthy. So what, I'm broke? I'm good for now. Something will happen. Something always does." She stopped talking to allow the server to put their plates in front of them. They both had BLTs and fries. Another server followed with their drinks. After they left Michael picked up his glass. "A toast."

"To what?"

"Tomorrow," he said, raising his eyebrows. "C'mon."

Leslie picked up her glass. "I'll drink to that. To tomorrow." She took a sip and smiled at him.

Gulp. I wish she'd stop doing that, he thought as he smiled back.

They had a nice leisurely lunch; it was only when the table service started to get ready for dinner, they realized how long they were sitting there. "We need to go, Leslie. I think we're in their way."

Leslie's head swiveled around and looked at the empty tables. "You're right." She stood up. Michael rose and ushered her out to the bright afternoon light. The wind picked up and blew the dusty leaves around. He opened the door, seated her, and got in the driver's side.

"Thank you, Leslie. I can't remember the last time I had so much fun." He smiled, but a shadow passed over his face. He pulled out and started back home. Leslie looked at his profile.

"It's okay, you know," she said.

"What is?"

"Having fun. Without Emily."

"I know, but sometimes I feel guilty; about having a good time when she's not here."

"From what you told me about her, I think she loved you enough to want you to go on and have a good time whether she's here or not. She had no choice but to follow the path laid out for her, and you walked by her side the entire way. She was blessed, in that way, to have you. Now, I think she'd want you to find somebody to walk with you when the time comes."

His eyes were bright with unshed tears. "You're absolutely right. It's so damn hard, though. It feels like I'd be replacing her."

"No, you're not. You have two beautiful daughters. You'll see her looking at their faces. Or the way they act. She might think she left you with the best of everything."

Michael glanced at her and smiled. "Thank you, Leslie. It's been so long that I think I'm the only one who remembers her. It makes me sad, though."

"It will probably never go away, the pain of losing her. Or the joy of being her husband."

He drove them home, his psyche soothed by Leslie's innate grasp of his thoughts. Michael was embarrassed about the amount of grief he held in his heart, an unending source deep inside. He felt differently after talking to Leslie. She felt his sadness and acknowledged it, something most people avoided. They all thought he should be over it by now. It was ancient history, something that happened so long ago that it was pointless to talk about it now.

Leslie didn't minimize his pain, and mentioning it removed some of the guilt that weighed heavy on him for years. He somehow fused her death and his pain together, and that was wrong. He should be able to think of wonderful things, and precious memories with love. Love they shared together. The clock ran out on them sooner than it should have, but she was the most incredible thing to ever happened to him, and she didn't deserve to be linked to pain. She was the greatest joy of his life and should be remembered as such.

It was almost dusk when they got home. He placed the pumpkins on his steps, and they made plans to carve them on Saturday. Each said goodbye and went home. Michael paused and watched her lock up. Once she left and went deeper into the house, he locked up his house and went to bed.

The next morning, he was shocked when he saw her at his door. It was a Saturday morning; the clear yellow light gave no clue to the chilly weather outside. He opened the door, still shocked to see her. "Come on in. Coffee?"

"No, I forgot to tell you I have a couple of kids I tutor on Saturday, but I'll be over about one o'clock.

"One o'clock?" he said, puzzled.

"To do the pumpkins? Or do you have other plans?"

"No. It just took me a second, but one is fine."

She turned and made her way to the door and left. Michael watched her Jeep leave, and he went to take a shower. Soon, he was out in the garage arranging his tools. He adored his tools. They were the old men's equivalent to blowing things up. Michael heard her Jeep pull in and peeked out of the window but didn't see her. Leslie came over shortly with a box rattling around. "What's in there?"

"Some tools to clean the insides."

He picked up a drill. He started it and looked inside Leslie's box. "Tools?" He said over the blasting noise of the drill. "You call those tools?" He turned the drill off. "Now, I've got *tools.*"

Leslie watched Michael work. He had the insides out in two minutes. She was enthralled by the whole process. The look on Leslie's face was nothing short of Rapture. He laughed at her.

"That was incredible. Look how clean it is," she said, her hair falling towards both sides of the pumpkin.

"Don't get your hair in there."

"Why? Is it hard to get out?"

"I wouldn't know," he said smiling and pointing toward his bald head.

She laughed. "Yes, why would you know? What do you want me to do?" he instructed her to the desk. "Use the pen and create six spooky faces."

Leslie got out her phone and googled pumpkin stencils, a number of odd ideas filled her feed. She sketched out the ones she liked. Michael stopped his drill to see if she had any faces ready. He had already leveled them and cleaned out the guts. She handed him the faces.

"Alien life forms? I'll cut two, and we can each have one."

"Are any of these of interest? Carving six pumpkins is a lot of work."

Michael's eyes lit up. "Nope. Any excuse to use them is fine." He got out his band saw, put his goggles on and fired it up. He smiled and turned his back to her. Five minutes later he asked her opinion.

"You're finished so soon?"

"Skill plus power yields quick results."

He was finished in no time. Leslie cleaned up as he went, and other than his power tools his workshop was returned to its pre-gourd condition. "I'll be finished in no time flat. I'm going to take a quick shower. I've got enough wood for one more burn, and it's supposed to be a nice night out. We had a late lunch, but I have some hot dogs if we get hungry."

Michael hurried. He wanted to surprise Leslie and have all the jack-o-lanterns lit when she came back. From what he felt so far, Leslie was the type of girl who delighted in the simple. If she walked over and he arranged the lit pumpkins in a display, she'd be thrilled. Way more thrilled than warranted. The smaller the gesture, the greater her pleasure. He knew there was no future with her. He was her father's friend. *But it was nice to be able to do something and not feel like it was fodder for the dump.*

He stepped back to the house to see how it presented itself when Leslie came around the corner. He saw her before she knew he was there. The look on her face was priceless. Her mouth opened, and she gasped. "You like?" he asked.

"Oh! You scared me! These pumpkins look so good." Leslie said, smiling. Even in the late evening light, he could see the flames dancing in her eyes. Michael reached out and took the tray she was holding.

"They're brownies. I didn't do so great on the appetizers, so I switched to dessert."

"Take a seat. I'll get us a couple of glasses, and we can drink to the end of daylight savings time."

"Is that this weekend? I wasn't aware."

"I don't know. I think it's in a week or two."

Michael sat down and poured them each a glass and sat silently as he looked at the fire.

"Are you ok?" Leslie asked. "You're being awfully quiet."

"I'll be right back. I've got something for you." He went in the house and came out holding a piece of paper. He sat back down and laid an envelope on the stump. On top of it was a joint and a white Bic lighter. Leslie looked at the items. "What's up with this?"

"It's a joint and another letter addressed to you at my house. We could get high and open it, or open it and get high."

"Are you some kind of pothead?"

"No. I admit I picked it up after my wife died. It was the only thing that calmed my internal chaos. I never smoke alone, and usually just on Thursdays, but you're the perfect partner. You get so mellow. No stress. No drama. No commute. Right next door."

"What's the envelope?"

"Leslie Nelson in c/o my address again."

"I think I'd like a hit before I see my mind-fucked mail."

"What's that mean?"

"It means this is supposed to be another piece of a puzzle, but I'm not supposed to figure it out just yet. It could be one of those people who are really angry at Paul and thinks I know more than I do. Maybe I should relocate out west near the boys. So, yeah, light that bad boy."

Michael lit the joint, took a big hit, and passed it over. After they were done, he put it out and grabbed the envelope. He passed it to her, and she held it by her thumb and forefinger. Leslie tore open the envelope and pulled out another news clipping. It was her leaving the courthouse after she was freed. Again, a newsprint article with a red heart drawn around her.

Leslie stood up and put the paper in the fire, a with a whoosh it flamed out. She sat back down but didn't speak. After a while, she said, "if the sender's intent is to scare me, he's a bit late for that. I was arrested by the FBI. I'm not sure there's anything to be gained by harassing me other than some petty revenge." *Why the hearts, though?* Leslie thought. *If it was hatred that drove the letters, she would be Xed out, crossed out, or blackened out. Not a heart unless it was a message. A message they wanted to rip her heart out.*

"I don't get it. What purpose does this serve? Maybe somebody got the house number wrong, and it's no more complicated than that. You know how much news coverage I had. Maybe it's a stalker with a mad crush on me? You know how nutty people can be. Maybe someone kept seeing me on TV and think I was sending them a secret message; that I was in love with them. That's why the hearts."

"You know, Leslie, if they have my address, they know approximately where you are. You could be being watched by some lunatic. You need to be careful."

"You think? That's pretty extreme."

"All bets are off. You have no idea who it could be. It could be some nut job. You need to be careful and aware of your surroundings. Maybe the hearts are just a disguise, so you think it's harmless. It's harmless until it's not."

"Should I be scared?" Leslie asked as if the idea just occurred to her.

"Probably not. You just need to be careful." Michael said, trying not to alarm her.

Leslie and Michael sat until the fire turned to embers and both went home, beat and ready for bed.

***

Leslie went home and checked all the doors and windows. She was locked in for the night and went upstairs to bed. There was nothing to watch on TV, she read until she was sleepy getting up once to look out the window, but the street was quiet. She turned the TV on the timer and fell asleep before it went off.

The next morning, she sat having her coffee and looked on her computer, perusing her favorite gossip sites. She was getting old. So many of the young people had names she didn't recognize.

Leslie looked at her email. Another load of unwanted digital correspondence. She started to click/delete, click/delete. Occasionally, something different; her friend Jess wanted her artichoke dip recipe, and her alma mater wanted money. She had been unsubscribing as fast as possible, but nothing stopped the deluge. She got a request to join other people creating a fund to spend on fine art. *What do they do? Have twelve investors buy a Picasso, and each get a month with it?*

Leslie was glad she didn't have enough money to consider investing in art. *That one's for Paul to figure out,* and remembered there was no Paul. It felt like a piece of her broken heart migrated and got stuck in her chest. She started to cry, to sob gut-wrenching sobs. The tears did nothing to rid the blockage caused by that piece of her heart.

Leslie sat back and stopping crying; she took dish towel, wiped her face, and closed her eyes. She tried to calm herself with the breathing techniques she learned at Yoga. After fifteen minutes, she felt better and opened her eyes. Leslie was trying to figure out why she broke down. She hadn't cried about Paul in a while, and the sudden outpouring of tears surprised her.

She was married to Paul for almost thirty years. Leslie didn't care about the money or the circumstances in which she found herself, she missed *Paul.* Love isn't a tap to be turned on or off.

Leslie couldn't help it. She still believed her husband loved her. Leslie grieved for her past, for her sons' loss of a dad, for the blank space in front of her. Everything she loved was a lie, except for the boys.

If some weirdo was stalking her, she did not want to point towards her boys and decided to stay put. *Whoever it was will get bored and go bother someone else.* Leslie thought. She shut the computer down and stopped thinking about Paul. It didn't matter if he loved her or not, he loved money and power more.

***

A knock on the kitchen door interrupted her introspection. It was Michael and she waved him in. He came in rubbing his hands together. "It's a little chilly out there." He looked up at Leslie and noticed her puffy eyes and sad demeanor. "You okay, Leslie?"

"Yeah, I'm okay. Just got stuck in the past for a minute. What's going on?"

"I've to run an errand, and I thought you might want to come along."

"Yes, I'd like to get out of here. Let me grab my jacket." She grabbed her coat, and they went outside. "You're right. It is quite brisk out here. Where are we going?"

"It's a surprise. C'mon, we'll take the truck."

Michael pulled out and started to drive.

"Not a hint? A clue?"

"The Farmers Market. This is the last weekend, and then it closes for the season."

"What's at the market that's so important?"

"Pumpkins. I need a couple more."

Leslie laughed. "Pumpkins? Halloween's this week. If you wait a few days, they'll be giving them away."

"You'll like these pumpkins. They're different."

The crisp fall morning warmed a bit with the bright sun, and when they got to the market, it was a beautiful day. They parked and walked to the stalls. Leslie stopped at the first stand. It overflowed with orange orbs of all sizes. "What size? You have your pick here."

"Oh, no, no. They're much better back here." They walked to his preferred stand. "Right here."

"They are the same color as the other ones." He took her hand and pulled her to the back, the farmer nodding hello to Michael. He took Leslie over to a pen containing puppies. "This color. Which one looks good?"

"The two females the guy is coming back for. Only the male is left." Michael picked the puppy up. "What do you think, Leslie? He's a handsome devil."

Leslie glanced at the puppy, but the mother's whine caught her attention. She looked like she was part Australian Shepherd and a mix of some sort. She was distressed as Michael handled her baby and continued to cry. Leslie knelt and tried to soothe the dog.

"Shut up, you damn dog. You take the male, and I'll take care of her." The farmer called over his shoulder.

"What do you mean, 'take care of her?'" Leslie said.

"Lady, somebody dumped this pregnant dog off at my barn. She ain't mine. I figured the pups would go easy from here, but I don't need another dog. I don't *want* another dog. So, she'll go the way animals go when they ain't wanted on a farm."

Michael put his hand on Leslie's shoulder, but she pushed it away. She stood up and looked at the farmer. "Does she at least have a name?"

The farmer looked at her. *Another whiny bleeding-heart liberal do-gooder,* he thought.

"Look, lady, we try not to get too attached to the ones, you know, we can't keep. Too bad. She's a real sweet dog. Smart, too, but I got no place for her."

Leslie blinked a few times, and Michael sensed a storm brewing. He put the pup down with the mother and took her arm. "Leslie," he started to say, but she pushed his arm off.

"What are you going to do, Mister? Take her out behind the barn and shoot her?" Leslie's voice raised up louder. "Is *that* what you do?"

The farmer looked at Leslie with pity in his eyes. City people didn't understand a farm's finite resources, and if he fed every stray dog, he'd go broke, but she looked like a nice lady.

Michael was wondering if in fact bringing Leslie here was such a good idea. He didn't think it through. *Everybody loves puppies,* he thought.

"Lady," the farmer said, "she's a real nice dog. I wish I had somewhere she could go, but I don't."

"I'll take her."

"Leslie," Michael said. "Think this through. I brought you here to look at the puppies, not to get a dog. Do you even want a dog?"

"I want this one. Even if I don't keep her, I'll find her a good home. She doesn't deserve to go behind the barn. It's not her fault the original owners didn't get her fixed and dumped her, and it's not her fault the farmer can't keep her. She can stay with me. It's lonely at night, and I want this dog."

"If you say so, lady, she's yours. She's a good dog, and I'm glad she found a home. Do you still want the pup?"

Michael didn't see how he could get out of it, so he said yes, and they left with two dogs, one more than he planned on, but he should have known it was in Leslie's DNA to not walk away.

***

"She's a nice dog," Leslie said as they headed home. Leslie insisted they wait for the other two pups to go so the mom could kiss them goodbye. The farmer said Lady, you can wait if you want, so she and Micheal sat and played with the puppy where the mom could see him. The man came for the females, and the mom licked them both. She started to show signs of stress, but they distracted her by having her follow her son to Michael's truck, and she jumped in after her pup. With Leslie, the cab was crowded, all squished around each other. Leslie stroked her dog's silky fur. She switched to scratching the dog's ears. "She needs a name. Anything come to mind?"

Michael said "Lady."

"She is dainty. I love her. Lady's a good name. What made you think of that?"

"The farmer kept saying, okay, Lady. If you want, Lady. Whatever you need, Lady. Okay, Lady."

"I know, but he was talking about me."

"Okay, Lady."

Leslie looked at the dog's tail. Tremulously wagging, a tail wagging with hope. Her dainty face and large luminous eyes turned up at Leslie. With all the shitty people in her life she had no reason to think Leslie was any better, but she looked at Leslie still with hope. A place where she was wanted, and where she wanted to be, where people were kind. She never understood her role as a dog. She was barely a year old.

Somebody gave her to a friend, who traded her to someone who dumped her when she when going to have puppies. She made a bed in an empty stall, and that's where the farmer found her. He wasn't a cruel man, he knew she was going to have them any minute. He gave her water and food until it was time to go to the market. He brought all six, two boys and four girls.

The dog could tell they were taking her babies and was quite distraught. The farmer took another. Where were her babies? She cried despite it making the man mad at her when her faith was rewarded by the nice lady who knelt in front of her and fell in love.

"Well, hello there, little momma." Leslie said, smiling at the dog. She thumped her tail with the conviction yes, she did find her home.

"What are you going to name him?"

"His name is Rex."

"Rex is good. It means King. How come you named him that?"

"It was the first name I thought. It worked, so Rex he is."

"Michael? Did you plan on coming home with a dog?"

He glanced at Leslie. She was in the moment, enjoying the day and the dog in her lap. Rex didn't like being the odd dog out and was climbing over her legs and on his mom. "No, I honestly thought you'd like to see the puppies, and that would be that. Lady, there, is a sweetheart. Rex is going to take a bit of work."

Leslie took out her phone and took a picture, sending it on to her dad. Look what I got! She wrote. A few minutes later, Michael's phone rang. It was Bill Phelps. Michael answered and said he was on his way home from the Farmer's Market. Yup. It is. I'll call you later.

Michael pulled into a pet store. "You need to treat her for fleas and ticks. She's been outside, and you don't want those in your house." They bought the dogs some food and treats, beds, and the flea treatment. Located next door was the Doggie 'Doos Salon, and they had time to give her a bath with critter-ridder shampoo. Lady was afraid of everything, but she was mostly afraid the lady was going to change her mind and leave her there. Her fears were not as bad as before, but she was still nervous. Her new owner stood right by and watched all the grime she'd been cased in rinse down the drain. "You are going to be the prettiest girl ever!" Leslie told her, and Lady was happy she pleased the lady.

All set. Lady was the perfect name. After her bath, she pranced around as if she was showing off. *See how pretty I am?* She seemed to say to Leslie. *And I'm all yours.*

They got home and Michael helped her bring the dog supplies into Leslie's kitchen, but Leslie was absorbed by her new pet.

"Bye, Leslie. Wish me luck."

"Why do you need luck?"

"Because yours must be housebroken, Rex here has a way to go."

Leslie laughed. "See you tomorrow. Want to take the dogs for a walk in the morning? Okay, see you then."

He laughed and headed home with his new dog.

"Come on in, Rex. This is your new home." Michael watched Rex smell his new environment. He went to hike his leg up, and Michael clapped his hands. A startled Rex stopped and looked at him. Michael scooped the puppy up and brought him outside. The dog went back to sniffing around and emptied his bladder. Michael leaned over and handed him a training treat and heaped praise upon him going potty outside. Just what Michael did not want to do. The puppy seemed smart, once crate-trained, and with regular exercise should catch on quickly.

As soon as Michael got inside, he sat at the kitchen table. *I'm gonna need a gate,* he thought, or else my whole house is going to be one big urinal. Right now, Rex was taking a nap. He dialed Bill Phelps.

"Hey, Bill."

"Michael, what's this about a dog?"

"I took Leslie to the Farmer's Market to look at some puppies. I thought, what's wrong with that? Everybody loves puppies."

"She got a puppy?"

"No, I got the puppy. Leslie took the mom. The farmer told your daughter that once her puppies were gone, she'd be taken care of the farmer's way. Once she figured out it was a slug to the head, she was adamantly not going to leave her behind. I ended up with the puppy. You don't want a puppy, do you?"

"That's my Leslie. Righting wrongs whenever she sees one. It sounds like she's happy."

"She is. The mother was so upset they kept taking her puppies away, but she found a kindred spirit in Leslie. We stopped at the pet store, and they had an opening, so she's nice and clean. At the market, she looked really grubby, but she cleaned up nicely. Pretty dog. Seems really sweet, too."

"Thanks for keeping an eye on her. That situation with Paul knocked her for a loop. It seems like she's getting her back on her feet. I'll be home the weekend before Thanksgiving. The week after I'm taking Billy around and turning over the accounts."

"Well, hurry up. I'm afraid of what will happen if we go to the zoo."

***

Michael worked on house-breaking Rex, who grew daily. Lady may have been a little lady, but Rex had paws the size of dinner plates. He was a big, exuberant puppy. They took the dogs each morning for an hour's walk to tire them out so Michael could get some work done. It seemed as soon as he started Rex would get his head stuck in a paint can or something equally annoying and distract him.

One morning after their walk, a truck labeled Evergreen Fence Company was parked in Bill's driveway. "Surprise!" Leslie said. "My dad is getting the yard fenced in for Lady."

"Lady? That dog is stuck to you like Velcro. She doesn't need a fence."

"It's for you, too. If you want some free time, stick him in our yard. He can play with Lady or sleep on the deck." Leslie laughed.

"I'd like to make a big stink and say if I wanted a fenced-in yard, I'd get my own, but I'm just going to say thanks and leave it at that."

"I know the plan was to see if I wanted to get a puppy, something to keep me busy, but I ended up with Lady. And you ended up with the puppy. I feel bad about that. I didn't know it was for me. But I got Lady. I don't think I could care for a puppy. I'd forget to let it out. Or in. But Lady gives me something I didn't know I needed, something that cares about me. Paul's rejection of me hit me hard, and Lady just loves me. A puppy wouldn't be mature enough to give me that. If it isn't something you want to do, he's a beautiful puppy. We could find him a good home."

Michael looked down at his feet, Rex lying on his back chewing his shoelace. He looked at the fence. "If I could put him over there when he's driving me crazy, that's huge. He's pretty much housebroken, and it's nice to have him laying at my feet while I watch the news, so he can stay for now."

"That's nice.

"You all set for Halloween?"

"I've got the pumpkins on the porch rail. I wanted to light the walk with them, but little kids are barely smarter than Rex. I can just see some kid's costume catch on fire because he wanted to see what's inside. I used the battery-operated tea lights instead." Michael said.

"I wanted to place them on the steps, but you're right about little kids. I think I'll put mine on the railing, too. I'm just going to sit on the stairs and give out candy. I've got a couple of bags. Do you get many trick-or-treaters?"

"To be honest, no. Halloween's not a big deal anymore. It's not like it used to be, we used to get mobs. Now, parents don't want their kids exposed to strangers. Or sugar."

"That's sad. How about we put all the pumpkins on my porch, and you sit with me on the steps? I'll have my light on, and you won't have to."

"Do you want some wine? I've got a bottle. I also have another joint if you're interested."

"You know, you are really a bad influence," Leslie said with a smile.

"No. You are. I hardly ever drank or smoked except on Thursday nights."

"You're probably right. I met Paul the summer going into my senior year of college. I was doing an internship at his firm, and when we got together, we never partied. I didn't have a chance to develop any bad habits. He was older, and had been in a frat, so I'm sure he did his fair share of partying but was over it when he met me. He grew up with alcoholic parents and didn't drink as a rule. He could take it or leave it, and I didn't care.

"I'm sorry if you've fallen into my arrested development. I was never a beer drinker. I knew a lot of people who partied, but I was so intent on making sure I didn't flunk out I never went out much." Leslie confessed.

"Really? You were that bad a student?"

"No. I was there on an academic scholarship. I was worried I'd lose it, so I studied a lot."

"I'll get the pumpkins. You get the candy and glasses. Meet you back here in five."

Leslie came to the door and Michael asked her to wait before she came out. He went to the door and told her to walk to the street without turning around and not peeking. They were to the curb when he told her to turn around.

"Oh!" she said and clapped her hands together. "Look at it! It looks great!" Michael lined all the pumpkins in a row across Leslie's front porch railing and lit the tea lights. It did look small-town chic. The large number of them with these precision-cut faces were impressive. Michael watched the rays emanate from her joy. He secretly felt pleased he helped put them there. She stood staring at the display, a smile across her face and her hands clasped at her chest.

It was a nice night out, only a light jacket was needed. They sat on her steps with candy for the kids and wine for them. They also smoked a little weed, so they both had a mild buzz. Michael wasn't sure what he wanted to do. Tell ghost stories and try to scare her or ask her to expand on her life with Paul. Being a man, he decided he wanted details about her marriage.

"You said you met your husband while you were in college, and he was a partner in a firm. Did you get married right after you graduated?"

"It was kind of strange. I guess I never had a serious boyfriend and his interest surprised me. I wanted to go to college in the city to see what it was all about. The best financial aid package was from NYU, so I left this little pond of a town and dove right into the ocean. I had room and board covered, but I had to buy my own books and any extras. I did have money socked away for books, but there wasn't much left for fun. I was so poor. When I had to work in an office, I tried to borrow clothes from Jenny, but she didn't have much, so a lot of it was from a thrift store." Michael saw her smile in the dark. He wanted to ask her if it was because she was thinking about Paul but decided not to interrupt.

"I never told Paul. He would have had a fit if he found out that's where I shopped. I met him in the elevator. He was just making small talk, and said something like 'going out for lunch?' I told him I was going to the corner store for a slushy. He thought it sounded good and came with me. I saw him here and there, but he was high up the corporate ladder, and I was an unpaid intern. I didn't believe him when he said he was interested. I mean, come on.

"I asked him why, and he said I wasn't like other girls. I was different, like the girl next door. Unpretentious. I was in the beginning, but he had an image to uphold, and I needed to dress comparable to the other wives. So, this sweet kid from the sticks morphed into a typical Manhattanite. I think when I lived in Senecaville with the boys, I was happy. I was just Leslie Phelps from upstate. After they left, we sold the place, and I ended up back in the city and back to my urban version. That's how it was until the Feds knocked down my door. You know the rest."

"The rural life seemed to agree with you."

A car drove by beeped and somebody yelled, "Love the pumpkins!"

A couple of kids ran up ahead of their parents. "Trick or Treat!" They yelled. Leslie asked them about their costumes and put some candy in their bags when one of them saw Lady.

"Hey, can I pet your dog?" the bumble bee asked.

"What dog?"

"That one," he said and pointed at Lady.

"Oh, her. That's my cat. She's dressed like a dog for Halloween."

The parents finally made it up the walk. "Hey, you guys," the mom said, "slow down. Did you say thank you?"

"Thank you," they said it like they practiced it all afternoon since they came home from school.

"You're welcome," Leslie said with equal enthusiasm.

"Can we pet her dog, Mom? Can we? Can we?"

"Yes, her name is Lady. She's my cat in a dog costume but she's a very sweet girl." The two boys loved up on Lady, and Lady loved them back.

"Come on boys. We need to get going," the dad said, sounding like he already had enough. They went down the walk and the echos rang out of their. "Goodbye, Lady!" It echoed down the street and faded away.

"They were nice," Leslie said.

They discussed bringing Rex out, but because they couldn't predict his behavior, he was left crated inside.

"Yes, they were," Michael agreed. He debated asking any more about Paul. It was really none of his business and he didn't care that much. They didn't have much time to get into any kind of deep conversation with kids coming sporadically. Everyone loved the pumpkins including a few cars that beeped their approval. Some of the parents stopped to visit, commenting on how things had changed.

"I remember running wild and egging houses," one dad reminisced. "Hardly anybody out tonight." Michael said.

"What's that?" his young son said.

"Egging houses. You see how we only go to houses with the porch light on? When I was a kid, if a house didn't have its light on, we threw eggs at their house and drew on their windows with soap."

"That's mean, Dad. I can't believe you did that."

"You're right, which is why we don't do it anymore. People only give out candy if they want to, the ones with the lights on. We leave the other houses alone."

"What did you do if you got caught?"

"Run like hell!"

The woman decided to put a stop to the dad's memories of days gone by lest the son get some ideas of his own. "Your Dad was a very naughty boy. Thank you very much but we need to get going."

"Bye! Thank you! I like your pumpkins!" The boy said.

"Good thing the mom shut him down before he got to the part about smashing pumpkins," Michael said.

"Why you little hoodlum, you."

"Not really. It was part of the desire to blow things up. It was for educational purposes."

"I bet," Leslie answered. She looked up and down the street. It was absent of any more trick-or-treaters, and she checked her watch. "Eight o'clock. I think it's time to shut it down."

"Just a second." He pulled something out of his back pocket. It was another letter. "This came the day after you got Lady. You were so happy I didn't want to ruin it for you." He extended it to her.

"Got your lighter? I'm not interested in what it says."

"I do, but I think you should look at it just to be on the safe side."

"I guess," said Leslie. She ripped the envelope and pulled out the familiar newsprint. It was a picture of her in her jailhouse sweats being escorted by the FBI with the familiar red heart outline. She sighed. "I don't get it. I don't get any of this. What's the point?"

"It looks like somebody is fixated on you but happy to admire you from afar. Otherwise, I think they would have made some sort of move. Have you noticed any strange cars or people hanging around? Did you ever feel like you're being followed?"

"No. Not at all. My life is so small I would notice something out of the ordinary." Leslie put the paper back into the envelope. She stood up, took the lighter and set it on fire. Leslie watched the flame lick up to the postmark.

"It could be some teenage boy with a serious crush on you."

She returned his lighter. "Put this one in the record books and call it a night."

He walked her to the door and helped extinguish the pumpkins. "Good night, Leslie. Don't forget to look under your bed for any monsters."

"Very funny. Don't let the bedbugs bite."

"Don't kid about those. Goodnight, Leslie."

"Goodnight, Michael." She said as she shut the door. He heard the lock turn and went down the stairs. She turned the light off after he crossed into his yard, secretly pleased she waited until he was out of view before she turned it off. He sat on his front steps finished the joint and thought about his next neighbor.

He liked Leslie. A lot. More than he thought he should, and there were more than a few reasons. Her dad was his best friend. *It's weird to make new friends as an adult with people you actually like not, ones you tolerated through your spouse,* he thought. *Then you lose your spouse and become the odd man out.* After what is considered a sufficient period of mourning, the wives brought out an available woman they conveniently just 'happen' to know.

He was abrupt in his honesty. Michael did not decline an invitation and told the host if his attendance was so he could meet a woman, 'no pressure,' tell him now. He'd go, but if the intent was to spring a surprise date on him, he left. Michael lived that way for years and saw no reason to change.

Leslie came from out of the blue. She wasn't searching for somebody; she was trying to hide. She was a fugitive. A felon. A dangerous woman. Since sex mostly occurred in his mind these days, he indulged in looking at her that way. Wanted by the Feds. On the run. And he caught her only to get caught up in her web. He shook the image out of his head. *This is some good weed,* he thought. *It's like I'm writing the script of some B movie.* Michael got up to go inside and glanced at Leslie's to make sure the downstairs was dark. He crossed back into her yard, took one of the pumpkins off her porch, and smashed it on her front walk.

***

The next morning his phone rang while he was having his coffee and surfing the web. Nobody ever called him this early. It was Bill Phelps.

171

Wondering what he wanted, he answered. "Morning Bill. What can I do for you on this fine morning?"

"Michael. It's Leslie. Somebody smashed a pumpkin on the walk, and she thinks it was deliberate."

Michael started to laugh. "It was deliberate. I did it. It was supposed to be a joke. We were talking about how times have changed as far as egging houses and smashing pumpkins. Now, it's so sanitized. I'll go over and clean it up and apologize. I didn't think I'd scare her like this. Let me go over now. Bye, Bill."

"Thanks, Michael."

Michael laughed under his breath. Leslie must have a hair trigger. He felt bad he should have realized she'd be spooked. The more he thought about it, the worse he felt. Michael knocked on her back door. Leslie walked into the kitchen and hurried to the door. Leslie unlocked it and pulled it open. "Michael, come in. I think someone is trying to send me a message. I-" She was wildly waving her arms around.

Michael put his hands on her arms to still them. "Leslie. Stop. It was me. I wasn't thinking. I thought it would be funny. I'm sorry. I forgot about how it would look to you."

"You did that? You?" The scared look in her eye turned to anger. "What were you thinking?"

"Leslie, I wasn't thinking. I swear. I'm sorry. I'll clean it up. Let me go get a shovel."

"I almost had a heart attack. I don't know if you saw the postmark, but the letter was from Miami. What's up with that? Why does someone from Miami keep doing this?"

"I didn't see it. No wonder you were spooked. I'm so sorry. I'll take care of it right now." Michael said, and high-tailed it out of there. He got his shovel and put the pumpkin, or most of it, in the pile of leaves left in the road for the town pick up. Michael thought about going next door and apologizing again but went home instead. The postmark was a valid reason to put her on edge. Whoever it was wasn't backing down.

In his opinion, it was somebody her husband screwed over. There were no threats in any of them, just someone playing head games with her. Going to the police was a dumb idea. She burnt all the letters and there was no proof of anything. If she was wound that tight, he didn't have the emotional resources to deal with her. He was too old to be caught up in this kind of scenario. Sad but true.

Leslie was initially frightened. *Who would do that? Is someone watching me?* She called her dad and told him about it, but he told her it was Halloween, and she did have four pumpkins sitting right there. He'd call Michael and have him check it out.

When he got home, he called Bill and apprised him of his lapse in judgment.

"What did you do that for?"

"It appealed to the teenage boy in me. I apologized but I don't think she wanted to hear it. I have to go walk my dog. He thinks he lives at your house. Lady's teaching him some manners. Goodbye, Bill."

Michael went over, leash in hand and knocked on her door. Half of him thought she'd kick Rex out and tell him to both stay in their own yard, the other half she'd be curt and say as few words as possible. He was surprised to see she acted as if this morning didn't happen.

"Oh, is it time for our walk already? Let me grab my jacket and the dogs." She came back with her coat on and Lady right on her heels; Rex right on top of her afraid he'd be left behind. They put the leashes on and headed out the door. "I think we are getting the last of the good weather. A cold front is supposed to come through and bring some snow."

"Snow? Isn't that a four-letter word?" Michael said, glad she wasn't bitching him out for acting like a sixth grader.

"Yes, it is, because shit, fuck and golf were already taken."

They walked down the driveway and stopped to look at her pumpkin-stained walk. "Sorry about that," Michael said.

"No, I'm sorry. I overreacted. The letters aren't threatening or anything. They may be sending them to you because they don't really know if I'm here, or think your address is my dad's. How would they know you've even given them to me? I've decided it's probably someone pissed at Paul and acting out. The best they can do is scare me. Okay. Mission accomplished. I was scared, but not anymore."

"I think you're right. What's it been? Almost two years. If a person was intent on hurting you, they would have done something by now. So, let's forget about it and enjoy our walk. I'll get the hose out when we get back and clear that off."

"No need. The rain can do it." They reached the corner. "Right or left?"

"Let's go left. We always go right."

"Left it is," Leslie said as she stepped off the curb. She walked ahead with Lady, who pranced right along.

He was following behind her, a view he couldn't fully appreciate because Rex was trying to pull his arm out of the socket. "Stop it, Rex! Stop."

Leslie turned around. "Here. Let's trade dogs."

"Sure, but he's a handful," Michael said as they switched leashes.

"You take Lady and walk ahead of us. I think Rex's problem is he wants to catch up with Lady. Okay. Go."

As soon as they started off Rex pulled on the leash. Leslie called out "Stop!" Michael stopped and turned around to see what she was doing. Leslie tightened up the leash until he was right next to her, so Rex had nowhere to go. When he lunged forward, she yanked on the leash and started turning him around doing figure eights until he stopped pulling. "Okay, let's walk."

They got about five steps, and he started pulling again. She stopped and repeated the exercise. "Let's try it again. This time it was ten steps, he started pulling and she stopped and did it again. Leslie repeated it five more times. "Your turn, Michael. The whole point is to establish who's leading. You have to teach Rex it's not him. Every time he pulls, stop and do the figure eights. He won't know which way he's going. You do. It's just telling him you are in charge, not him. Keep doing it until he stops pulling. He's a smart boy, he'll get the message. If he wants to catch up to Lady that will only happen if he doesn't pull."

They started off again. Michael had to stop a few times, but by the end of the walk, Rex behaved himself.

"That was impressive, Leslie. Where did you learn how to do that?"

"When we lived in Senecaville it was near a horse barn, and after the boys were in school, I decided to learn to ride. Depending on the horse you may have to lunge her, which is holding the rope and letting her run-in circles, and then reversing it. All that did burn off excess energy, so she was too tired to misbehave. If you were riding her and she wouldn't obey, you got off and did the figure eights to show her who's in charge. I figured it would work on dogs, too. It does."

"Thanks. Now I can enjoy taking him for a walk. Before this, I really didn't like him very much. It's getting better. He likes his crate, and he loves his toys. Now that I can walk him, or send him to your house, I think he'll won't be such a pain. How do you stop him from chewing on my shoes?"

"Put them on the top shelf of your closet, Leslie advised. "He's a puppy, and that's what they do."

After their walk they went to Leslie's house. He sat on the deck and threw the ball for Rex, something he enjoyed until his arm got tired. She came out with two mugs of hot chocolate. He reached out and took both mugs so she could sit next to him. Rex sat in front of Michael, quivering with anticipation, the saliva-soaked tennis ball at Michael's feet. He looked at it covered with spit.

"What do I do now?" He asked Leslie.

"Are you kidding me? Here, hold my cup." She found a good-sized stick and threw it. Rex picked it up and came back, only he sat on the ground blissfully chewing.

"Didn't you ever have a dog? It's not rocket science. They aren't that smart. It's either food, water, or boredom. He likes to chew, so get him some chew toys and hide your shoes. Take him for a walk and tire him out. Find a doggie daycare or put him in my yard with a big stick. A tired dog causes no trouble."

"We did have a dog when the girls' were small. Fluffy. It was one of those little yappy dogs that looked like a dust mop. My wife picked it out and took care of it. It didn't like me. She growled at me whenever I got near my wife."

"Yes, those little dogs are annoying if it's not yours. Rex, here, is a mutt, so he doesn't have any breed-specific problems like bad hips, his issues are behavioral. Those can be trained out of him fast because he's just a puppy. Go look up some training videos. When does he get fixed?"

"Next week."

"Once he gets neutered, he'll calm down a lot."

"Maybe because I have some, I feel guilty about removing his."

Leslie took a sip. "Men." She shook her head. "You guys are so off base. Just because you check out a woman's boobs doesn't mean we sit around book club and discuss your junk. Like, boy Joe is really something, his balls are almost down to his knees."

Michael almost choked on his hot chocolate. "Leslie. Never joke about a man's balls!"

"Never again. Promise." They sipped their hot chocolate.

"Leslie, you are one big surprise."

"How so?"

"Mrs. Nelson was quite a city slicker. Manicures, haircuts with…What do you call those stripes?"

"Stripes?" she looked at him, confused. "You mean highlights?"

"I don't know, but probably. Dressed to the nines. High heels. Now look at you. You've let yourself go. You need a haircut. Your roots are showing. You have a dog. You're a totally different person."

"I think Mrs. Nelson was a big phony." Leslie said. "I only looked like because that's what all the other wives looked like. I was happiest when I lived in Senecaville. I was just another mom with kids who played soccer. I only got presentable when I knew I had to attend some function.

"Leslie Phelps is who I am, who I've always been but got sidetracked by Paul. I still can't process it, Michael. He left me after all this time. He lied to me. He said he loved me, the bastard. How come I didn't see it? I wasn't one of those girls fishing in the big pond for a rich husband. That was the furthest thing from my mind. I was there to get a degree and a job. He just plucked me out of my life and put me down in his.

"I never got a chance to decide what I wanted to do. I went from my parents, my dorm, to Paul's. I did work before I got married, but I lived with him." Her soft brown eyes looked into his. Michael wasn't sure why she was telling him all this. "Maybe if I lived on my own before I got married, I'd have a better sense of self. Better late than ever. Now I have a chance to figure out who I am. Or who I am now."

"Leslie, the way your dad talked about you, or rather your lifestyle, I hesitate to say I thought you be some high society bitch who wouldn't know how to change a lightbulb, but I was wrong. You aren't like that at all, you have incredible skills. Horses and dogs. You should open your own dog training school."

"If I could, I'd become a groomer slash trainer. If I was younger, I'd make the investment. Now I prefer to work part-time doing the prep classes. My expenses are minor. I get health insurance through my dad, and I drive his car. I suppose things will change when he gets back, but I'll worry about it then. You done with your hot chocolate? It warmed my insides, but my outsides are cold. I think I'll go in now."

***

"Rex, come. Michael said, but Rex didn't move. He lay in the grass looking at him but not moving. "Rex, *come*." He repeated louder but Rex ignored him. Michael was getting frustrated. "COME!" but Rex did not.

Leslie came outside with a little baggie containing dog treats. "I'm not sure who I'm training here, you or the dog. Here's a trick that works on both dogs and little kids. Bribery." She handed him the bag. "Take one out, come back to Rex and don't show him the treat, make a fist and let him smell it. He'll be curious enough to pay attention." The dog got up and looked at Michael. "Now go back and turn to face him. Open your hand and call him." The dog walked over to check out Michael's open hand and took the treat. "Now, give him a lot of attention for being a good dog, and repeat the word 'come.' In the short term he'll come because he's a puppy. After a while he'll obey because you've conditioned him to. Put the treats in your pocket when you're out with him and give him a treat and a lot of attention when he behaves. Go back to the figure eights if he's naughty and reward him when he stops."

"I'm serious Leslie, you need to start a dog training school."

"I'm not training Rex, Michael. I'm training you. I'm freezing and going back inside. Talk to you later." She went inside, and he tried the come command with a treat a couple of times. Rex was a fast learner and Michael was able to direct him inside.

Well, I'll be. Leslie Jean Phelps, ex-con on the run trains both men and dogs, he thought. *The FBI would be lucky to hire her.* He figured Rex might be tired enough to take a nap in his bed and let him get some work done. Once in the garage, he ran to his bed and went to work on the leftover half-eaten chew.

Michael started running a loud saw, wondering if the noise would freak Rex out but the dog was oblivious to anything but the chew. He was working on a channel running down the middle of the split log, varying the depth to mimic the pattern of a creek bed. The goal was that once prepared he would fill it with resin and let it cure. The legs were simple boards cut with a half-circle to match the rounded part of the log. In the end, it would be a fully functional coffee table with what looked like a stream running down the middle. He considered making matching end tables but would need to go back to the lumber mill for wood.

He spent a few hours working peacefully when Rex jumped on Michael to alert him that his nap was over.

Michael brought him out and he did his business, rewarded Rex with a treat and a number of good boys. They went inside and Michael reheated leftovers and fed Rex. He decided that Rex getting a walk in would make for a peaceful evening, so he grabbed his leash and hooked the dog. He was going to see if Leslie wanted to go, but he thought Rex got so excited around Lady he was hard to focus. Michael filled his coat pockets with some reward treats and they set out.

He was correct, Rex was more reasonable without Lady. Michael found the treat and reward system worked. Rex would even sit at the corner until the light changed. Initially, Michael was wondering how long he needed to keep Rex before he could find him a new owner, but he found a certain sort of therapy walking him. It allowed him to go out and absorb Mother Nature. There were other people out with their dogs, and they were very social, talking to him. Michael didn't know exactly what was missing from his life after Emily died.

He knew Emily would be furious if she thought she was the reason he closed himself off from the rest of the world. There wasn't much to be interested in besides poker night and lunch at the diner, but Rex changed that. He was out meeting people, a skill he thought he lost, struck mute after her death. Dog people were very friendly as a group, some runners had high-maintenance breeds that only hours of exercise made them tolerable. They ran by with a wave but never stopped.

The night was turning dark when they headed home. Lady was a beautiful dog, but Rex must have taken after his father. His coat was sleek and dark except for a white blaze on his chest and four white feet. He reminded Michael of a seal. Overall, he liked Rex. Walking Rex was a way to get some exercise, and a way to meet people. He needed the exercise more than he needed friends, but it was an enjoyable way to go out and appreciate God's green earth. Michael was heading up his driveway when he heard Leslie's door slam as she came out on the porch.

"What? We weren't good enough to come along?" Leslie yelled.

"No, but I wanted to work on his behavior. He gets around Lady and loses his manners. A lot of guys are like that so I can't hold it against him."

"Can we still walk in the morning?"

"Absolutely. This was a training mission. You can tell me if we made any progress."

"I'm freezing. See you in the morning?"

"Dress warm. It's supposed to drop into the thirties tonight. Bye, Leslie."

"Bye, Michael."

Michael brought Rex in and gave him some water. He was trying to decide if he should feed him. It probably would have been smarter to feed him before their walk. Michael sat in his recliner and while debating what to do Rex came over and flopped at his feet. He looked at Michael with love in his eyes and fell asleep, deciding for himself about dinner. Michael put his feet up, turned on the TV and looked for something good to watch. He found something, a documentary about monsters of the deep. A man, his dog, and TV. *What's not to love?* He asked himself, but his mind kept drifting to Leslie.

She shared quite a bit about her marriage to Paul. It seemed like he checked in and checked out, treating his family like a hotel. Her sons seemed to know what they wanted to do for a living, and it didn't seem like Paul minded them moving to the other side of the country. Most men like him wanted an heir to follow in their footsteps, to appreciate what his hard work had wrought and to carry on his legacy.

It seemed like having a part-time dad was enough for the boys. Leslie raised them right, and when it was time to go out on their own, they had a vision, a direction, and followed it. She was proud of her boys even though they were men. Before she settled here, she was out there with them. Leslie didn't stay, not because they ignored her. It was the opposite. She felt she was in their way and distracting them from their work.

Leslie missed the east coast and her family. Her dad was at the age where people referred to him as spry. Bill Phelps was sharp as a razor, but the human body had its limits. His joints ached from sitting in planes for too long, and sleeping in a different bed every few nights meant he was never getting a decent night sleep. Bill was even looking forward to Leslie being there. There was a certain distance between them once Paul entered the picture. She was his Leslie now, and Paul took his sweet little girl and turned her into a cosmopolitan urbanite. It was all a farce and when Leslie called her dad for help, she was the Leslie he knew and loved.

A few more weeks and it would be Thanksgiving, and Jenny offered to host it at his house, so he'd get some relief from traveling. The week after, he'd take Billy to the key accounts and turn them over, creating a wide block of free time. He physically needed a long rest, and afterwards a long unbroken stretch of time in Florida. Maybe Leslie would be around and could come with him. Bill would like that. She could read a book at the pool, and he'd play golf. They'd meet up, have dinner and watch TV. He'd pay her salary as a companion. He thought that was a great idea.

Michael's plans usually involved traveling to see his daughter Marcie and her husband Steve in Cincinnati. They were the house flippers. They had a local cable TV show and there were rumors of a national cable network being interested in picking it up. Those rumors were always there but nothing concrete ever happened. Marcie and Steve's niche was reclaiming old homes, upgrading them in functional use but preserving their heritage. The were filmed a lot at junkyards and houses set to be demolished. Those were the best. Historic woodwork, old mantles made of marble, and field stone fireplaces they would take apart stone by stone. A local realtor funded them, using their work as a marketing piece of investing in the city. They traveled and collected a lot of inventory they stored in a barn located on their property. Michael's two grandchildren were doing a semester abroad and wouldn't be there.

His other daughter, Carly, was a traveling nurse. She was unmarried and happy about it. She had a contract through the first of the year and was unavailable for Thanksgiving. He thought the effort and expense wasn't worth it to go to Marcie's and have it just be the three of them, and he didn't want to leave Rex. He was a big doofus ready for anything, but it was more on his end. He liked having a dog, Rex in particular. It was decided they'd all come there for Christmas.

He was hoping to wrangle an invite next door for Thanksgiving. Bill would be home, Billy Jr and his wife Stephanie, and even Leslie's partner in crime, her sister Jenny. Her husband was on call and the kids were invited to their friends. Once again, promises were made for everyone to be there for Christmas.

Michael joined Leslie and Lady for their morning walks. He liked to take Rex out alone in the evening for training. Rex was just about ready to let them come along. When he was around Lady, he took his cues from her and was mostly well-behaved unless a squirrel came across his path. Michael knew to tighten up the leash and make him sit until he forgot the squirrel and wanted his treat.

"Very nice," Leslie complimented him. He felt inordinately pleased to show Leslie his success. Sometimes they'd have serious discussions about the state of the world or talk about the latest hot reality show. They argued about whether or not the genre jumped the shark.

"Don't you think after twenty years or so, everyone worth discovering had already been discovered?"

"Probably. I wait until the finals before I watch." Leslie said. "That reminds me. Charlie's movie is the Friday Night Creature Feature on the Graveyard Channel. Want to come over and watch it?"

Friday night? Hell yeah. Try not to act like an idiot, he told himself. "Uh, sure. I have no plans. Is this your big starring role? You were the ingenue?"

"It's 'The Zombie Zoo.' The basic premise is that Zombies are all dead. Whatever made them Zombies no longer exists, but what's left is kept in a zoo as a tourist attraction. Feeding time is especially crowded. A solar flare shorted out the power grid and the automatic power panel in the zoo's security system failed. Now the Zombies are out looking for fresh meat.

"The only thing to do is take them out one at a time. I have two lines. But it's Beast vs. Beast. It's pretty funny. But yes, Friday at nine. Want to come over for dinner first?"

"Dinner? Movie? Friday? Love to."

"Okay. It's a date. Come around six."

***

Michael couldn't help but be pleased with the invitation. He had a genuine affection for Leslie. They liked the same things, and never ran out of things to talk about. He daydreamed they were closer, but occasionally reality would seep in, and he questioned if Leslie would ever be interested in an old, fat bald man. He wasn't exactly fat, but the solid physique he never had to work at grew soft with age. He recalled her statement about a man's saggy balls and his belly prevented him from seeing his. He checked in the mirror once and decided that they looked fine, but he never looked again.

He wondered about Leslie's body. He was sure gravity took its toll on her, too. Her boobs must have sagged since she had two kids and also had bit of a paunch. From the back, her bum looked wider but not as large as most women her age. She mostly wore jeans and didn't fuss with make-up, and her self-cut hair was growing out but still looked lopsided. Leslie looked human and her bright smile made her approachable. She always looked you in the eyes when she talked to you.

The fresh fall air was sliding low into winter norms requiring hats and gloves. They walked quickly and didn't talk much. They went inside her

183

house afterward for hot chocolate and conversation. The dogs lay on one of the braided rugs in a patch of sunlight from the dining room windows.

They sat, using the warmth of the hot chocolate to heat the mugs and warm their hands.

"What's going on? Any plans for Thanksgiving?"

"Rex can't travel, and they won't. I'll see them at Christmas." He shrugged but didn't look too torn up about it.

"Why can't Rex travel?"

"Because I said he can't."

"Are you gonna sit around eating a turkey sandwich watching football in the dark?" Leslie teased.

"Or find a movie. I'm not that into football."

"Are you into turkey?" She invited him to come over and bring Rex. "Have Thanksgiving dinner with us."

"I really shouldn't impose. It's your family's Thanksgiving after all." Michael said, looking down at his boots.

"Oh please. You have to come. We're having it here because my dad needs a break from all the travel. I'm sure he'll be happy there will be someone too polite to say, 'Hey Bill, put a cork in it.'"

"So that's enough to earn a Thanksgiving dinner with all the fixings?"

"That's all. Steffi makes a hell of an apple pie. Pumpkin Cheesecake."

"And nobody will be mad I brought my dog?"

"No, I'm sure somebody will be mad, but fuck 'em."

Leslie always made him laugh. He should go. A small step towards a larger goal. "Leslie, I would love to come over for Thanksgiving. Thank you. What time? What should I bring?"

"Noon if you're into mimosas. Dinner's at three. Wine. Some beer, too. Wear your colors."

"Colors? What colors?"

"Your team colors."

"Which one's my team?"

"I don't know who's playing," Leslie confessed. "Just wear blue. You look good in blue."

Michael felt his scalp flush red at the compliment, unsure if it was a compliment, but he was happy about the invite.

He peeked out of the window on Thanksgiving Day. Once another car arrived, he went over carrying a bag of beer, wine, and some champagne. He knocked on the back door and Leslie waved him in. When he gave her the bag full of beverages, she pulled out a bottle of champagne. "Yay! Look what Michael brought. You go into the living room and see my dad. I'll bring you out your mimosa. It's that way," and she pointed her finger.

"Yes. It's in the same place at my house."

"Don't be a wise ass. Keep Rex out of the kitchen. He's counter height and that's dangerous. Let him hang around Lady. She'll keep him in check."

He brought Rex into the living room. Bill got up to shake his hand his hand. "Nice to see you, Michael. You know Billy and Jenny. Lady got up and greeted Rex. "She's his mother? What was the dad? A Great Dane?"

"Could be. Someone dumped her off at a barn. The farmer brought her and the pups to his stand at the Farmer's Market. Lady watched him give her pups away and got very distressed. Leslie got involved, and she bonded with her. I ended up with Rex. He's just a puppy, so if he gets obnoxious, I can take him home. Leslie said it was okay if I brought him."

"He seems like a fine dog to me." Bill said. "What's your take on the game?"

Michael knew enough to fake it. "What's the line? Who's the favorite again?" Bill and Billy got in a heated argument about the outcome of the game. Jenny came out from the kitchen, wiping her hands on a dish towel. "I didn't come all this way to hear you two argue." Leslie followed and handed a mimosa to Michael.

"Where's mine?" Billy Jr. said.

"In the kitchen with your wife," Leslie answered.

"Ah, the sweet sounds of home," Bill said. "Leslie, would you mind?" He said as he stretched out his hand with his empty glass.

"I'd be honored, Dad." Leslie took his glass and looked at her brother. "Get your own, Spud." She said as she walked by him.

"Steffi? Could you come out here please?" Billy yelled.

"Get up and make it yourself." She yelled back. They had been married a long time and had that close couple shorthand.

Leslie came back with her father's drink and almost dropped it. Somebody took it from her as she clapped her hand over her mouth in shock. "Boys!" she screamed. "Look, everyone! It's the boys!" and rushed over to hug them both at the same time.

They squeezed her back and untangled themselves. "Mom, give us a second to take our coats off. We're happy to see you too." Somebody took their coats and Leslie looked at her 'boys'. They were men and had been for a long time. She couldn't help it; tears filled her eyes. Charlie hugged her and passed her to Will. "Aw, Mom we wouldn't have come if we knew you were going to be like this."

"Like what? I can't be happy to see my sons?"

Michael stood up and freed the couch so the three of them could sit. "Here. Why don't you all take a seat," he said.

"Michael. Meet my sons, this is Charlie, and this is Will. Boys, this is our next-door neighbor, Michael Caldwell." They shook hands hello.

"Charlie, is it? Your mom made me watch Zombie Zoo. Well, we watched Zombie Zoo. She didn't make me watch it. Well done."

"You think? Zombies are pretty much played out, but we had the budget and time to make it, so we did it on the fly off an old script."

"Your Mother is quite the actress. I think she wanted to end the movie after her scene."

Leslie approached with their drinks, trying not to eavesdrop. They saw her coming and stopped talking, which immediately put her radar up. "Here," she said, passing out the drinks to whoever was closest. "Why did you just stop talking? Are you talking about me?"

Charlie said, "we were talking about your acting career."

"I said I thought you were big ham," Michael added. Both of her sons were trying not to laugh at Michael's delivery. He was spot on.

"How would you know? You were snoring up a storm after fifteen minutes." Charlie and Will exchanged looks. When she was with them out west, she was so uptight, but home agreed with her. She seemed much more settled here, like before when they lived in Senecaville. Their mom was always so nice, making a casserole for a neighbor if they had a baby, or baking brownies for new families moving in.

That's who they remembered, but when she came with Jenny, she seemed fractured. Brittle. She would sharply cut from one subject to another mid-sentence. It was very concerning, but Jenny said Leslie was overwhelmed by it all and processing it in small bites. Jenny was right. That last month she seemed better, smiling and joking around. Their grandfather called often, and when she said was going home, they put her on a plane and went back to business like before. She settled at her dad's place and was apparently making friends.

✳✳✳

Charlie and Will talked about their father's behavior at length, and neither of them could come up with an explanation for his actions. He was their *dad*. How could he do this, steal all this money and take off with another woman? Leave his wife shit outta luck? He was a creep. Their father was a *creep*. Leslie liked to think they were too far away to catch any fallout, but she was wrong.

There were a number of big-money players who got taken in by Paul Nelson, famous in LA as well as NYC, but the Nelson Brothers were poor, and few people made the connection. Sometimes people figured it out and pressed them about it, and their stock answer was they hadn't been back in ages and hardly talked to him. If he were rolling in dough, none of it rolled their way. The FBI gave them financial colonoscopies, too. Their *dad* was a bad guy.

Stephanie came out and announced, "Dinner in thirty." And went back in the kitchen. Leslie followed, and the guys made small talk and slowly headed over to the table. Will was more intensely interested in sports than Charlie. When younger, they had a similar build, except maybe Will was denser. Charlie had Leslie's coloring, light sandy brown hair with the dark ring circling the amber of their iris.

Once puberty kicked in, Charlie was taller but Will broader, and as adults Charlie still remained taller, and Will worked out with weights, he had more bulk in the form of muscle. He still took after his Aunt Carla, with his dark hair and thicker body. Will's hair was long, black with loose curls, and he had a perfect jaw. No weak chin for him. Leslie wondered if it was the pressure among the undiscovered talent to present themselves as having an edge nobody else had. He certainly had movie star good looks, but whether or not he could act remained to be seen.

The women started handing dishes out, and the men set them down. They all took their seats, said grace and a collective Amen. Leslie usually did it. She didn't mind. Her dad was a religious man, but he wasn't one to show off. Leslie sat at the foot of the table, her sons on either side. The dishes got passed by and everyone took their fill. Everyone started to eat, and four different conversations broke out. Looking between her sons caused a little catch in the center of her chest.

"What's wrong? Why aren't you eating?" Charlie asked. Will nodded.

"I'm in shock. How did you get here?"

"Grampa. He called and asked us to come. Said he'd pay for our flights, so we said sure. We're driving down to the city tomorrow. Someone wants to see Will. Will has an appointment," Charlie laughed.

"Appointment? With who? Why? Are you up for a part?"

Charlie laughed again. "With an agent. A *modeling* agent."

"Modeling? Did you get an offer?" Leslie sounded surprised. She had no idea he was interested in modeling.

Charlie laughed again and Will told him to knock it off. "It's a one-off kind of job. It's a shoot for a book cover."

"A Romance novel. They're looking for some dark, swarthy guy to play a pirate." Charlie laughed. "It's for a dark-haired Fabio."

"I'm not just saying it because you're my son, but I can totally see that. Don't shave for a few days and you'll look swarthy. Explains the muscles."

"A job's a job. California's expensive, and a lot of decisions are based on looks, so I work out. Everyone else does. I think I should get a spray tan to emphasize the swarthy look. What do you think?"

It was Leslie's turn to laugh. "That's a lot of maintenance. All that just to be competitive."

"I don't mind. I like to work out. Somebody needs to make money." He shot a look at his brother.

"Hey, I work. Maybe not as visible as you, but I pay my bills." Charlie turned to his mother. "I've been working a number of behind-the-scenes jobs. From a go-fer up to a P.A., That's fine with me. I want to know everything there is to know about the industry. I'm getting an education of the business as a whole." Charlie said, teasing his brother. "Will's getting a makeover."

"All a mother wants for her children is to be happy. I'm glad it's working out."

They turned back to the table and the other conversations. Everyone talking all at once, Bill and Billy jr. were arguing about football. Jenny was talking to Michael about kids going away to school and roommate drama. Stephanie talked to the boys about their adventures in Hollywood, and movie stars. Leslie sat there and felt overcome with with emotion for her family. Paul wrecked a lot of peoples' lives, but none here.

Her Paul couldn't be that guy, that cheating, stealing, lying rat bastard. Paul gave her the two miracles of her life: her sons. *How could such a dishonest man sire two beautiful boys? When exactly did Paul change? Did he change or was he always a dishonest creep? Did he really love her? Did he ever love her?* Thoughts she had in the past rose again in her mind, but they were rhetorical and always would be. Leslie would always doubt if he ever loved her. Her heart said yes but her head said no. The people at this table were her family, and her gratefulness threatened to spill down her cheeks.

"Leslie? Are you okay?" Michael asked. He saw the raw emotions cross her face and wasn't sure she landed on a good one.

His question startled her. She thought she was alone in her thoughts, but her feelings bubbled up and made them obvious to anyone watching. "Oh, I was just being grateful having my family all here."

"Even me?" He joked.

"Yes, even you." Michael almost choked on her answer.

The food and the football lasted well into the evening. Michael chose to go, saying Rex needed a walk to burn off the calories Bill fed him under the table. Leslie and Lady walked him to the door.

"Thank you for inviting me, Leslie. It was nice to spend it with family, even if it wasn't mine. Your sons are great kids. You did a good job with those two."

"I'm glad you came. It was a nice time, wasn't it? We still on for our walk tomorrow?"

"You don't want to spend the morning with your boys?"

"They're not leaving until later, and Lady needs a walk. *I* need a walk after all I ate today. I'll see you tomorrow morning. Regular time?"

"Regular time. See you then." He said as he exited and took Rex for a walk. The night was dark and cold enough to see your breath, he walked at a brisk pace and thought about Leslie. He couldn't help it. The more time he spent around her, the more he liked her, and that was wrong. He was too old for her. Leslie was a young, vibrant woman who deserved to go dancing, not sit next someone in a rocking chair. Michael walked faster and got home. Rex went and flopped in his bed while Michael took off his boots. He fought the urge to look out his kitchen window and spy on his neighbors.

Michael sat in his recliner and watched TV. He let Rex out for the night and went upstairs to bed.

The next morning while he was having coffee, he heard a knock at the door. Michael got up, opened the door and welcomed Leslie inside. "Still cold out?" He asked, mostly because he wasn't sure what to say.

"Yeah. Make sure you wear a hat. You don't want frostbite on your melon."

That last bit smarted but he did put on a brown knit hat before they left the house. Since the idea of her scared him, the last thing he wanted to do was make a move on her. He figured her sons would make for benign conversation. "Your sons. You really didn't know they were coming?"

"No! I was surprised they came all this way."

"They're so excited to see you. They seemed like nice boys."

"They are. Very nice boys. Although I often wonder if there are crossed wires somewhere that will appear sometime in the future. Like their father. I never saw it coming. Neither did anyone else."

"I don't know what to say. What do they think about their father?"

"I thought most of Paul's clients were on the east coast. Apparently not. Some big Hollywood players got suckered, too, but the boys live in a pretty low rent district and no connection was made linking them. Some people put it together, but like I said they're pretty poor, and their story of they don't speak to him and had no idea what he was doing wasn't questioned because it was the truth."

Michael couldn't help himself. He brought up Paul. "What do you think about Paul? Do you still love him?"

They stopped at a crosswalk. "Do I love Paul? That's a hard question to answer. I never confronted him. We never split up. He walked away and didn't consider how what he did would impact me, or he didn't care. That Paul, I hate. There is no explanation on earth he could give me that would allow me to forgive him for the shit I went through for the six months after. The year after. But the Paul I married? I waited and waited for him to come help me, but he was gone. I still love him but in an old boyfriend kind of way. There's so much history there I'll never forget. He gave me my sons. Why do you ask?"

Michael took a deep breath. "Yesterday at your house the only couple was Billy and his wife. Usually, there are always married couples, one single woman, and me. I'm invited specifically to even the count. I go because it's a pretty good meal. I don't have to cook. I'll talk to the woman like, 'Hi, how are you? Just so you know there is no possibility of romance with me. I have herpes' and leave it at that."

"You don't." Leslie paused to consider the possibility. "Do you?"

"No. Not in the slightest." He laughed. They relaxed and walked on. "Single men in this age bracket are attractive party guests. There are always unattached women on the hunt."

"On the hunt? For what?"

"Male companionship. At this age no kids at home and no exes in the picture. Pilates and yoga get boring after a while, and they look for an eligible bachelor to appreciate their hard work."

"You're not interested in that?"

He looked at her and laughed. "Female companionship? No thanks."

"What I meant was, aren't you lonely? Wouldn't you like a woman to hang out with?"

"For a long time, I felt like I would be cheating on Emily, so I avoided situations completely. Maybe because so much time has passed, I don't feel that way anymore. I'm not sure what to expect at this point of my life. Getting Rex was probably the best thing I could have done. I have to take him out twice a day. Feed him. Be responsible for something other than myself. It's good. I walk him and meet people. Dog people are very sociable."

"Yes, dog people love other dog people, although some are real assholes. They have untrained, undisciplined dogs, and if it's aggressive to another dog, it's never their dog's fault. You need to keep your eye out for them."

"What about you? Do you ever get lonely?"

"Me?" Leslie looked at him, surprised at the question. "I never thought about it, but probably. The house can get pretty quiet when everyone's gone, and rather than face it I leave. I've picked up a few more students to occupy my time, but I don't really enjoy it. Getting Lady did a lot for me, too. That thing with Paul crushed me. I had love, gave love, and ppppffft! No love. He took more than money from me. I'm not sure what's next in my life either, but having Lady helps. Having you helps, too."

"Me?"

"Yes, you. You've been a very good friend to me."

I'd like to be more than just friends, Michael thought. Instead, he said, "I'm glad I've been useful."

"Bbrrr. I'm freezing. Let's head back."

They walked the rest of the way quickly and in silence. Once they reached their driveways, they parted ways and Michael said he was going to Wegmans later. If she needed something let him know.

Her talk with Michael stirred up emotions she thought were long dead. The implosion of her marriage with such force flattened everything else in her world. She felt numb and desolate when she was alone. Questions with no answers circled her brain at random moments. Without provocation, she would start to cry. It didn't matter if she was alone or in line at the grocery store. Tears would flow. Once, the cashier called her manager about a lady who wouldn't stop crying holding up her line. The manager took her and her cart aside and offered to help. Leslie apologized using the excuse of a death in the family as the reason for her behavior. She signed up for home delivery and hadn't gone back since.

Did she still love Paul? Michael asked her. I don't know. I wish I didn't, but we were together a long time with much more good than bad. When she thought of him it always went back to their early years, years she thought were happy. It was as if her mind blocked out any memory of him since he sold the house in Senecaville. His desire to cash out the money that place was worth rather than keep it like Leslie wanted might have been a red flag. Never before did he disregard her feelings so blatantly. *God, I wish he didn't bring up Paul. I know I should hate him and want his head on a pike, but all memories lead back to that lemon slushy.*

Leslie and Michael continued their daily walks and she'd go with him on their evening walks as well.

She learned about raising girls, something she had no experience with. From what he told her, she should consider herself lucky. Girls were willing to go at it over boys or something simple like nail polish.

"Maybe because my boys were so close in age, they grew up sharing everything. If one boy was good at math, the other was good at sports. One impressed the teachers, the other, girls. Charlie was the creative, intellectual one. He's a master conversationalist and subsequently manipulative as hell. He'd ask for twenty dollars and walk away with fifty. He was also good at basketball but didn't play because the coach didn't like his attitude. Charlie had no reason to bleed on the gym floor. The coach wanted that kind of commitment, but Charlie wasn't interested.

"Now Will, is a year younger and totally opposite Charlie. He was much more consumed with his looks, and good at any sport he played. Popular. Between the two of them, there isn't a problem they can't solve. They loved their dad, and he was a good dad. He worked a lot when they were little, but he was always present in their lives. I don't think they like him much anymore, mostly because of his treatment of me. He ghosted them, too."

"Did you ask them if they received any anonymous mail?"

"No, I didn't think to. They didn't mention any, and I didn't want to tell them about mine. They'd be worrying about nothing."

"It's been a while since you've got one, too. Maybe your secret admirer moved on."

"It has been a while. Have there been any high-profile ladies in the news lately?"

"No, I try to pay attention as little as possible during the nightly news. The world looks bleaker and bleaker every day. Here, watch this. Rex, sit. Stay."

Leslie noticed a large dog coming towards them. They were far enough off the walk the man and his dog could pass with no trouble. She took Lady and stood next to Michael. When the strange dog neared, he started growling. The dog lunged at Rex and bared his teeth. The owner pulled his dog back while trying to regain his balance, but he wasn't steady enough. The dog was closer this time and if he lunged again, he could sink his teeth into any one of them. Leslie pulled a small can out of her pocket.

"That dog takes one step closer to me and I'll pepper spray the bastard. Two more steps and I'll pepper spray you, you asshole. He needs one of those prong collars if you can't control him. Take him to obedience class or walk him in the park away from people. That dog has one in the chamber and a loose screw. He's going to bite someone. It's only a matter of time."

"What the fuck do you know, lady?" the guy said, pissed she was giving him shit.

"I know enough when that dog hurts someone it won't be his fault. It'll be yours. You think that you're so smart and so strong that dog's going to listen to you. He won't. Now leave, or I'll spray you just because you're an egomaniacal jerk."

"Fuck you, lady," he said as he wrestled his dog back into control. Leslie gave Michael Lady's leash. She turned toward the man and extended her arm straight, pointing the spray directly at his face. "Say that to me again and you'll be the one who's fucked."

He yanked on the dog and dragged him into the crosswalk, crossing the street and cursing. He kicked the dog when he was on the other side of the street that was the spark that lit the fire in her eyes. "Hold Lady," she said and started across the street.

"Leslie! Stop!" Michael yelled after her, but it was too late; she was already on the other corner. The man turned around, unsure of what she intended to do. She got up right next to him. Even the dog looked unsure of what was happening and stayed back. Leslie still held the spray in her hand and yelled in his face. "The only thing wrong with that dog is YOU! What are you, some kind of hard ass? You're going kick the dog and show him who's boss? What an asshole. You're lucky I'm not holding my phone because I'd call the police and report you for animal cruelty." The man and the dog backed off and headed in the opposite direction, and Leslie ran across to Michael.

"Leslie. What is wrong with you?"

"Nothing. He made me mad, kicking the dog like that."

"You could get hurt making a guy like mad." Michael admonished her. "Don't do that again."

"I can't promise you anything, but I am getting a little old to be chasing strange men around. I can barely keep up with the ones I know," Leslie said with a wink.

Michael felt his heart skip a beat and winked back.

***

The weather turned sharply colder at the beginning of December. Her dad and brother were traveling until Christmas. He would be finished with his life on the road and sharing his home with Leslie and her dog. It was something he was secretly looking forward to. He didn't know what Leslie's long-term plans were, but he was in no hurry for her to leave. Bill knew that was selfish, she should be out building a new life and future. After her years of being a big-city wife and her time as a guilt-by-association thief, he thought she might want to stay awhile and get her legs firmly planted beneath her.

Leslie had no plans to go anywhere. Her life was sectioned into semesters, and she had no commitments beyond them. She was looking forward to her father's return. When she was younger, they were very close. *I need to find the chess set,* she thought. It was something they both enjoyed doing. Until then she passed her time with Michael and Rex. He came over once a week for pizza and a movie.

Michael was happy at the invite, but once he got there, he got nervous. They sat next to each other on the couch. Leslie would tuck her legs under her and cover them both with a blanket. At this point Michael would fumble. *Should he put his arm over the back of the sofa and gradually let it drop until he had his arm around her? Should he lean closer to her? Put his hand on her thigh? Why not grab her and give her a kiss?* But he remained immobile and mute.

It was so smooth and easy with Emily none of these questions ever entered his mind. Leslie was one ball of confusion he couldn't untangle, afraid if he tried and failed, he would never be able to leave the house again. His preoccupation with Leslie was concerning to him. Michael liked her, her liked her a lot. Knowing that any attempt he made to go further than friends would put the two people he liked the most, Leslie and her dad, in a position to tell him to go home and stay there. *Getting old sucks. Why do the same problems that plague teenage boys still affect him at his age? Does it ever stop? Will I be chasing old ladies around a nursing home someday?*

"C'mon, Rex, let's go for a walk. Just you and me. No girls allowed." Rex trotted over and Michael attached his leash. He grabbed his coat and gloves. Leslie's comment about his melon caused him to grab his hat and put it on. "Ready, Rex? Let's go." They headed out into the chilly evening air and started off.

They took a long walk and when he was good and tired, they started back in the dark. He was on the corner and noticed Leslie turned on her front light. There was a man standing there. Judging from the brown cap he wore and large envelope under his arm, Michael assumed it was a delivery. He was surprised to see when Leslie opened the door the guy entered inside and quickly shut the door behind him.

Leslie heard the doorbell and wondered who could be at her door this time of night. She looked out the window and saw a delivery guy with an envelope and figured it must be something for her dad. Leslie opened the door only to have the man push his way in and shut the door. "What the?" Leslie said. "Get out of here right now! There are cameras everywhere and if I scream it will trigger the alarm. Now go!" She went to go around him to open the door, but he pushed her back and took off his hat.

She looked at him, and her mouth dropped open in shock. She blinked her eyes a few times to clear her vision. "What the fuck? You've got to be kidding me! Paul, is that you? Paul!"

***

He had a full beard, longer hair, and a dark tan. He was heavier. Paul always was lean and lanky, missing a gym session was not in his usual behavior. He was a handsome man, meticulous about his appearance but the man in front of her was neither. He was scruffy and ill-groomed. Leslie always thought Paul was vain about his appearance, he wore custom suits and never had a hair about of place, but this man was almost unrecognizable. Leslie looked into his familiar eyes. *Damn. It is Paul.*

"Paul. What are you doing here?" His answer was to grab her in his arms and kiss her. She tried to push him off her, but like a wilted plant devoid of water suddenly finding itself in the rain, Leslie collapsed against him and kissed him back. She wanted to hate him. She wanted to take a steak knife and stab him in the heart, but his kiss brought back all the good things they were, things Leslie missed and wanted again. The thoughts swirled in her brain in no particular order, leaving her dizzy and disoriented. She felt weak but pushed him off her. Paul led her to the sofa, sat her down, and sat next to her, not releasing her hand.

"Paul. What are you doing here? You really need to go."

"Go? That's my plan, only you're coming with me. I came back to get you."

"What? *Go* with you? You're crazy. You have no idea what you put me through. I went through hell for almost two years, branded as an accomplice. I had nothing. You took *everything*. I was flat broke like all the others you stole from, yet I was in on it, that I knew what you were doing. You asshole." The shock of seeing Paul was starting to wear off, and she was getting angry.

"Leslie, let me explain."

"Explain what? Nothing you say will change the past."

"Didn't you get the money I left for you? The fifty grand I left in your suitcase. That was to support you until I came back and the money you had in Senecaville. I left it there for you."

"The FBI was watching me so that money I couldn't do much with without raising up red flags. I still don't understand what happened. When did you become a scam artist? That isn't the man I married. *You're* not the man I married."

"Leslie, let me explain. It wasn't on purpose. I started moving money from one account to cover another. Some of the tech stock tumbled, and some real estate investments didn't go as planned. I was going to repay the shortages, but I ran out of time." Paul said, his hands resting palms up on his knees.

"Sounds like you were skimming off the top to me."

"Actually, I banked commissions I didn't earn. Maybe a little more. I was going to repay the money once the business turned around, I swear. Money was coming in so I could cover the debt on top, but like I said, I ran out of time. One of the other partners got involved, and I had to make money for her or else she was going to turn on me. She was blackmailing me, and it reached a point where the company called in accountants to look over the books because the discrepancies were becoming obvious, so I had to run. Mary Alice, too. She's as guilty as I was."

"I don't know which is worse, cheating an old lady out of her pension or cheating on me."

"I didn't cheat on you. We did have to leave at the same time, but she went her way, and I went mine. I think she's in Southeast Asia somewhere. I went to Cuba so I could be close to you."

"Cuba?"

"The extradition laws aren't enforced in Cuba. I also have a yacht moored in case you want to travel, but unless you want to go to the other side of the world, Cuba is our best shot at not being discovered. Or prosecuted. I'm on the hook for millions of dollars here. There's no way to track it down; it's held in untraceable offshore accounts, but if I get caught, that's it for me."

"I wish I could say I'm happy to see you, but I'm not. I'm furious. You abandoned me and the kids. How could you do this to them? Your sons. You walked away from them, too. Exactly who are you, Paul Nelson?"

"It doesn't matter. I'm your husband, and I've come to take you to paradise."

"Paradise? I don't think so. I've got news for you, Paul. You are no longer my husband. It was easy. If the FBI couldn't find you, I wasn't going to either. It was proof I was unable to serve you the papers so it was quick and clean."

Paul's eyes started to water. "We're not married? I love you, Leslie. I've always loved you."

"How the hell was I supposed to know that? You disappeared without a whisper, and I was left to deal with the FBI raiding the place at six a.m. My life was hell. They put me in handcuffs, Paul, handcuffs. People spit on me. I was under house arrest. I felt so bad for all the people you screwed over, but conveniently all your assets were tied up in an estate trust and untouchable.

"Oh, yeah. Your lovely sisters tried to kick me out of the apartment. My home, Paul. I only got to stay there because that's where the Feds wanted me. If your family was able to evict me sooner, I would have spent the time in jail because I had nowhere else to go. Fuck you, Paul, and your family, too." Leslie said, bitterness lacing her voice. She wrenched her hand back.

"Leslie, don't be like that. I am so sorry." He reached again for her hand. "Melly, I can believe, but Carla? I can't believe you thought I left you forever. I only kept you in the dark so you'd be safe. You couldn't be held liable for something if you were ignorant about it."

"Well, thanks for that but I didn't get the memo."

"You didn't get my mail?"

"What mail? I didn't get anything from Cuba. *That* I would have noticed."

"No, but in order to do what I did, it was a very orchestrated process. I had to make friends with some not-so-nice people. I sent clippings from the papers, with a heart around you, and paid someone to mail them from Miami. I had them sent to the house next door, so if someone was checking your mail, it wouldn't raise a red flag. I can't believe you didn't know it was me."

"You? Why would I think they were from you? You left me holding the bag. You left me at the mercy of the Feds, for God's sake. Those papers scared the shit out of me. Who would know where I was? I thought I was being targeted, that someone was stalking me. You were one of those people who lost everything thanks to you and feel you owe him his pound of flesh. Wow. He sought vengeance, but he never got the opportunity."

"Better for him. I'm not worth the misery of prison."

"You know what, Paul? Fuck you. I never want to see your face ever again." Leslie said with fire in her eyes.

"Leslie, don't be like that. I'm sorry."

"So you think that's all it's going to take? I'm sorry? I'm sure everyone you stole from would be very happy to see you in prison. The more miserable, the better." Leslie said, irritated. Lady hopped around, needing to go out. Leslie walked to the back door and let Lady out. Her movements triggered the motion-sensitive lights. She wandered around, smelling the ground for the right spot. Leslie watched Paul rub his nose.

"When did you get a dog? You know I'm allergic to dogs, don't you?"

Leslie let Lady in and gave her a treat. "She lives here. You don't," she said, looking him in the eye. She turned and walked out of the room. Paul followed after her into the living room. Leslie sat on the couch, Lady next to her. Paul took a seat in the matching chair. He rubbed his eyes, they were starting to itch.

"I can't believe you got a dog. I'm having a reaction to it." Paul said in a scratchy voice like he had a hair caught in the back of his throat.

"I hope you brought your own EpiPen; you're not getting any help from me, and I won't dial 911 either."

"Leslie, don't be like that."

"Like what? Having the nerve to go on without you? What did you expect me to do? Throw myself off the Brooklyn Bridge?"

"Please, I thought you knew. I thought you'd find the money and mail and put two and two together. I'm sorry I couldn't share more, but I didn't know who was watching."

"Exactly. I didn't either and was scared shitless this whole time." They sat in silence. The only noise was of him trying to clear his throat. After a while, Leslie spoke. "Well. What's next?"

"We stay the night here, and tomorrow a car will pick us up. Where we are going after that is of no importance to you. The less you know, the better off you are."

"I'm not going anywhere. You can't make me."

"Here's the deal. If you don't come, I'm taking the dog, and when I get far enough away, I'll dump her. Maybe it'll get hit by a car and you'll never see it again."

Leslie gasped. "You wouldn't. You're not that kind of guy."

"'Desperate times,' and all that. I'm not as flexible as I used to be. I'm not a lot of things I used to be. If you push me up against the wall, Leslie, the dog, comes with me. Paul lifted the corner of his shirt and flashed the pistol on his hip. If you don't come, you will just have to take your chances and keep your mouth shut. Once I'm in the clear, I'll call you where you can find her. Or her body. Any hint of trouble, she gets it. I'm not the kind of guy who'd shoot a dog, but I'm capable of a lot of things I never thought I'd be. The best way to keep it safe is to come with me to be sure."

"You wouldn't," Leslie said but thought this new Paul seemed like he would and mail her Lady's dead body. "I'm going to get a drink. I'm only going as far as the kitchen. You can come along if you want."

He got up and walked alongside her. "What? Don't you trust me?" Paul looked at her. Her face went from sad to indifferent. *I can't believe that's Paul. My Paul.*

"I have to feed Lady," Leslie turned her back to him and prepped her dinner. She tried nonchalantly to look for her phone. After she put the dish down Leslie swung her gaze around, looking for her phone. She remembered the last place she saw it was on the table and casually glanced there.

"Nice try, Leslie, but your phone isn't there. I had to disable it. Even if you find the phone, you won't find the battery. Let's go sit down and watch TV."

"I have to let Lady out. Want to watch?"

"Of course. I haven't forgotten how smart you are, Leslie. You'd probably send out an S.O.S. using the porch light." Leslie opened the door and let Lady out. "I would have if I thought about it." Lady came back inside, and they went back to sit in the living room, watching the Nightly News but not speaking.

***

Michael went inside his house, welcoming the warmth after the cold night air. He looked out his window into Leslie's living room and saw her arguing with the man. He was no longer wearing his hat, and he looked a bit scruffy. Michael checked the road and her driveway, but there was no vehicle or delivery truck in view. The street was quiet and empty.

Who is this guy, and what does he want with Leslie? Michael thought. He dialed her phone, but it went right to voicemail. He looked in her window again, and she was seated on the sofa. The look on her face gave nothing away. She was no longer arguing with the man. *Maybe the guy left,* he thought, and stopped looking in his neighbor's window.

Michael fed Rex and let him out to do his business. He could see in Leslie's kitchen, but it was empty. He exited the kitchen, turning off the light. They watched TV for a bit. Rex sacked out by his feet, tired from his long walk. When he stood up to go to bed, he looked at Leslie's house one last time, but all was quiet. Michael turned the lights off and went up to bed.

***

Leslie studied Paul's face, trying to find a trace of her husband, but it was hard to find anything. "So, what do we do now?" Leslie asked.

"I'm hungry. Let's order a pizza."

"A pizza? I wish I could help, but you broke my phone."

Paul took his phone out. Leslie expected him to have the latest high-tech model, but he had a simple phone.

"What's a good place to get a pizza around here? One that delivers?" Leslie gave him the information, and he called. While they waited, the silence drove

204

Leslie crazy. She felt compelled to ask Paul questions to see how much of him was still in there.

"Paul, talk to me. What happened to you? To us? What was so bad you had to leave?" Leslie's tight voice wavered.

"Leslie. Please. It's like I said, it was very simple. I was playing chess. I moved money around and took a little off the top for me. One day, I moved a little too much and needed to get the money replaced immediately. I planned on paying it back, but Mary Alice wanted in, or else she'd blow the whistle." Paul stared off into the distance.

"I did what I could and was tipped off. The hammer was going to fall, so I ran. I left. I always had an escape bag packed. I got us new IDs, New passports, new identity cards, new everything. I can't believe you didn't know I'd be back for you."

Leslie looked at him and saw exactly what happened. While uncommon, she'd heard about them. Ponzi schemes. Knowing Paul, he was smart enough to go on for years. But why? Was it the thrill of the win? Paul certainly didn't need the money, so why risk his life, his career, and his family just to meet some arbitrary metric he set for himself? What an asshole. *What a selfish asshole. Playing with everybody's money but his own,* she thought.

A knock on the front door signaled the delivery driver. Paul paid the guy in cash and set the pizza on the coffee table. They included paper plates and napkins. He walked with her to grab a couple of drinks out of the refrigerator. She handed him a Diet Coke and brought hers to the table. Leslie sat down, and Paul gave her a slice. It was her favorite topping, ensuring nobody else wanted a piece. He remembered. Black olives and banana peppers.

She raised her eyes and looked at him. "What? Did you think I'd forget your topping preferences? We were together a long time, Leslie. I love you. You made a huge impact on my life, on me. I remember everything about you. It's not like we've been apart that long." He smiled at her. "You are as beautiful as ever."

"Well, thanks, I guess. I feel like I've aged twenty years since this all started." Leslie said and took a hard look at Paul, trying to remember his weaknesses. *He was incredibly vain, and the perception others had of him was important and played right into his ego. He loved power and, liked to be the alpha male, and had no problem stepping on somebody else to advance himself.* Leslie decided to cater to that, to acquiesce and play dumb. *I'll just be little old me, the country bumpkin from upstate, and defer to him so I can buy some time until I can figure a way out of this mess.*

"How's your pizza?" he asked.

"Good. Do you want some rum for your drink? You never did like the taste of diet soda."

Paul picked up his can and sipped. "No rum, thanks. I need to keep my wits around you."

"You look so different, Paul. I hardly recognize you. You look like a hippy compared to the corporate investment lawyer I married." She saw him glance at his reflection in the mirror hanging above the writing desk and frown. It was ironic. The mirror over the desk where her parents used to pay their bills was now casting back a reflection he wasn't proud of: the image of a thief.

"So, where did you go?"

"I grabbed the bag with the legal dupes, packed a carry-on, and left. I took a midnight flight to Paris. You were sleeping. I kissed you goodbye and *Ubered* to JFK, where I caught the first flight out. It was going to Europe. I arrived at Heathrow, had a layover, and a connection to Paris. I used the layover to get a ticket to the Turks and Caicos under my new identity. I bought a hat and a cane and kept my head down so if my image was caught on security there was never a clear shot of my face. I changed clothes, put on a fake mustache and limped out of the men's room, went to my gate. I was gone from the US before the shit hit the fan."

"But why, Paul? Your family had loads of money. You didn't lack a thing."

"You know about my parents. My mother's side had the money. When I was at boarding school, I was considered a pauper. Yes, there was the place in the Hamptons and the apartment, but it was all tied up in a trust. I wanted my own. I wanted to be able to buy and sell those rich assholes from Bennington. Only I had to leave before I was finished."

"You mean before the Feds broke down the door? I was asleep, and all the pounding on the door woke me up. I had no idea what was happening. They were looking for you, but you weren't there. I thought you were in the gym downstairs. I kept calling your phone, but you didn't answer. They put handcuffs on me, Paul. *Handcuffs.* I went to jail in my pajamas." *Let that sink in.* "You wore a phony mustache? That sounds ridiculous. Nobody could tell?"

"That's one thing about having a disability. People don't look at you. If they showed my photo to anyone, the doddering old man with a cane would have been the last person they'd think of, and if anyone was asked to describe him, I was an old man wearing glasses."

"Glasses? Since when did you start wearing glasses?"

"I bought reading glasses at the gift shop. I even flew coach."

"It sounds to me like this wasn't a spur-of-the-moment decision, Paul. It sounds like a perfectly planned exit strategy."

"It was, but I considered it a contingency plan. I didn't think I'd actually need it. By the time it got discovered, I figured we'd be retired with no forwarding address."

"What about Charlie? And Will? Did you figure on walking away from them, too?"

"I didn't think that far ahead." His toned turned dark. In that moment, she saw the real Paul. A man who would walk away from his family for money. Any guilt he felt about leaving his family behind wasn't visible.

That asshole. That Bastard, Leslie thought. *Just be cool and keep him talking.* "It's too bad you didn't come earlier. The boys were here for Thanksgiving."

"How are they? How do they look?"

"Good. Great. They had a meeting in the city. They were staying at one of Charlie's friends and slept on some blow-up mattresses on the floor. Personally, I think they're getting a little too old to live like college kids. They should have contacted their Aunt Carla to see if they could crash a couple of nights in their childhood beds, in their childhood home."

Paul grimaced at the thought of his sons sleeping on someone's floor. They were too good for that.

"What's going on with the apartment? Why couldn't they stay there?"

"After I was released from house arrest, I packed a bag and went to stay at Jenny's. The apartment was the way the cops left it. I don't know if your sisters fixed it, but they really trashed the place.

"I sold all my jewelry and gave my lawyer all the money I scraped together, as well as what you left behind. I don't know what legal mumbo-jumbo he used to gradually give it back. I got an allowance. At my age." Leslie sounded disgusted. "My dad gave me a credit card.

"As far as the apartment, the law really did a number on it. They sliced open all the cushions and mattresses. They cut the linings of all your suits and jackets, looking for clues. Oh, and for some reason, your office door was locked, so they kicked it in, busted up your desk, and emptied all your files."

"My files? My antique desk?" Paul sounded stunned. He never counted on them tearing apart the apartment.

"Why does it matter? It's not like you're ever going back there. One more thing. You stole the doorman's retirement account. You took Ed's money, and he blamed *me.*"

"Oh. Ed," was all he said.

"Yes, Ed. I thought at least they could sell the apartment and furnishings to recoup a little of the money, but it seems all your assets are tied up in a family trust, so nobody on your side took a hit, just people like teachers and doormen."

Paul got up and started pacing. "It wasn't supposed to be like this. Nobody was supposed to get hurt."

"*You* didn't know where the money was coming from? You, the financial guru? I'm not buying that, Paul."

He suddenly faced her. "Stop! Stop it, I said! You don't have to buy it! It happened. Now we have to leave here."

Back to us. I better settle him down. "After I left Jenny's, we went to LA and visited the boys. Will was living in the guest house of a fancy mansion of some movie star. I forget who, but they were on location. Jenny left, but I stayed. Charlie even cast me in his movie."

The change in subject mollified Paul. "Charlie. How is he? Still making movies? Is he making any progress in the film industry?"

"He's happy with the progress he's making. There are a lot of jobs behind the camera, and he's exploring them all. He's doing side jobs. I think he directed a music video and the movie I was in. He's just happy to be in the mix."

Paul smiled thinking about Charlie, out there young and making his mark. "And Will? What's he doing?"

Leslie laughed. She could see a little regret in his eyes, missing his boys see their way to their future. "Will? He's doing fine. In the beginning, he got a McDonald's commercial. He also had a small part on a soap. The meeting they had in New York was for him. An agent saw him and recommended he meet with an agent for print work."

"Print work? What's that?"

"Not that you'll be passing by any newsstands, but he's a model for book covers. Will's a pirate for a romance novel called 'Fire on the High Seas.' He's put on a lot of muscle and takes after your sister Carla. He's got long black curly hair, and with a spray tan and beard, he makes for quite a sexy pirate."

Paul sat down and thought about his sons. He loved them and missed seeing them grow into men. Will taking after his side pleased him greatly, and with regret he would never see them again. Leslie could see the emotions wash across his face, and she couldn't help but feel sorry for him.

"Didn't you think about this at all? Was the money worth what it cost you? Your career, your life, your family?" Leslie asked him. "We were happy. I loved you, and you loved me, or so I thought. We had enough. Why did you want more?"

"Weren't you listening?" He said harshly. "I made a mistake. We had all these clients with millions of dollars. I didn't think anyone would notice. Our lives weren't supposed to change at all."

"Losing a hundred sixty million dollars is more than a bookkeeping error. You had to know, you had too. You're a smart guy; it would be discovered. You had all your fake documents ready to go."

"No!" he said as he slammed his fist on the table. "I had *our* documents ready. You're coming with me. It doesn't matter how far it's gone. It's where we go from here. Tomorrow a car will pick us up. I've changed my mind. I can't leave you behind. It's too big a risk I don't trust you. I'll leave the dog, but you are coming with me. You love me. You'll forgive me after a while."

Leslie figured she needed to calm him down. "Relax, Paul. You've got it covered. I'll go if I can take Lady."

"The dog stays. You're coming. You know I'm allergic to dogs. Like I said, I can put a bullet through it's head to show you I'm not fooling, so don't push me. You may never see her again." Paul threatened.

"OK, Paul, OK. I'm coming."

"I wish you were coming because of me, not to save some stupid dog." He sneezed three times.

"Who knows, Paul? I know we can't go back, but maybe in time I'll understand. I'll get over it."

That seemed to relax him. "Give me a chance, Leslie. I'll make it up to you."

"We'll see. I'm tired. I need to go to bed before my hip gives out. We'll talk again tomorrow." Leslie insisted she leave the room. She could not take one more syllable out of his mouth into her ear. She wanted to go to bed and headed to the stairs. Paul stood up and grabbed her arm.

"Not so fast, Leslie. You're sleeping down here with me. I love you but I don't trust you. Go do what you have to do in the bathroom. I'll be out here, but I'm not closing the door. I wouldn't be surprised if you tried to climb out the bathroom window. You're much too resourceful. I remember that much about you, Leslie."

Leslie forced a smile. "Yes, you know better than to leave me alone. What are you going to do? Tie me to the couch?"

"No. My arm. If you move, you'll wake me."

"You will not."

"Yes. I'm tying you to me. If you move, I'll know it."

"Well, let me go in the bathroom. When I'm done, I have to let Lady out."

"You'll have to wait for me." After she finished up, he tied a rope around her wrist.

"What's this for?"

"So, when you let the dog out you don't go with her. Be right back." Paul returned and they went into the kitchen and let Lady out. Michael was in his kitchen, and he saw the light go on as Lady went out. He looked into Leslie's kitchen window as was his habit. Michael saw the back of her head and the man across from her. He looked at the man's face, but he did not look familiar. He met all her family at Thanksgiving and the man wasn't present. Michael watched her turn off the light and go into the living room, the man close behind. The lights turned off and the house was now dark. Michael went to bed and had a restless night, worrying about Leslie.

Over at Leslie's, she and Paul were tied together at the wrist. She had the couch, and he was in the recliner.

Leslie thought this was a good time to have a heart-to-heart talk with Paul.

"What's the plan, Paul? For tomorrow?"

"We wait for a phone call. It will tell us when to be ready for a ride to the airport."

"Isn't that dangerous? To go through the airport with a woman tied to your body?

"When you take a private jet, things are a lot more relaxed."

"A private jet? Are you kidding me?" Leslie scoffed at the idea of such excess.

"What's the point of having millions if you going to fly coach?"

"How come you have that cheap-ass phone? I figured you'd have the latest in technology."

"This?" He took the phone out of his pocket. "It's a burner phone. Once our ride comes, it's no longer useful." Paul continued talking about the plan to exit the country, filling in with details and specifics.

Leslie let him ramble on and decided she was too tired to listen. She wished he would just shut the fuck up and go to sleep.

***

Leslie didn't sleep that well, tied to Paul. It seemed like every time she opened her eyes Paul was awake, looking at her. She shut her eyes and faked being asleep. The night dragged on. Finally, the sky brightened enough that sunrise was sure to follow. She sat up and looked at Paul, sitting there staring at her.

"Will you stop looking at me," Leslie said. "I have to go pee and probably let Lady out."

"Okay, let's go." Paul stood up. Leslie stood too and started towards the bathroom, still tied around her wrist. "Is this really necessary?" she held her hand up.

"Just until our ride comes."

"When will that be?"

"When my phone rings." He ushered her into the bathroom and followed after her. He followed her into the kitchen. She took care of Lady and looked at him. "Coffee?"

"Thanks." Leslie made a pot of coffee and set two mugs down. She got out the half-and-half, put that down and sat. "If you want sugar, it's in the cupboard up there." She pointed to a high cupboard and poured herself a mug. She sat opposite Paul, and he watched her. "Will you quit looking at me? I don't like it."

"I can't help it, Leslie. It's so good to see you. You're even prettier than I remember."

"Yeah. I'm a real looker." Leslie said over the rim of her mug. The steam rose to her eyes but didn't cover her flinty glare. "What do we do now?"

"Wait."

"Wait?" Leslie groaned.

"I know, Les, you were never one to sit around." Leslie brought the mugs to the sink and washed them out.

She turned and walked back into the living room. After they took their seats, she turned on the news. "Let's see if there is any news of an escaped felon on the loose."

"I don't think so, but let's..." Paul said and, his voice floating over her head. Leslie was worried she was going to fall for him again. It was like magnets drawing through him pulling her up close. They could end up igniting a passion like an A-bomb, a big mushroom cloud contaminating everything nearby, but she just didn't have the motivation to chase her tail enough to prove to him she loved him. *Fuck that.*

***

Michael was up making coffee and he could tell by the silhouette there were two people in Leslie's house.

He called her phone again, but it went directly to voice mail.

Michael put his coat on and grabbed Rex's leash. He adjusted his hat as he left. He walked down the driveway, went up the steps into her house, and rang the doorbell twice. Finally, the door pulled open, and the man was standing there. "Hello. My name's Mike, I'm Leslie's dog walker. Is Lady ready to go?" Lady sidled up next to the strange man and looked very happy to see them, wagging her tail in anticipation. Mike bent over and scratched her ears. "Hello there, Lady," he said as he tried to look into her house and find Leslie, but he didn't see her. Michael looked up at the man. "Is Leslie around? She owes me for last week," he asked to buy time as he stood up.

"No, she's packing. I'm an old friend of hers. We go way back. In fact, we are going to the wedding of a couple of old friends."

"Does she need me to watch Lady while she's gone?"

"No, we're going away for a while and Leslie wants to bring her. Thanks, but I think we're good. I walked her earlier this morning." He sneezed and closed the door in Michael's face. *Huh. A man who looks like ditch digger and wears a Rolex watch,* Michael thought.

Micheal turned and walked down to the sidewalk. He headed the opposite direction of his house in case the man was watching him. Michael took a turn around the block and was soon in front of his house. He gazed at Leslie's house, but it was quiet.

Micheal hurried up the driveway and entered his house. He filled Rex's water bowl, sat down while still wearing his jacket, and pulled out his phone. He googled a few sites and discovered his instinct was correct. He called the police, spoke to a detective and told them what he found out. Michael didn't know what time they were leaving, and they asked him to watch the house. They were sending a car over to sit on it until they could develop a plan and get the pieces in place.

Michael sat in his dining room looking at Leslie's house. He wondered if Leslie wanted to go with him and he ruined her chances by calling the cops. Michael knew he had to do it. That's the kind of guy he was. He got out his laptop and looked at the tons of pictures the man's name called up. A car pulled up and parked on the other side of the street, not directly in front of her house, but close enough to observe any traffic in or out.

There was no activity for a while, and Michael hoped something would happen soon before they left.

Suddenly, the place blew up. The FBI appeared out of nowhere in riot gear and a SWAT team swarmed the house. Michael went out and watched them kick the front door in. Minutes later, they ushered Paul out of the house swearing and spewing threats against her. "You bitch, Leslie, I'll get you for this!" Michael heard him say as they dragged him off, put him in a car, and took him away. There were still others milling about her house.

Leslie and Lady stood in her driveway. She appeared in a state of shock and the number of people trying to talk to her was overwhelming. Michael walked over and when she saw him, she started crying and ran into his open arms. He embraced her and rubbed her back trying to settle her down. Someone handed him a box of tissues and when she stopped crying, he gave her some to clean her face.

"How did they know he was here?"

"I'm afraid it was me. I pretended to be your dog walker to get a good look at him. When he wouldn't let me talk to you, I knew it had to be him. I wasn't sure if you'd be happy to see me. You two could have been working on an exit strategy, but the way he hurt you before I couldn't let go. He deserved it. I hope you can forgive me."

"Forgive you? I could kiss you," and grabbed his head until their lips met, and she kissed him like a woman would. Not a thank-you kiss, or you're the best kiss but a kiss with hunger and longing. Her lips were the match that set him on fire. He pulled back. "Um, a, Leslie I'm not sure this is a good idea. I'm too old for you. You're just kissing me because you're grateful."

"Says who? I can kiss whoever I choose, and I choose you. I was wondering if you were going to make a move. I guess I needed to call in a SWAT team to get your attention."

"But Leslie, you don't know-"

She cut him off. "I have adult kids, you have adult kids, approximately the same age, so you can't be that much older. I don't care if you're too old. I don't even know what it means. I'll pick out the best rocking chairs I can find, and we can sit and watch the world go by from your front porch."

"Maybe watch the waves roll in from our lanai in Hawaii. I'm not that old."

Leslie kissed him again. A police officer approached them. "Sorry to break up the party, but you're needed at the precinct to make a statement."

"Who's going to watch my house? I'll have to bring my dog. I have no front door."

"One of these guys can stay here until we get back. Just so you know, you're going to have to fix it yourself."

"Are you kidding me? You guys kicked it in. You should fix it."

Michael spoke up. "Don't worry, Leslie, I'll do it."

The officer led them to his car. "I hope you don't mind, but you'll both have to sit in the back."

Lady jumped in and they slid in after her. The cop shut the door, and Leslie smiled at Michael. "Did you ever make out in the back of a police car?"

"No. I've never been in the back of a police car."

"Well, I have. It's better with company. You want to make-"

She couldn't finish the sentence, the words swallowed by his lips. "mmmmmm," he said.

"mmmmmmm." she answered.

✳✳✳

THE END

Acknowledgments

I'd like to acknowledge Forest Blakk, who never gave up on his dreams. A good person, with great music, and a lovely wife.

Thanks for showing me if you believe in yourself enough you can accomplish anything. You should really check out his music.

About The Author

After retiring from Corporate America, she spent her free time volunteering until Covid-19 made those activities obsolete. Not one to sit around and watch Days of Our Lives, she decided to write a book. She wrote a couple, so depending on which one hits the shelf first, this could be her debut novel. She is an empty nester of two adult daughters. One husband, a dog, and a cat remain.

Regarding any questions, criticisms or comments you may have, feel free to reach out at www.cynthiaakingbooks.com